The Shellfish Grift

A Coastal Cowboys Novel
by

Mike Rose

Cover design by Karen Snave
Set in Arial and Iowan Old Style
by Tristan Steffe

Paperback ISBN: 9798991205801
Ebook ISBN: 9798991205818
Library of Congress Control Number: 2024915397

For my family, for everything you did and everything you do. A luckier man than me does not exist.

For Susan, I love you.

I

A Good Sunset Ruined

Sunday, October 9

IT WAS THE BLUE HOUR, that time of day before dawn when
the sun is still below the horizon. The sky overhead was rich
with color, the marshland suffused with bluish light. Soon
there would be a golden glow reflecting in the calm waters of
Banks Channel, sounds rising from the marshes, singing a tune
no voice could ever match. Tranquility that can only be found
at the coast. Usually.

The air always felt colder on the water than what the weather-
erman said, especially in the early fall mornings. Alex Spencer
III knew this, having spent a lot of his early years on a boat with
his father. He was prepared. Willie Covington, on the other
hand, was not. Willie spent most of his life avoiding boats and
the water, even though he lived at the coast. It was for tourists
and rich people, he thought, neither of which he liked. But here
they were, on a boat somewhere in the Intracoastal Waterway
just before sunrise.

"Why the fuck are we out here so early?" Willie complained. "It's fuckin' freezing."

Alex hated having Willie there with him, but ever since he made the mistake of telling Willie about the gold when they were sitting around smoking weed, he was stuck with him. "I told you, Willie, fishermen get out before the sun is up. If we want to catch this Bratton guy, this is the best time. Besides, maybe he won't be as drunk or mean as the last time we spoke to him."

The last time they met with Holt Bratton, he threatened to turn them into chum for shark bait.

"I figure if we can catch him checking his oyster farm, we might get him in a better mood. Maybe make him an offer he likes."

"I still don't get why we have to buy up these oyster lease things, let's just find the gold and take it."

Alex sighed. "It's my brother-in-law's plan. He knows what he's doing."

Alex slowed the boat as they crept down one of the finger creeks off the waterway into the marshes. Alex prayed he wouldn't bottom out.

"Stop, stop right there, you stupid motherfuckers!" The shouting came from a man standing nearly chest high in the water. "What the hell do you think you're doing?"

Alex killed the motor and let the fourteen-foot skiff float a bit. He watched as the man started moving towards them faster than he thought someone could move in the water. Holt Bratton was a big man, nearly six-foot-four and easily 280 pounds, most of it muscle. He was wearing camo chest waders and a black tactical fleece cap that made him look even more menacing. As he approached the skiff, Holt's eyes narrowed.

"You two motherfuckers again? Do you know how close you are to my water columns? If you damage my oysters, I'll pound you into fish food. I thought I told you what would happen if you bothered me again."

Alex stood at the edge of the boat. "Mr. Bratton, I just wanted to…" Before he could finish, Holt was at the boat. He grabbed Alex by the shirt and flung him overboard in one quick motion. The move caught Alex by surprise, and he ended up on his back as he hit the water. It was only about four feet deep, and Alex sank to the bottom quickly. Before he knew it, Holt reached down into the water and yanked him back up.

"I ain't sellin' to you, and I better never see your ass in these waters again, you got me?" He dropped Alex and turned to Willie, who was still on the skiff. "Goes for you too, dipshit."

With Holt facing Willie, Alex reached into the skiff and grabbed a rod holder installation wrench his father had left on the boat. As Holt began to turn around, Alex swung the wrench and struck Holt, catching him on the temple, enough to stun him. As Holt stumbled back, Willie took advantage, jumping on top of Holt, pushing him face first into the water.

"Help me hold this big sumbitch under water, Alex," Willie shouted.

But Alex froze, watching in horror as Willie held Holt's face underwater until his body finally went limp.

"What are you doing, Willie? We aren't supposed to kill him."

"You're the one who clubbed him, Alex, this is on you." Willie looked around, seeing Holt's jon boat near the marsh. "Help me drag him over closer to his boat. We'll make it look like he fell out and hit his head."

The sun was rising as the two finally got back to the skiff. Alex started the outboard, and they slowly worked their way back out to the waterway, looking to see if there were other boats, potential witnesses.

"This is bad, Willie," Alex whimpered. "You killed that man. Jack is gonna be pissed at me," he continued, referring to his brother-in-law.

Willie looked at Alex. "You hit him, dumbass, you killed him. You best remember that before you go running your mouth to anyone." He had never killed anyone before, but he felt a rush of adrenaline.

Willie took a deep breath to calm down. He looked at Alex, softening a bit. "Relax, Alex, everything will be fine, especially once we get the gold."

CHIEF ROB PHILLIPS sat down in front of the television, wings and beer on the coffee table, Buffalo Bills kickoff just a few minutes away, when his phone rang.

"Sorry to bother you, Chief," Sergeant Shaefer said, "but we just got a call about an unattended boat out near Howards Creek."

"Did the caller say it looked damaged?" The chief knew some-times owners abandoned damaged boats in the marshes so they didn't have to deal with them.

"Negative. They seemed to think it was a perfectly good boat."

The chief rubbed his forehead. Probably some dumb kid play-ing out in the marshes and didn't properly anchor the vessel. Topsail Beach Police didn't have its own boat, so he knew they would need help. "Call Pender County Sheriff's Department, and see if they can bring their boat out to investigate. Make sure they come by and get you first. If there is anything to this, I want you to contact me immediately."

"Yes sir."

Chief Phillips shook his head. "I'll be lucky to make it to half-time," he mumbled.

It was two hours later when Sergeant Shaefer called again. "We got a floater, Chief."

ORVILLE DENTON WAS a North Carolina State Senator for thirty years before retiring. The Republican senator spent the last ten years of that time as President Pro-Tem, meaning if legislation got passed, it had to go through him first. He was a shrewd negotiator, which belied his eastern North Carolina country background. Even the Democrats from the urban areas of the state knew they had to make Orville happy if they wanted any chance at success. His influence survived even after leaving office.

Denton's family made their fortune in tobacco when it was truly the cash crop. In the years after the decline in tobacco use, Denton did what he could to help eastern North Carolina farmers, including subsidies and more lenient regulations on pesticide and fertilizer use, despite the impact on water quality. His backroom dealings regarding hog farming were among the more egregious acts. He was a master at keeping his hands clean while reaping the benefits of every ethically questionable move he made.

Denton had spent most of the morning at church, a ritual he continued even though he was no longer running for office. He really didn't like church, but a politician had to get the church vote or lose the election. Now it was a habit. Besides, if he didn't go to church, his wife wouldn't make the Sunday meal. He sat at the kitchen table, having just finished a meal of fried pork chops, collards, grits with red eye gravy, and biscuits. He was working on his second piece of chocolate pecan pie. He was a big man with a big appetite.

Denton could hear the television in the next room. His wife was watching Fox News, which she kept on most of the day. He had just taken a huge bite of pie when his phone rang.

"Eunice, turn that shit down," he yelled as parts of pie flew from his mouth. "Good lord, I'm a god-fearin' Republican, but even I can't stand all that bullshit."

He answered his phone, "This is Denton."

"Senator Denton, it's Deputy Barnes."

Orville didn't recognize the voice on the other end of the line right away. After an awkward pause, the man spoke again: "From the Pender County Sheriff's Department."

Orville had informants all over the state. It was hard to keep up sometimes. "Of course, son, whatcha know good?"

"Well, sir, you said to call you if anything peculiar happens, and I'm not sure this falls under that category."

"Spit it out, boy, I ain't gettin' any younger."

"Sir, we had a local show up dead today, a floater. It's strange 'cause he's one of those oyster farmers in the water all the time."

"Shit happens, son. What makes it strange?"

"Word is he had quite the bump on his head, like someone hit him." The deputy hesitated for a second. "I'm sure it's nothing."

That fuckin' peckerwood, Jack Fleming, Denton thought.

"Are they thinking foul play? Who's involved so far?"

"Nobody said foul play for sure, sir. The medical examiner is talking to the sheriff and the Topsail Beach Chief right now. I figure we won't have a preliminary evaluation until tomorrow. Full autopsy may take a while."

"Deputy, I need you to make sure you tell the medical examiner that this was accidental, you got me? Tell him it's from me, he'll understand."

"Yes sir." There was another pause. "Senator Denton, the sheriff's election is comin' up next year, and I plan to throw my hat in the ring. I sure could use your endorsement."

"Of course, son. We always need a good man in office." I could always use another puppet, Denton thought.

Denton hung up the phone and called out to his wife, "Eunice, I need you to help me pack a bag, I gotta go to Raleigh. And for the love of Jesus, turn that shit off the TV."

MATT SHEEHAN ALWAYS enjoyed the sunset at Topsail Beach. Whether watching from his office at town hall, or from his spot at the southern end of the island, gazing at the sky as it exploded in colors of orange, gold, and purple over the water made Matt appreciate the serenity of the coast, particularly on this barrier island.

Matt and his closest friend, Dan Trekor, sipped on Irish whiskey. It was Matt's turn to choose the music, and he went with one of his favorites: David Gray's *White Ladder* album. They were on the deck of a two-story home built at *The Point*, a 150-acre tract of mostly undisturbed land located at the southernmost tip of Topsail Island.

The house was part of a small complex consisting of two 5,000 square foot homes, two smaller guest houses, a fenced-in swimming pool, and a boat house near a six-slip private marina. Slaggers Inc., owner of the property, converted one of the 5,000 square foot homes into labs and offices for the University of North Carolina Wilmington to use for various marine studies.

The sun had dropped below the horizon when Matt's phone rang. He looked at the display. "It's the police chief."

"On a Sunday," Dan replied, "that can't be good."

"Hey Chief."

"Hey Boss, I'm sorry to bother you on a Sunday night, but we pulled a floater out of the water today. I wanted you to hear it from me first before word got out."

Shit, just what we need, Matt thought. His initial assumption was a visitor caught up in a rip current, or someone just drunk and stupid.

"Do we have an ID yet?"

"Actually, we do. It's Holt Bratton," Chief Phillips responded.

Holt Bratton was a local fisherman and a general pain in the ass to the police department. Charges usually included drunk and disorderly conduct, fighting, and domestic violence. He was always accusing the police department of abuse of power or brutality, a real class act. But when it came to the water, he was no novice. A longtime fisherman and boater, he was more at home on the water than on dry land. Even blind drunk, the guy was unsinkable. He survived hurricanes. It doesn't make sense, Matt thought.

"Do we know if it was a drowning, or is there more to it?"

"We won't know for sure until an autopsy is done," the chief responded, "but it appears that he fell out of his boat and drowned. It is a bit strange, though, because he was out in Howards Creek, not the ocean. The waters were pretty calm. My guess, he just had too many." There was a pause on the line. "Boss, I can deal with any press that may come, but can you tell the mayor?"

Matt groaned. Mayor Davenport was a good man, and certainly had the town's best interest at heart, but Matt knew the mayor would turn this into a shitshow if he didn't get to him first.

"Coward," Matt responded to the chief.

Chief Phillips laughed. "You just have a way with him. Isn't that why you're the town manager?"

"Yeah, I'll call him now, before the coconut telegraph gets a hold of it. Were there any locals already at the site?"

"No sir, we kept it pretty quiet, but I'm sure someone saw police cars and the ambulance, so questions will be coming shortly."

"Thanks, Chief."

Dan looked over at Matt as he hung up. "What's that all about?"

"Police found a dead body in Howards Creek."

"OK, but why call you?"

"Well, I am the town manager after all."

"Does that make you an expert on police investigations?"

"Of course not," Matt said. "But I oversee all town departments, police, fire, public works, all of it. Anything big that happens, I need to know."

Dan smirked. "So, you head up a bunch of departments you know nothing about, is that right?" he asked.

"I'm more of a generalist. I depend on good department heads to handle the day-to-day work."

Dan laughed. "Whatever, it sounds more like a scam to me."

Matt gave a wry smile. "I suppose every good town manager has a little bit of con artist in their blood."

With the peacefulness of the sunset ruined by the call, Dan took off. Matt called Mayor Davenport as promised to explain the situation. The hierarchy of Topsail Beach, like most North Carolina towns, started with the mayor, the chief elected official. A good mayor sets the tone for the town. Then there were the board members, also elected by the residents. Their job was to set policy. The town manager implements that policy. At least, that's how it should work. Sometimes elected officials got in the way.

There was little for Matt to tell at this point, just that Bratton was dead and that further information would come after the medical examiner could take a look. It appeared to be a drowning. The mayor wanted to get in front of the issue, sending out notice to residents about the drowning, but after a long conversation, Matt convinced him that it was an open investigation and should not be discussed beyond recognition that it happened. Sometimes Mayor Davenport tended to overreact. Some thought it was his way of showing everyone that he was in control, but on an island full of Type A personalities, Matt knew it was just the status quo.

It was Matt's job to keep the mayor in check, keeping a lid on what happened until more was known. He could only hope it worked.

WILLIE COVINGTON SAT on a tattered and stained couch inside his rented house. He was staring at his hands as if they were random objects, not attached to his body. He was thinking about earlier that morning, how those hands held a man underwater until his mortal soul left his body. Willie had taken OxyContin earlier, but he wasn't sure if his euphoric feeling was drug related or adrenaline still rushing through his body.

Willie never killed anyone before. As a matter of fact, for all of his bravado, he avoided violence whenever he could. He was usually on the wrong side of beatings. As a small-time drug dealer, he generally preferred to deal with stoners or rich pussies, so that he could be the bully for a change. Alex Spencer was a great example.

All his life, Willie was told he was a loser. As a child, his mother would introduce him as her "botched abortion." His story was disturbing, but sadly not that uncommon. Willie's mother was an addict, meth being her drug of choice. If she thought she could've traded Willie when he was a baby for meth, she would've taken the deal every time. She never beat Willie, she just neglected him, which left much deeper scars.

Willie never knew who his father was. For that matter, neither did his mother. It could have been any number of men, none of which had a single redeeming quality. With no father-figure in his life, and a loveless mother, Willie was truly alone from the start.

When Willie was young, he and his mother moved into a rusted, dilapidated single-wide mobile home in one of the rural counties outside of the Wilmington area. The middle of the trailer sagged, and there was no heat or air conditioning. It smelled of soiled clothes and rotting food, which could usually be found in the sink. There was only one bedroom, which his mother used to entertain her guests. Willie slept on the couch at the opposite end of the trailer.

He had no friends in school, often getting the shit kicked out of him by the other kids. In his teen years, he was gangly, all arms and legs and no muscle. He had a bad case of acne which left his face scarred in adult life. His mother died when he was sixteen, so he quit going to school and lived in the old trailer alone. No one in the school district ever bothered to try and find him. He would work odd jobs to get enough money to eat, until his mother's former dealer, Jukes Grubbs, brought him on to sell his poison to the "stupid cracker high schoolers" that were afraid to buy from a large black man.

Eventually Willie moved back to Wilmington, continuing to move product for Jukes, occasionally supplementing his income with petty theft. He was still skinny, although he did finally add some muscle to his upper body. His hair was oily, his teeth stained from cigarettes and poor dental hygiene.

Now he sat in his house, thinking about all those people who thought he was a loser. Just like the fucker, Holt Bratton.

"I am the badass now, motherfuckers," he shouted, even though there was no one else in the house. "Fuck with me, and you die."

MATT TOOK OFF FOR HIS CONDO in downtown Wilmington along the Cape Fear River. On the drive, he couldn't shake the feeling that something wasn't right about Holt Bratton's death, but he convinced himself to let it go. He didn't want anything making his life more complicated than it already was. Screw it, he thought, I'll worry about Topsail Beach tomorrow.

On the way home, Matt decided to call his daughter, Sedona. She and her husband had left to go to Montana a few days earlier. They would spend the next several months there operating an outfitters company before returning to Wilmington in the spring. Their time in Montana was one of the many reasons Matt hated winter. When Sedona was growing up, she and Matt were very close, but Matt went into a deep tailspin after his wife and Sedona's mother, Hannah, died. Sedona was left to care for herself and her younger brother, Tanner. Resentment grew and the relationship frayed. It took a long time for Matt to rebuild trust, and it was still a work in progress. There was a lot of pain to heal. Matt couldn't help but feel that those winter months in Montana were his punishment, not by Sedona, but by God. Sort of like the Greek story of Persephone.

Sedona answered on the second ring. "Hey Dad, finished with your sunset viewing?"

Matt smiled when he heard his daughter's voice. "Am I that predictable, Dawg?" Matt called her by his nickname for her, short for Mad Dawg. It came from her softball days. Hannah hated it, saying Sedona was too beautiful a name to be wasted. Matt only called her that when it was the two of them.

"Yes, you most certainly are. As a matter of fact, it's been about a week since me and Jed got here, so this would be the 'Why did you have to go to Montana?' phone call."

"No, no, that's not why I called. I was just thinking about you. But since you mentioned it, there are better ways to make a living."

"Enough, Dad." Sedona chuckled, but got serious quickly. "I'm actually glad you called. Jed and I have something to tell you."

Panic filled Matt's chest. "You're not moving to Montana permanently, are you? Jaysus, Mary, and Joseph, tell me that's not it."

"No, Dad, it's not that." She paused for just a moment. "I'm pregnant."

Emotions ran through Matt like a freight train. Excitement, confusion, concern filled his head.

"You still there, Dad?" Sedona asked.

"Yeah, I guess I'm in shock. When did you know? How far along are you?"

"Two months or so. I'm due in April."

"Two months! You knew for two months and you're just telling me now?"

"Easy old man, don't have a coronary, my child needs his grandpa."

"I don't understand, why didn't you tell me? Have you told anyone else?"

"So far, just TJ knows."

"Tanner knows?! Why would you tell him and not your own father?" Matt quickly changed course. "And why are you in Montana? You should be here, taking it easy."

"This is exactly why I didn't tell you. Jesus, Dad, I'll be fine here. Can't you just be happy with the news?"

"Oh, Sedona, of course I'm happy for you. I'm thrilled. I just worry is all. I think it would be better for you and Jed if you planted permanent roots in Wilmington. You can supplement the shop with another sideline. I know Jed loves working on making bourbon, maybe start a distillery."

Sedona laughed. "Just like that, right? Nothing to it."

"Start-up funding is easy enough. Slaggers would love to invest."

The other end of the line got quiet, and Matt instantly knew he crossed a line. When Sedona spoke, her tone was edgy. "I'm not having this conversation with you, Dad. I don't want anything to do with that company."

"But Sedona—"

"I gotta get this place set up," she interrupted. "The kitchen is a wreck. But we want you and TJ to come out here for Thanksgiving. Whatcha think?"

Matt knew this conversation was over. "I think that would be fantastic. For now, you just take care of my future grandkid." Matt let out a little sigh. "Love you, Dawg."

"Love you too, old man."

After his conversation, Matt decided to go to Mad Mole Brewery for a beer on his way home. Mad Mole was a frequent hangout for Matt, because it had had some of the best beer around, and it was also environmentally friendly. But mostly for the beer. Might as well go for the one, he thought to himself, and toast the grandfather-to-be.

Monday, October 10

Senator Jackson Fleming started his day at 7 a.m. sharp, every day. Anyone who worked for or with him knew that and made sure they were there on time if they wanted to see him. Once the week started, it was a whirlwind of activity, and Fleming hated for anything to get off-track. And in state politics, it's damn near impossible not to get off-track.

Fleming looked out the window of his office in the North Carolina Legislative Building in Raleigh. It was one of the better offices on the second floor, one that normally came with seniority. His black hair had a sprinkling of gray, the only evidence of aging on the forty-five year old. He still looked as if he only had to shave twice a week. He had square-framed glasses that helped add dimension to his round face, and he always wore a perfectly tailored suit for his slim, 5'6" body.

Jack Fleming won his first election at age twenty-five, one of the youngest ever elected to the North Carolina House of Representatives. He was smart, ambitious, and had the backing of several well-to-do benefactors. He was also driven to constantly improve his standing, even if it meant stepping on people on his way up.

By the time he was thirty, Fleming was elected to the state senate, but his sights were set on the Governor's Mansion even then. Over the next fifteen years, he made the right friends and worked his way up the ladder of influence in the senate. He found himself as chair or vice chair on several of the more prestigious committees. His knowledge of the political system, as well as his sometimes charming, often persistent personality enabled him to advance in the ranks quicker than most. It also didn't hurt that he married into one of the more wealthy and prominent real estate families in the eastern part of the state.

Fleming represented New Hanover County, which included the city of Wilmington, but he wasn't born and raised in eastern North Carolina. This worked both to his benefit and detriment. He often needed the support of his fellow legislators from the region to help push his agenda, but he despised working with them. Fucking farmers and fishermen, he thought. Working class people were not in his circle of friends, but he could put on a show with the best of them. However, those farmers and fishermen were not as naïve as he thought, and they knew how to work the system as well. It made for an uneasy and unnatural balance. Those who paid close enough attention knew that this "man of the people" was in fact in it for himself.

It was late in the long session of the General Assembly, although this session looked like it may extend close to the new year. Fleming sat behind his custom-made maple desk. It was a statement piece according to Fleming, who felt like the furniture provided by the state of North Carolina was too industrial looking, beneath the dignity of the office. The baroque desk was indeed an architectural statement, complete with secret drawers. It barely fit in the office, was extremely impractical, and definitely Fleming. He claimed that his personal funds paid for it, but some thought otherwise.

Before he could settle in, his administrative assistant appeared in his doorway. "Your brother-in-law is on the line."

Fleming rolled his eyes and sighed. "Did he say what it's about?"

"No sir, just that it was urgent."

Fleming rubbed his temples and sighed again. "Thanks, Sylvia. Would you close the door on the way out?" Fleming picked up the phone. "What do you want, Alex?"

"This isn't necessarily bad, Jack; I mean, it could work to our advantage," Alex Spencer III stammered.

"What isn't necessarily bad?"

"Holt Bratton is dead...didn't you know?"

Fleming hesitated. "What did you just say?"

"Bratton is dead," Alex repeated.

"How the fuck would I know that? What's going on, Alex?"

"Me and Willie went to see him to get him to sign over the lease to the shellfish land near Topsail Beach. That big sonufabitch refused and started pushing me around, threatening to kick my ass. He threw me into the water. He was full out crazy, Jack."

Fleming blew air out of his mouth. He tried to calm his voice. "What exactly happened, Alex?"

"Willie did it. I mean, I hit him in the head with some tool off the boat, but Willie held him under the water until he was dead. It just happened so fast I didn't know what to do, so we left. I heard later that the cops found a floater. They think he drowned."

Fleming sat back, balling his fists in an effort to stifle his initial impulse to punch a hole in the wall. How can anyone be as inept as this moron, he thought. How many times had he told Alex not to be directly involved in any negotiation with the lease owners. And why in the name of God was Willie Covington involved.

"When did this happen?"

"It was early yesterday morning, before sunup."

Fleming could feel his blood boil. "And you're just telling me this now?"

"I wanted to tell you in person, but you had already left to go to Raleigh," Alex answered. The truth was, he went back to Willie's house after it happened to get high.

"Why were you even there, Alex, this isn't supposed to involve the company." Fleming was referring to the family business, Coastal Property Group. "You should not be directly involved. Does anyone know you went to see him?"

"I... I don't think so, except Willie."

God, what a moron. Fleming pounded his fist on his forehead. He spoke slowly. "Pay fucking attention here, Alex, as if your life depends on it. You were nowhere near Bratton yesterday; you were at whatever dump Willie lives in."

"Doing what?"

"I don't know, Alex, just think of something, you idiot. Make sure Willie knows too. So help me Jesus. Also, I don't know a Holt Bratton, never heard of him, understand?"

"Ok, ok, Jack, I got it. But it's gonna be fine. We'll still find the treasure."

Fleming closed his eyes. "Shut up, Alex, just shut up. Hire someone reputable to negotiate the leases. And make sure you keep Willie out of this!"

MATT PULLED HIS TRUCK into a parking spot across the street from the town hall around 8:15 a.m. The building represented the history of the island and the town. During World War II, Topsail Island was home to the Army for "Operation Bumblebee" developed to study and train with rockets. After the war the army left, and the island was mostly a fishing village, with small fishing shacks and boat docks dotting the island. It wasn't until much later that the town became a vacation destination. There were still only around 400 year-round residents, but the summer population swelled to over 5,000, thanks to all the vacation rental homes. This was the reason why Topsail Beach needed to be a fully functional municipality, and why Matt Sheehan had a job as town manager.

Matt stepped out of his truck, stretching his 6'2" frame skyward. Although fit for his fifty-three years, he felt the kinks that come with age. He was second generation Irish-American, with angular features including a strong jawline, high cheekbones, and a slightly upturned nose. He still had a full head of chestnut brown, thick, wavy hair, but the sides already had a significant amount of gray. His neatly trimmed beard had as much red as brown, but again, gray had begun to invade the chin area.

It was his deep-set eyes that drew people to Matt. Not in the way Paul Newman's eyes made women swoon, or piercing eyes that reached into your soul. Matt's eyes made people stop and reflect. They were laughing eyes, kind eyes, empathetic eyes when they needed to be. Whatever magic they held, looking into his eyes ultimately made people trust Matt almost immediately. People were drawn to him.

He walked into the reception area of town hall with its patchwork of fixes and minor renovations. The space was decorated with two chairs that had the whole "beach feel" design, and the walls were painted what was best described as a teal green, or "Topsail Beach Green." It was the adopted color of the town. Two pictures hung on the wall: one an aerial of the barrier island, the other a photograph of a bear that found its way on the island several years before. As Matt walked in, he was greeted by Kelly Robbins, the town clerk.

"Good morning, Mr. Sheehan, did you have a good weekend?"

Matt shrugged. "Morning, Kelly. It was pretty good until last night."

"I heard from the chief this morning. Hard to believe Holt would drown like that. I thought the SOB was indestructible."

Matt grunted as she continued.

"Well, not to pile on, but you already had a few calls this morning. Miss Evelyn would like to see you about the pickleball courts. It seems there was another dispute this weekend about court etiquette."

"Jaysus, Mary, and Joseph, these octogenarian pickleballers are the biggest pain in my ass. Can somebody tell them they are not playing the world circuit?"

"Mr. Sheehan, you know pickleball is the center of the Topsail Beach universe, way more important than water quality, beach nourishment, or other silly town operations. You need to get your priorities straight." Her tone was perfectly sarcastic.

"You also had a call from Gus Eberhart, and of course, the mayor wants you to call him right away."

"Anything else, oh bearer of joyous news?"

"Not yet, but the day is young!"

Matt was expecting the calls she mentioned, except for the

one from Gus Eberhart. Gus was a longtime resident who did a lot of water-related odd jobs, like boat shuttle during the season, charter boat fishing captain, and small dredging jobs for private docks and marinas. He was mediocre at best at these jobs, but he was a world class complainer, one who felt like the town never did enough to help businesses like his. His problems were always someone else's fault.

As expected, Eberhart got right to the point, which in his mind was why the town wouldn't solve his problems. "Matt, I got three dredge projects going on and nowhere to place the spoils. Why hasn't the board of commissioners stepped up to address the problem. As usual, the town refuses to help local businesses!"

I walked right into it, Matt thought.

"I'm not following you, Gus," he responded. "What does the town have to do with it?"

"You know damn well the Army Corps won't let us use their spoil islands anymore. We need a place to dump the excess sand and silt. What I'm asking is why hasn't the town built its own spoils island?"

Matt knew the US Army Corps of Engineers had eliminated easements from their sites several years prior, claiming they were running out of space for their own dredging needs along the Intracoastal Waterway. It was a shitty move, but not a local government call. "There are several private and state-owned sites Gus, plus you can truck it inland...."

"Do you know how much trucking adds to the costs?" Eberhart shouted. "And the state sites are becoming harder and harder to access. They want beach-suitable sand only, and who determines that? They got new rules coming down on us all the damn time. I need Topsail Beach to create a spoil island, or at least help with costs, but I know you won't because the town doesn't care."

And there it was. Matt paused to choose his words carefully. "Gus, you know the town has to follow the same processes private companies follow. Same permits, same sand quality, same environmental requirements. That includes not just randomly creating a spoil site in the marshes. And as far as using taxpayer money to subsidize your business, the last I checked your boat was not registered in our county."

Eberhart hung up on Matt. Matt was sure this would not be the end of it, since one of Gus' projects included dredging the docks for the local historic preservation society. But there was something Gus said about the difficulty of accessing state spoils sites that stuck in Matt's mind. He made a mental note to look into any issues regarding the use of state-owned sites, since that could affect the town down the road.

Next up, the Great Pickleball Battle.

JACK FLEMING WAS STILL FUMING from his call with his brother-in-law when his assistant stuck her head in the door. "Senator Orville Denton is here to see you, sir."

"Here? I don't have a meeting scheduled."

"The senator said he didn't need an appointment. Said you should be expecting him."

Fleming shrugged. "I have no idea why he's here, but send him in. And Sylvia, would you cancel any appointments I do have today? I have some family business to attend to."

"Yes sir."

The large man waddled into Fleming's office and sat down in one of the chairs in front of his obnoxious desk. He smelled of fried food, and Fleming was sure he heard him fart as he sat down. This man embodied everything Fleming found repulsive. He could not understand how the man who currently sat in front of him ever garnered the power and influence he had.

"My Gawd, son, this desk is sumpin," the man said in his deep southern drawl. "You compensatin' for a small tallywacker?" He laughed so hard he started coughing. It was all Fleming could do to hide his disdain.

"Good to see you, Orville, what brings you here?"

"'Senator Denton', or 'sir' if you rather," the man said. "I'm not sure I like you enough to be first name friendly. Ain't you gonna offer me a drink?"

Fleming furrowed his eyebrows; it wasn't even noon. "I don't keep any alcohol in my office, Senator Denton, sorry."

"Course you don't, ya peckerwood, but I was talkin' 'bout tea or water." Denton shook his head as he spoke. He couldn't figure out how this arrogant bastard was rising in the ranks. It's why he didn't run for re-election. At first it was just the uppity liberals from Charlotte, Raleigh, and Asheville that got on his nerves. Now all these elected officials from across the state seem to think their shit don't stink, but he knew better.

"I came by to see how everything's goin'," Denton said.

Fleming gave him his best smile. "Just fine, Senator, everything is moving along as planned."

"Is it now, son?"

Fleming hated the condescending way this redneck talked to him. His smile dissolved as he spoke. "Of course, I have my best staff writing up legislation, and I already have several key senators on our side. You have nothing to worry about."

Denton leaned forward in his chair. "That ain't what I hear at all," he hissed. Fleming could smell his breath. "I hear you got a dead body down in Pender County."

Fleming's eyes flashed a startled look, thinking: how does this guy know so much? He recovered quickly. "I'm not sure what you're talking about, sir."

Denton thought, what was it that my mama used to say when she met up with an idiot? Oh yeah, bless his heart. "Let me help you out, the old boy they fished outta the sound, he happened to be an oyster farmer. He had his own leased area and everything."

Fleming started nervously shuffling papers around on his desk. "Oh yeah, I heard about that, drowning I believe."

Denton slowly stood up and leaned over the desk, looking into Fleming's eyes. "Never interrupt me, son. They found the boy had been bashed on his head. Thought it kind of peculiar, so they figured they would check to see if foul play was possible. Jog your memory now, boy?"

Fuck, Fleming shouted in his head. "No worries, Senator, I'll take care of it. We're still good to go."

"I have my doubts about that, boy. I already took care of the problem." Denton took a deep breath before continuing, "All I asked of you was to get some legislation passed, and we'd all get what we want. I would control the dredge, and you would get my support in the next Governor's race. I told you this plan of yours to get control of oyster leases was unnecessary and probably stupid, and it looks like I was right."

"Control of the oyster leases gives us more influence on where dredging takes place, plus we can use those leases..."

"Let me stop you right there. I don't want to hear nothing

else other than 'yessir' from you. Clean up your house, son, or I will. That includes dealin' with your brother-in-law. We on the same page?"

"Yes sir," was all Fleming said.

Denton turned and walked toward the door. "Bless your heart, motherfucker."

MATT AND KELLY SAT at the conference table in his office, across from Ms. Evelyn Patton. Ms. Patton had been living in Topsail Beach since the early 1980's. She was a long-standing member of the only church in town, a board member for the local historical society, and president of the Women's Bridge Club. And now, local pickleball advocate. Needless to say, Ms. Patton carried a lot of influence in the town.

She walked into the office with a scowl on her face, but she softened as she accepted a cup of coffee from Kelly.

"Pickleball is a serious sport, Mr. Sheehan," Ms. Patton said. Her quiet, almost gentle voice made it hard for Matt to connect the topic to the person. "When our group goes out to play, we follow the rules as established by the USA Pickleball Association. So, you can imagine how frustrating it can be when groups of people are out there just hitting the ball all willy-nilly with no regard to the sanctity of the sport."

Matt refused to look at Kelly, fearing he would break down laughing. "I can certainly understand your frustration, Ms. Patton, I surely do. But you have to understand that these are public courts, free for anyone to use. As long as they aren't being destructive or threatening, they can reasonably use the courts."

Ms. Patton seemed to ignore everything Matt said. "We would like you to post these rules at the courts." She handed him a hand-written list of what he assumed came from some website. He figured she didn't print it out because she had never actually hooked up a printer.

"Ms. Patton, even if the commissioners adopted these rules, we have no way of enforcing it."

"You can use the police to arrest the little bastards." Matt raised his eyebrows. Ms. Patton reached across the table and patted Matt's hand. "I know you can do it, you're such a sweet man. Sooner rather than later, OK?"

With that, she got up and left, saying goodbye to both Matt and Kelly. After a moment, Kelly looked at Matt with a huge grin.

"I believe the Pickleball Mafia just sent you a message."

"I feel like I should expect a shark's head in my bed tonight," Matt said. "This day is already in the shitter, and it's not even noon."

DAN TREKOR SAT IN HIS OFFICE at the Slaggers compound looking over the financials for The Salt Marsh, a restaurant that was one of several subsidiaries of Slaggers Inc. Matt and Dan originally set up Slaggers Inc. as an offshore shell company to hide some ill-gotten gains, but as time went on, they were able to parlay that into successful, legitimate businesses, all without revealing who actually owned Slaggers Inc.

It was a large office, well-appointed but quite comfortable

in a business casual way. While it included the standard office desk, it also had a sitting area off to the side, allowing for a more informal conversation area. There was a wet bar in that corner as well.

It was just before noon when one of the UNCW grad students, currently doing research at the compound's facilities, knocked on Dan's door. The door was open, but Brittany knocked anyway.

The October morning had warmed up, so Brittany was wearing a pair of shorts and a bikini top. That was not unusual, but the concerned look on Brittany's face was, Dan noted.

"Mr. Trekor, there is a lady outside looking for you or Mr. Sheehan, I think?" she said meekly.

"You think?" he responded, eyebrows raised.

Brittany hesitated a bit, as if wondering how to say the next sentence. "She wants to know where 'the shanty Irishman and his dirtbag friend' are. Those were her exact words. She's kind of scary."

Dan tightened his lips, trying to hide his smile. "Did she say anything else?"

"No." She hesitated again before adding, "but she did call me sugartits."

Dan covered his mouth as he tried to stifle a laugh. "You can send her to me."

Brittany stood in the doorway for a little longer, looking down at the floor.

"Anything else?" Dan asked

She shuffled her feet, continuing to look down. "Is Tanner in today?"

Dan couldn't help but smile wide. All the female grad students wanted to know when Tanner was around. "Yeah, he's around here somewhere. Do you want me to tell him you're looking for him?"

Brittany turned red in embarrassment. "No, no, I'll find him later. I have to go back out in the field."

As Brittany turned to leave, the lady walked up from behind and startled her. "Jaysus, Sugartits, I could die from exposure by the time you get your ass in gear." Brittany stared back at her in sheer horror. "That's your cue, darling, bye bye."

Brittany looked quickly at Dan, then turned to leave, wanting out of the office as quickly as possible.

Katie Kenny stood in the doorway of Dan's office, all five foot six inches of her. Like Matt Sheehan, she was second generation Irish-American, complete with short auburn hair and amazing large, emerald-colored eyes. A small group of freckles crossed the bridge of her nose, a poster child for Ireland if ever there was one.

"Well, hello, Katie, it's been a while. Glad to see you haven't changed. Come on in and have a seat."

"You don't seem to be surprised, almost like you were expecting me."

"Oh, I am very surprised, shocked in fact. But the way Brittany described my visitor, it could only be you."

She smiled. "What gave me away?"

"I dunno, 'Shanty Irishman, dirtbag friend, sugartits', pick one," Dan responded.

She shrugged and changed the subject. "Surrounding yourself with coeds I see. Aren't you and Matt a little old for that game? Seems borderline pedophilia, you old goat."

Dan laughed. "It's not like that, Katie, not at all. The university uses this property for environmental and marine research, and we're happy to oblige. Plus, Matt and I know our limits, trust me." Dan looked at her for a moment, amazed that the years had been so kind to her.

After a few seconds, Dan continued, "What are you doing here?"

Katie pouted, her lower lip jutting out slightly. "'Hello Katie, it's so good to see you. How've you been? You look great, I hope everything's going well.' Jesus, Trek, have you lost all your social graces?"

Dan raised his hands up defensively. "Hello Katie, it's good to see you, how've you been? Blah blah blah. What the fuck are you doing here?" He hesitated for a moment. "And how did you know to come here?"

Katie rolled her eyes at Dan. "Really? Slaggers Inc. 'You know my name, look up the number?' How many times did you and Matt sing that stupid song in college? I doubt the Beatles sang it as much as you two. Once I heard some company named Slaggers owned land on Topsail Beach, it didn't take long for me to figure it out. How you two feckin' morons are still alive amazes me."

"OK, I know the how. Still don't know why you're here."

"A girl can't come for a visit?"

"After nearly thirty years, no. It's my experience that there is always a reason. And by the way, you look amazing."

About that time another man walked into the office. "Dan, have you seen my dad? I texted him, but he didn't answer. We've got a problem with some newly proposed legislation..." He stopped when he realized someone else was in the office. "I am so sorry to interrupt. I'll come back later."

Katie stared at the man intently, almost like she'd seen a ghost. Her mouth was open slightly as she stared, eyes wide and at a loss for words. Dan smiled again, and began to speak.

"Katie, I would like you to meet..." he didn't get to finish.

Katie raised her hands towards her mouth. "Matt's son," she said.

The young man looked confused, but extended his hand. "Tanner Sheehan, nice to meet you." Katie took his hand, but continued to stare. "No doubt you are your father's child," she finally said.

Dan shrugged. "Matt was a bit softer at that age, but I guess there's a resemblance."

"Shut the fuck up, Trek," Katie responded. She turned back to Tanner. "I'm Katie Kenny, an old family friend. Pleasure to meet you."

"Well, if you're an old family friend, I look forward to talking to you more. Will you be staying in the area for a while?"

Dan interrupted, "We're not even sure why she's here."

"Would you shut the fuck up, Trek, Jaysus," Katie replied.

Tanner smiled at the banter. "Either way, I look forward to seeing you again."

"Same," Katie responded. As Tanner turned to leave, Katie called back. "Oh, and Sugartits is looking for you."

Tanner laughed as he walked down the hall.

"It was a long drive from Charlotte, and I'm hungry," Katie told Dan. "I would love some good seafood if you know a place."

"I think I know a place. How about I take you there, my treat."

"That sounds great. I can follow you in my car."

Dan snickered. "We're not going by car, darling."

They walked to the docks on the sound side of the property. Dan helped Katie step into his Carolina Skiff, and they took off down Banks Channel towards the Intracoastal Waterway. The water was calm, and Dan took the ride slowly so that they could enjoy the sun and breeze. He maneuvered around other boats' wakes, so that Katie wouldn't be bounced around.

They arrived at the dock of the Salt Marsh, and Dan pulled into a slot marked reserved. Katie noticed the sign as they tied down the boat. She looked at Dan and raised her eyebrows. "It's OK," Dan said, anticipating the question, "I know the owner."

"Let me guess, is it possibly owned by Slaggers Inc.?"

Dan shrugged and led her up the dock towards the building. Before they got to the door, they were greeted by the hostess. "Hello Mr. Trekor," she said, her wide smile showing off perfect white teeth. "We weren't expecting you for lunch today." She glanced over at Katie. "Just the two of you?"

"Hi Emma, yep just the two of us. How's business been?"

"Last week was really busy, especially for the shoulder season." She was referring to the period after Labor Day, but before winter. Still some tourists, but not peak season. "If we stay clear of any storms, I think it could be one of our best years."

"Fantastic. Sounds like the Salt Marsh will be able to stay open the whole offseason."

"Looks like it, I know the staff hopes so. Your usual table?"

"Yes, thank you. And let's go ahead and order two shrimp burgers with plantains on the side." Dan turned to Katie. "I don't usually order for others, but I know you are going to love the shrimp burger."

"I also have beer from Mad Mole Brewing for you. I know you'll want the amber with the shrimp burger today. How about you, miss, can I get you a drink?"

"Well," Katie said with slight exaggeration, "It sounds like Mad Mole is the way to go, wouldn't you say, Mr. Trekor?"

Emma smiled and led them to a table on the porch overlooking the water. Once she left, Dan shook his head at Katie and sighed.

"What?" She looked at him with feigned innocence.

Dan looked at her, eyebrows furrowed slightly. "Katie, why are you here?"

"Would you relax, Dan, I'm here looking into an issue for a cousin of mine. He has an oyster farm or some damn thing, and there's an interested buyer. He asked me to check it out. When I found out you guys were down here, I thought I'd say hello."

"And?"

"And to see Matt, OK? Goddammit, Trek, what's the problem?"

"The problem is, he hasn't seen or heard from you in nearly thirty years. It wasn't exactly easy for him when you left. He's been through a lot of shit in that time."

"It was a long time ago, Trek, and I was hurting too. I'm not the banshee you're making me out to be." She blew out her breath. "I loved Matt, whether y'all believe that or not. We were moving in different directions."

Katie took a moment to compose herself. "I know he married, and I know she died. As of today, I know he has a son. What else am I missing?"

Dan gave her a slight smile, not really sad, more thoughtful. "A lot. Some of it very sad, but much more of it was great. He's in a really good spot now."

Emma brought over their shrimp burgers and beer. "Can I get you two anything else?"

Katie answered, a little too sharply: "No, thank you. We'll let you know if we need anything."

Dan looked at Emma apologetically. "We're fine Emma, thanks." He looked back at Katie with a frown.

"I'm sorry, OK?" Katie's eyes pleaded with Dan. "Go on with your story."

"Matt met Hannah in a bar one night, as he was running a small time con on some poor unsuspecting chump." Dan chuckled before he continued, "The poor bastard turned out to be Hannah's date, and she was happy to be rid of him.

"Matt was enamored with Hannah, the first person he showed any interest in since you, Katie. Hannah found Matt charming, as everyone does, but eventually she realized that he was a grifter. It didn't matter to her that his victims were all despicable people, she would not be involved with him. Hannah worked as an advocate for the Southeastern Conservancy and Environmental Law Group and was quite serious about her work. Much of what she did involved lobbying state and federal elected officials, so she could not be associated with criminal activity, no matter how noble Matt tried to make it sound. He had fallen hard for her, so he stopped conning people. He actually went legit. She found him a job doing investigations for another law firm where he could use his unique skills."

"Wait a minute," Katie said, "he went legit for her? That little shit."

"Matt learned a lot after you, Katie, maybe a little too late for the two of you," Dan responded. "Can I finish?"

Katie nodded as Dan continued with his story: "Matt and Hannah eventually got married and had two children; a daughter, Sedona, and a son, Tanner. They moved to Wilmington where Hannah could focus on coastal environmental issues, her passion. Matt's skills at getting people to trust and believe in him, and therefore confide in him, well, they were in demand by several law firms. He could write his own ticket. But at the end of the day, Matt's universe revolved around Hannah and the kids. He was as involved in his family as anyone I ever knew. Family vacations, kids sporting events, the whole nine yards."

"Jaysus, Mary, and Joseph, spare me the Hallmark Love Story."

"You wanted the story, that's a part you really need to understand. They truly were that family. Shit, I kinda missed the old Matt, my drinking buddy and partner in crime. But he was happy, and I wasn't gonna fuck that up for him."

"So what happened?"

"Do you remember the stories that came out about hog waste in eastern North Carolina?" Dan asked.

Katie nodded.

"Well, Hannah was one of the leads working on that very issue. She had lobbied hard in Raleigh about the environmental threats that came with the hog industry, but many coastal representatives knew how important the industry was to the eastern part of the state, especially with tobacco taking a hit. Many environmental concerns related to the industry were being ignored. In order to make any impact, Hannah knew she would have to show the blatant abuses going on in the industry to bring more exposure to the problem. She found exactly what she was looking for with one of the largest hog farms in the state."

Dan looked around as the restaurant began to fill up inside. He wanted more privacy for the rest of the conversation, knowing it was going to be hard. They ordered another round of beer and moved outside to one of the picnic tables.

"Hannah had been getting reports of groundwater contamination, increased number of fish kills, and algal blooms identified by area riverkeepers. What I think was the final push for her was when they found out that ammonia levels in the area of the Nahunta Swamp were more than twelve times the allowable limit. Hannah discovered that though there were several sources, the most egregious violations came from a facility called Magnolia

Plantation. It was a hog farm owned by the Sampson Family, whose roots in eastern North Carolina go back to the 1700's.

"What Hannah found out was nothing short of horrendous. Magnolia Plantation was supposed to be treating the waste, claiming it was capturing methane to be converted to electricity. Honestly, I don't know the details, I just know it didn't work as well as they thought. But in the case of Magnolia Plantation, they were using the system to cover up other violations. The waste in the lagoons not only included hog manure and urine, but liquified pig carcasses, cast-off deli products, and God knows what else."

"So all this stuff was getting into the wetlands? Where in the hell were the regulating agencies in all this?"

Dan shrugged. "Regulating agencies are only as good as the support they get, and Republican leadership has cut most of the regulations. The Sampsons were very powerful at the time, and as a result, many of the coastal lawmakers looked the other way. Other state legislators weren't aware of the magnitude of the problem or just didn't care because it wasn't in their districts. All they saw was renewable energy from the methane, they didn't pay attention to the rest."

Katie felt a shiver. "I don't like where this is going."

"It's fucking heartbreaking," Dan replied. He took a big gulp of his beer, taking the moment to gather himself for the rest of the story.

"Hannah couldn't believe the abuses she discovered the more she dug into the matter. With the support of the Southeastern Conservancy, she went to the legislators first to try to get enforcement of existing laws, but also to lobby for greater regulatory requirements for the hog farming industry. When she couldn't make any headway with the coastal lawmakers, she took her platform to others, particularly the Mecklenburg County and Wake County delegations. That infuriated a lot of people, most notably the Sampson Family.

"Elijah Sampson was head of the family and often held court at his home with various powerbrokers in the state. Magnolia Farms was largely operated by his son, Jacob, deep in the family business as well. They knew they couldn't afford this kind of publicity, especially as they were working to increase their production of pork products and methane gas sales. The power companies would not want to be part of any environmental controversy, and the Sampsons were beginning to feel the heat. They stood to lose millions, and Elijah was not about to let that happen, especially at the hands of some environmental nobody. Elijah and Jacob knew they had to do something drastic to save the family empire."

Dan took another big draw of his beer before continuing, "Hannah was driving home from Raleigh after meeting with the Mecklenburg County delegation. She was going to meet with one of the riverkeepers in Duplin County, so she was driving on one of the two-lane back highways instead of I-40." Dan paused, wiping the tears from his eyes with a napkin. "Hannah's car was found half submerged in a swampy area off the road, her body trapped inside. Police said she fell asleep driving."

Katie put her hand to her mouth, and she could feel the tears well in her own eyes. She could see Dan's pain and felt sorrow for a woman she never met. She was speechless.

Dan was staring out at the water, although his mind was elsewhere. They sat in silence for what seemed an eternity until Dan spoke again.

"Matt was utterly destroyed."

"I don't think I want to hear any more," Katie said through tears.

"I don't particularly want to relive it myself, but you should hear the rest. You wanted to know what you were missing, well here it is.

"Matt went into a deep tailspin. He was drinking all the time, eventually losing his job. Sedona was seventeen at the time, Tanner maybe fourteen. Poor Sedona was a high school senior. She lost her mother, and her father was a basket case. Most of the time she was either dragging Matt out of bars or playing mother to Tanner. Matt went back to running small time cons to pay the bills, but mostly to pay his bar tab. This went on for months.

"I tried to help, but Matt just pushed me away. Hell, I even once tried to get him a hooker, figured maybe if he got laid, he would loosen up. Instead, he punched me in the mouth." Dan laughed a sad laugh, shaking his head at his own stupidity. "Even then, I didn't appreciate the depth of feeling he had for Hannah."

Again, he took a moment before continuing, "I would help Sedona where I could, but that poor child was drowning herself. Imagine having your mother taken away from you like that and then have your father lose it. I wish I had her strength."

"So where is she now?" Katie asked.

"She finally did what she had to do, or end up in the same abyss as Matt. She dragged him out of a bar one night and told him she was leaving. She said she was heading to college in Montana and if he had an ounce of love for her or Tanner, he would get his shit together. It wasn't a bluff, and he knew it. She left a week later."

Katie grabbed hold of Dan's hand; her tear-filled eyes wide. "Does Matt ever hear from her?" Her voice was almost a whisper.

"Oh, hell yes, they talk all the time. It's kind of annoying actually."

"God, you are a fecking tool, Trek."

Dan smiled. "I told you much of the story is really great," he said.

"So, is there more?"

"A lot. But for the sake of time, I'm gonna give you the abridged version. Once Sedona left, Matt got his shit together, basically. He stopped the con games, and he and I started our own business providing general consulting services to local governments. We handled things like grant writing, facilitation, shit like that. We were very good at getting two sides together to address anything from notices of violation to public-private partnerships. We were mostly middlemen, but if you claim to be a consultant, elected officials will hire you for anything. Matt was back to being a father to Tanner, going to all his baseball games, you know, just generally being there again. And he made that reconnection with Sedona.

"It was going well until one day, I guess about three years later, he got word from an anonymous source that Hannah's death wasn't an accident. Matt always thought the circumstances were strange, he knew Hannah wouldn't have been driving if she was sleepy, but he was too busy wallowing to think about it."

"Not an accident? Are you saying she was murdered?"

"That's right. Matt's source said Hannah was forced off the road, and intentionally blocked from getting out of the car. Hannah drowned, which is about the only thing the police got right. I can't even imagine what those last moments were like for Hannah."

Dan looked down at his feet, an ache in his heart he felt whenever he thought about it. He heard Katie sniffle and felt her hand rest on his shoulder.

"Anyway," he cleared his throat as he continued, "Matt knew this was the Sampsons' doing, but authorities wouldn't listen.

It was an accident as far as they were concerned, and it was not going to be reopened."

"Who was this anonymous source? Did Matt ever find out?"

"Nope. Over time we guessed it was some guilt-ridden witness or party to the crime."

"So what did y'all do?"

"Matt did what he does best. He got me and a few other old friends and devised the most brilliant con I ever had the privilege to participate in. It was a masterpiece."

"Oh shit." Katie's eyes went wide.

"The details are for another day, but Matt went straight after the Sampsons. In short, once the con was over, we had sent north of $75 million to an offshore account."

"Let me guess, Slaggers Inc."

Dan just tapped his nose with his index finger. "On top of that, when it was all done, Matt found a way to get both Elijah and Jacob Sampson charged under the RICO Act. Elijah died of a heart attack before serving time, but Jacob got twenty years."

"Did you guys feel responsible for the old man's death? I mean cons don't usually lead to fatalities."

"Elijah Sampson called for Hannah's death. The piece of shit got off easy. We know Jacob was at the site; the son of a bitch watched her die. That bastard is lucky to be in jail."

Katie took a deep breath. "At least Matt got justice for Hannah."

Dan's eyes went cold, almost as if cloaked in death. "Matt doesn't see it that way. Make no mistake, if Jacob Sampson gets out of prison, Matt will kill him."

ALEX SPENCER III KNEW what everyone thought of him. He heard the whispers. "Trust fund brat." "Lazy." "Spoiled...stupid...useless." It was "useless" that hurt most, even more than "stupid."

He was the youngest of three siblings: an older brother who graduated from Chapel Hill's Dental School and now has his own practice, and a sister who had a successful career in marketing before marrying a state senator. His parents were so proud.

Then there was Alex. Lazy, spoiled, useless Alex. But he wasn't lazy; he just didn't fit the predetermined role of a Spencer. He wanted to be a chef. From an early age, he spent more time with the family cook than he did with his mother. One year for Christmas he asked Santa for an Easy Bake Oven. He got boxing gloves and sparring lessons instead.

Even in his teenage years, he wanted to work at a restaurant, but his father wouldn't hear of it. He wanted to go to Johnson and Wales University for culinary school, but his family refused. If he wouldn't get serious about a respectable career, then his father would take him under his wing in the real estate business. Alex knew his father meant well, but they just didn't understand each other.

Alex tried to make it work, to make his father proud. But he hated real estate, and he was terrible at sales. From day one, he was the lowest rated salesperson on the team. "Lazy," everyone whispered. "If it wasn't for daddy..." "Useless."

In the end, it's why Alex started using drugs. If I'm always going to be looked at as useless, he thought, I might as well embrace the life. It's how he met Willie.

It's how he wound up in the mess he was in now.

FOR THE REST OF THE MORNING, Matt tried to focus on other town business. While his meeting with the 'Don of the Pickleball Mafia' seemed harmless, Matt knew the issue wouldn't die. It was only a matter of time before the group of dedicated pickleballers would put pressure on the elected officials, who would ultimately task Matt to come up with a solution. With all the other daily town functions, it had the makings of a busy afternoon.

Matt saw he missed a text from Tanner, so he gave him a call.

"I wanted to give you a heads-up, Pops," Tanner said. "A friend in the legislative building got wind of some draft legislation related to dredging and beach nourishment and thought it might be of interest. I've read it and believe it could have some serious repercussions on the Topsail Beach 30-Year Plan."

"How so?"

"In short, as written now it would impact state and federal funding access and use of private dredge companies."

"That can't be right, for one thing, this isn't the time to submit new legislation anyway."

"All I know is, something is in the works," Tanner replied. "I've sent a copy to Chris Taylor, and he agrees we need to discuss this now before it gets legs. He's on his way over to the office. Can you come by?"

Matt looked at his watch. "Yeah, I can come over. Tell you what, I'll pick up some sandwiches at the deli and meet you there."

Matt thought it might be a nice diversion from the other nonsense that started his day. He called in the lunch order, thinking he could just run in and pick it up.

Wrong again.

"I'm glad I ran into you, Mr. Sheehan." The unpleasant voice belonged to longtime resident Clara Yarbrough. "I have a bone to pick with you."

Mrs. Yarbrough's family purchased an oceanfront lot back in the 1970's with the expectation that the little island town would never change once they moved in, not an entirely uncommon thought among some of the older residents.

"Hi, Mrs. Yarbrough, it's good to see you. Unfortunately, I have a meeting to get to, so can we get together later?"

"The sandwiches are cold anyways, ain't they? Your people can wait a few extra minutes."

Matt knew this was a battle he wasn't going to win, so he just smiled. "What can I do for you?"

"I want to know why you still haven't done anything about all these people that park in the lot next to my house and then sit on my beach. I've been complaining about it forever, and I want something done."

Matt could see the owner of the sandwich shop snickering. "We've been through this, Mrs. Yarbrough. The beach in front of your house is public trust land, you don't own it."

"I own the walkway from my house to the beach," she said defiantly.

"Yes ma'am, you do. Is anyone using it that isn't supposed to be?"

"No, but they put the chairs and blankets out in front of it."

"They can, that's the public trust part. And the lot beside you is owned by the town for public access to the beach. People are allowed to park there."

She rolled her eyes and shook her head. "Well at least make 'em pay to park there, maybe that will keep those people away."

"I'm sorry, 'those people,' Mrs. Yarbrough?" Matt knew he shouldn't go there, but he despised the bigotry.

She looked around before she answered. "Yes, 'those people,' the undesirables. They come and trash our beach and don't pay taxes to the town like I do."

Matt had enough. "Look Mrs. Yarbrough, it's the town board who decides if we have paid parking or not. If I have anything at all to say about it, I would tell them not to do it. The beach should be for everyone. And by the way, they do pay taxes that, ultimately, we benefit from. And I have yet to see anyone trash our beach."

"You're useless," she said and stormed out the door.

"Life in a beach town," the shop owner offered.

Matt walked into the conference room at the Slaggers Compound, lunch in hand. The building was home to Southern Shores Consulting, the firm Matt and Dan started, now run by Tanner, who had expanded its services to include lobbying. He had taken the business to a new level, adding additional staff as well as offices in Morehead City and Raleigh. Southern Shores Consulting had projects for communities from Delaware to Florida and along the Gulf Coast to Texas. He was only twenty-five, but he already secured over $30 million in state and federal funds for Topsail Beach for beach nourishment. But mostly, Tanner made sure the company maintained an environment-first philosophy. He was a combination of his mother's passion and his father's ability to work the system.

Matt knew the best way for Topsail Beach to succeed was

to hire Southern Shores to handle its beach nourishment program. He conveniently danced around the ethical question of hiring a firm managed by his son. Technically, Southern Shores Consulting was a subsidiary of Slaggers Inc., and no one had traced the ownership of Slaggers to anyone in particular. It was not a con; Matt wasn't trying to fleece the town. In his mind, it was the right solution to an ongoing problem.

And it worked too. Topsail Beach had one of the most successful beach nourishment programs in the nation that not only created a wider beach but one designed to reduce the impact of storms and coastal erosion. It was designed to recycle its sand instead of mining it from offshore sites and had environmental safeguards such as sea turtle monitoring and improved protection for shellfish development. This made US Fish and Wildlife happy, which was always a plus.

On top of all this, it was much cheaper than the US Army Corps of Engineers' process, which made FEMA happier.

"Alright, what's so important that you had to call me away from town hall?" Matt asked, half-jokingly.

"What's on the agenda today, Pops, devising a plan on how to keep those evil day trippers away from the public beaches?" Tanner asked with a smirk. "I mean heaven forbid the people who help pay for the beach actually get to use it."

"Very funny. You know not everyone in this town is opposed to day trippers. Most understand that it is public trust beaches."

Tanner smiled. "We'll see when the paid parking is discussed by the board."

It was some good-natured ribbing, but unfortunately with a bit of truth. There were some residents, including an elected official or two, that thought Topsail Beach should be a private community, limiting visitors to those who rented homes, and not those who just come for the day. The argument was that day trippers don't contribute to the tax base, just place demands on services. What is conveniently left out was the amount of tax dollars the town receives from the state and federal government, paid by these day trippers. Like the $30 million the town received.

Tanner handed Matt a copy of the draft legislation. "This is the document I was telling you about," he said. "It's a draft, not even distributed to most legislators. The aide that gave it to me knew that even though it was in the early stages of development, it will have a huge impact if it moves forward."

Matt could only guess how Tanner commanded such loyalty in the legislative building. Sure, he was a lobbyist, but to get his hands on documents that are in the early stages of development was nearly impossible, especially if the proposal was controversial. Tanner would have to have aides that were more loyal to him than the representatives they worked for.

Matt read through the document twice, shaking his head. After the second time through, he looked up at Tanner and Chris. "What the fuck?"

"If this legislation, or some version of it, gets passed, it will likely destroy our program," Chris said. "Right now, we basically decide how and when to move forward with our projects, but this will force us to follow whatever state directive legislators choose if we want any federal or state funding."

"Who's sponsoring this bill?"

"No names attached to it yet," Tanner answered, "but it appears to be coming from Senator Strickland's office."

"That makes no sense, why would Strickland want this? He's got beach communities in Brunswick County that could be adversely impacted. I never liked the guy, but he's not stupid."

"Agreed, Pops," Tanner said. "We don't want this to gain any momentum. Let me ask around to see if I can get a better handle on it."

Matt rubbed his fingers across his forehead. "OK, walk me through this, guys. I need to be clear on the details if we're going to fight this."

"Alright," Chris started, "for a long time, the Corps was the only game in town for communities to do significant beach nourishment projects. There were a lot of reasons for this, but a big one had to do with the availability of dredges. As you know, we have to use US-owned dredges by law, and there are only a few US-owned private dredge companies big enough to handle major projects. It's not a huge deal for most North Carolina coastal communities because they already work with the Corps through their fifty-year project."

"Your point, Chris?"

"Our program doesn't use the Corps; we contract out the dredging. We can do that because we established an engineered beach as defined by FEMA to become eligible for disaster funds directly. Most importantly, our program is about half the cost of the Corps projects. It kind of pissed them off, but they had no basis to argue.

"Staff worked with the state to create the Inlet Recovery Fund, designed to provide funding for coastal communities to help keep the smaller shallow draft inlets open for boat travel, critical to the economy of the coast. We used those funds, along with federal disaster monies to get our program up and running. As you know, we've continued to use disaster funds and IRF funds to improve the process with considerable success, but not everyone was a fan."

Matt waved his hands. "I know all this Chris. What does this legislation mean to us?"

"Bear with me. You know the state built its own dredge, paid for in large part by the IRF, right?"

"Yeah, but I don't see Topsail Beach ever using it."

"I thought the same, unless this proposed legislation goes through. As I read this draft legislation, any state funds, including the IRF, are only available to communities that utilize the *Chinquapin* or are part of a Corps project. That certainly impacts our program financially."

Matt rubbed his chin. "That leaves us with just FEMA dollars."

"Keep reading, Pops," Tanner said. "It goes way beyond withholding state funds. It also limits any activity in federally designated channels, which includes our inlet and parts of Banks Channel. It regulates any FEMA disaster funds from storms. It even limits the use of federal and state spoils sites."

Chris shrugged. "As written now, it ends our program. We can't fully fund our work without these dollars, and access to federal channels is critical as a sand source," he said.

"Jaysus, Mary and Joseph, how the hell is this possible? How can the state legislate FEMA disaster funds, that's federal?"

"That part is certainly questionable, but remember that in a disaster all funds go through the state once FEMA determines eligibility. FEMA authorizes, but the state appropriates. I think that provision can be challenged, but who knows how long that would take."

Matt looked at Tanner. "You said it limits the use of spoil sites. How so?"

"In essence, it requires approval from either the Corps or the state to place dredged sands on the site. It also says that any new disposal sites that use state funds go to the Corps first. It leaves municipalities and private companies in a huge bind."

Matt shook his head. "What do we know about the dredge, Chris? Who pushed for it, who controls it?"

"In typical government fashion, lots of hands were in this pot, but it was spearheaded by Senator Denton. It was designed with the Oregon Inlet in mind, but ostensibly available for the entire state."

Tanner jumped in. "They awarded the oversight of the construction and ultimately the operations, including scheduling of the dredge to a former administrative staffer for Senator Denton, a guy named Dean Filben. Denton was huge in the push for the new dredge, which is coincidentally named the *Chinquapin*, likely after Denton's hometown. Seems he may have had a relationship with the company awarded the construction contract. Surprise.

"On top of all this, Filben is a brainless lackey. He has zero experience with dredging, beach nourishment, or pretty much anything for that matter. He is an arrogant prick with no redeeming value. And just plain stupid, dangerously so."

Chris chimed in, "If he is in charge of the dredge and its use, it will never be based on merit, only on spite and greed."

"How is Denton involved in all this, isn't he retired now?" Matt asked.

"He still wields a lot of influence, thus the appointment of Filben," Tanner responded.

Matt knew something was very wrong. This legislation made no sense. Why would Senator Strickland want this legislation when it could hurt his constituency, and why was Denton involved? Is this what Eberhart was talking about with the spoil sites? He needed more answers.

"Tanner, see what else you can find out from your contacts, like if any other elected officials are involved, if the Corps has a role, anything you think may be relevant. Chris, can you put together a comprehensive impact analysis for us if this goes through? Also, any arguments that show our program is far more suitable than the alternative. Most importantly, this stays with us. I'm not ready for the mayor or the commissioners getting involved."

"You got it, Pops," Tanner replied. "You got something in mind?"

"Just a lot of shit that adds up to nothing."

AFTER LUNCH, DAN WENT INSIDE to talk to the kitchen staff while Katie waited outside on the docks near the boat. It had been a while since she had been to the coast and had forgotten how the little things about it brought so much joy, the feeling of the salt air on her skin, the warm sun on her neck and shoulders. The sea breeze brought the smell of the marshes with it, earthy and slightly fishy. She smiled to herself as she remembered as a kid thinking it smelled like crab butts. She liked the feel of the floating dock gently rocking back and forth under her feet. There was something soothing about the motion, like an infant swaying in its mother's arms, safe and warm. She needed that feeling after hearing Dan's story, so she closed her eyes in hopes that all that troubled her would magically disappear.

The spell was broken when Emma, the hostess from earlier, came up to her.

"Did you enjoy everything, ma'am?" she asked Katie.

Jaysus, I'm ma'am now, Katie thought. "It was fine, thanks."

"Mr. Trekor is a great boss, always checking in on us, making sure we have everything we need. He made me manager even though I had no formal experience."

Emma paused for a moment, expecting some sort of response from Katie, but it never came. "Have you known him long?" she asked.

Katie was still trying to wrap her head around the earlier conversation with Dan. "Huh? Um, yeah, I've known him for years."

"You're very lucky," Emma said. She was looking down now, and Katie started to figure things out.

"Oh, darling it's not like that. We're just friends."

"I didn't mean..."

Katie cut her off, "If you're sweet on him, then make the first move. God knows he won't."

Emma stood there confused.

"Dan is a little old school," Katie said. "And by that, I mean he will see an age difference and feel like he shouldn't be interested even if he is."

"I'm not a kid," Emma responded. "It's not that big an age difference."

Katie began losing patience. "Look, if you like him, ask him out. I don't really give a fuck, I'm not a matchmaker." She realized how harsh she sounded. "Sorry, it's not my best day."

Dan came back out as Emma went hustling back in, eyes on the ground. Dan scowled at Katie.

Katie gave him her best innocent look with her big eyes wide. "What'd I do?"

He wanted to lighten the mood after their lunch, so Dan took Katie for a boat ride. There was a warm breeze from the southwest, and the water was smooth with very little chop, near perfect conditions. After such heavy conversation, Dan felt like a trip on the water would soothe their battered souls.

They left the Salt Marsh and took the Intracoastal Waterway towards Wrightsville Beach, but in the process, Dan turned the boat down some of the creeks that wound through the marshes. As they made their way in and around the area, Katie noticed how alive the marshes were, particularly with different species of birds. She also noticed what looked like small buoys in the water.

"What's with all the floaties in the water?" she asked.

"Some of them are crab traps that local fishermen set out," Dan answered. "Some of those markers are for oyster leases, probably like your cousin's place."

Dan slowed the boat down but made sure not to get too close to the markers. "You know, a lot of what Matt and I did as consultants emphasized environmental protections and causes, particularly with marsh preservation and clean water efforts. We developed partnerships with several non-profit agencies and worked on funding opportunities for things like living shorelines versus sea walls wherever feasible."

"I've read about the possible damage dredging and beach nourishment does to the natural habitat and that some experts believe it's a fool's errand trying to rebuild beaches that mother nature is just going to take anyway. Isn't that some of the work you guys do?"

"You've done some homework, I see," Dan said with a chuckle. "Yes, at least Matt and Tanner are more involved in those projects. They are pragmatic about their approach to issues, recognizing that there has to be a balance between environmental preservation and the realistic demands of development in the coastal region. It's a tough line to follow, but with every venture they take on, they look for a way to focus on the best environmental results."

"Don't take this wrong, Dan, but it sounds a little self-serving. Who is drawing that line between reasonable development and environmental protection?"

Dan nodded. "It's a fair question. Honestly, we try to involve parties on both sides of the spectrum and figure it out from there. I will say that as an organization, we will more often fall on the side of preservation if you want our involvement.

"But enough about the Matt and Dan story, what have you been doing since we last spoke, what nearly thirty years ago?" Dan said, his tone more amused than accusing.

"Cute. I see you haven't changed much, still an arse," she said with a smile.

"Just tryin' to figure things out is all."

"I know what you're trying to do, Dan, and I appreciate the subtle grilling. You're trying to protect Matt. I truly am here to help my cousin, but I want to see Matt. Maybe I need to."

Dan nodded before he spoke again. "Matt's more than a brother to me. When we met you in college, I knew immediately that Matt was done. And it was OK, it was like an expansion of my family. I loved you like a sister; I still do, I suppose. But Matt is part of me, his joy is mine, and his pain is too."

Katie started to respond but thought otherwise, deciding to answer his first question, "I went to Chapel Hill and got my master's in accounting. It turns out, I have a knack for forensic accounting, so I eventually started my own firm.

"I thoroughly enjoy my job, especially when I can nail some shithead white collar douchebag stealing from people in need," Katie said, her eyes lighting up as she grinned.

"What about family life?"

"Oh, you know, met a boy, had a daughter."

"Oh hell, another little you!"

"Claire is probably more like her father than me. She's in col-lege, UNC Charlotte believe it or not. We are close, although there are the usual mother/daughter conflicts."

"I didn't hear the 'got married' part." Dan rarely missed anything.

"That's because I didn't," Katie said. "Dennis is a good man and a great father to Claire, but it just wasn't right between us." She thought for a second. "Likely because my Daideo never approved of anyone other than Matt, probably because they were so damn similar."

"Daideo? That can't be your father, he hated Matt."

"Grandfather," Katie answered. "It's an Irish term."

Dan turned the boat down Topsail Creek, one of the cut-throughs connecting the Intracoastal Waterway and Banks Channel, and headed towards Topsail Beach. He slowed to nearly a stop and looked at Katie for a moment before he spoke. "Do you have a place to stay while you're in town?"

"Not yet. I'll just get a hotel room somewhere nearby."

"Nope, we have a guest house at the compound that you'll love. Your car, and I assume any luggage is still there anyway, right?"

"No, I can't," she responded.

"Yes you can. Besides, I think maybe it will be good for Matt to see you too. Might as well do it with a bang."

MATT PLANNED ON SPENDING the rest of the afternoon working on his monthly report for the board of commissioners but was distracted by all the recent events. His gut told him he was missing something, or several somethings. There were a lot of questions that didn't necessarily tie together, like how could a skilled fisherman like Holt Bratton fall off his boat and drown? Why was the state all of a sudden making it difficult for local governments and private businesses to use state-owned spoil sites? Where did this proposed new legislation come from?

Matt was staring out the window, lost in thought, when Tanner walked into his office.

"You OK, Pops?"

Tanner's voice snapped Matt out of his stupor. "Huh? Oh, yeah, I'm fine, just thinking."

"Well, are you ready for more bad news?"

"No," was all Matt could muster.

"Sorry, but I just got an email from FEMA; they are denying our request for funds for Hurricane Isaias damage to the beach. Actually, they aren't denying the claims, but they are greatly reducing the award amount."

Matt sat back in his chair and grimaced as if he had been punched in the gut. "What, why?"

"The email was pretty vague, saying we would get more information in a formal denial letter. But it says the calculations were inconsistent with those developed by the Army Corps of Engineers."

"It's the same fucking formulas and calculations we used on the last three hurricanes, all approved by FEMA," Matt exclaimed, his voice rising.

"Pops, I'm with you on this, but take a deep breath. There is an appeal process, so let's wait until we get the letter to see what exactly we're dealing with. Chris was copied on the email, so I will get with him to discuss next steps."

"What's the difference between our request and what is being proposed by FEMA, do we know that much?”

“I’ll need to confirm with Chris, but based on the amount of the award in the email, I would say it’s short by around seven million.”

“Jaysus, we were only asking around ten.” Matt shook his head. “I need to run this by the mayor and the board. Can you send me a synopsis of what we know and the next steps?”

“Already on it, Pops.” Tanner started towards the door. “Do you feel like we have a target on our backs all of a sudden?”

“I do now.”

Tanner smiled. “Don’t worry old man, I got your back.”

God knows he always does, Matt thought. But now he had another question to add to his list, why is the Army Corps of Engineers messing with the town’s FEMA money?

JACK FLEMING KNEW he had to re-establish himself as the one in charge. He needed to send a message to Orville Denton that he would deliver the votes to get the dredge legislation passed. Once he showed Denton that he could persuade the other legislators, maybe that prick would back off on the oyster leases. As far as Alex and Willie were concerned, he would deal with them later.

Fleming decided he would start with the representatives from the western part of the state. Those hillbillies would do anything for a chance to look relevant, he thought.

“Sylvia,” he barked at his assistant, “who’s the chair of the Appropriations Committee?”

"Bixby Lamont."

"Is he from the mountains?"

Sylvia rolled her eyes. "Yes sir, Transylvania County." But if you bothered to get to know your peers, you'd know that, she thought.

"Get him on the phone for me."

"Well, well, if it isn't my esteemed colleague from the coast," Senator Lamont said as he answered the phone. "Is this business, or pleasure?" As if he didn't know.

"Business, Bixby. I hear you're having trouble getting funding for some much needed snow removal equipment."

"Matter of fact, a couple of your boys from the eastern part of the state are holding it up. They say it's a local matter, not one for the state."

"I think I can make that go away for you, Bixby."

"'Preciate it, Jack. But Orville Denton told me he's already on it. So if this is about that dredge stuff, not to worry. I'm sure Orville will work it out."

Son of a bitch, Jack screamed in his head. He scrambled to salvage his pride. "Shit, Bixby, Orville's retired. Who knows if he has the clout to sway those votes."

Bixby Lamont laughed. "That's funny, Jack. Short of the Good Lord hisself, nobody outdoes Orville Denton. I'll let you know if I need anything from you."

Fleming slammed his coffee mug down on his desk, breaking the handle off.

"Everything OK, sir?" Sylvia ducked her head into the doorway.

"Just fine," Fleming responded, wiping up the spilled coffee.

IT WAS CLOSE TO SIX O'CLOCK, and Matt was ready for another sunset. He was still in his office, just finishing up the last of his staff report to the commissioners when Tanner walked in. He had gone back to his place to shower and change for the evening, which Matt assumed meant a night out. He couldn't remember the last time he went out on a weeknight. Oh, to be young and have that much energy, Matt thought.

Tanner walked over to the bar cart and helped himself to some of Matt's Slane, their favorite Irish whiskey. Matt was in awe with the grace in which Tanner moved. He still had the athletic build from his baseball days in college.

Tanner sipped his drink. "You OK, Pops?"

Matt smiled back. "I'm fine, just a lot to absorb in the last twenty-four hours."

"Whatever happens, we'll figure it out. You know I do my best work under the gun."

It was true, that boy could pull shit out of his ass like no one Matt ever knew, and he knew some of the best. Even in school, Tanner seemed to be the most prepared when he appeared to give the least amount of effort.

"Sunset is soon, want to join me on the porch?" Matt asked.

"I'd love to, but Brittany and I are headed downtown for dinner and drinks with friends in just a bit. Speaking of, do you mind if we crash at your place instead of driving back? You can use my place tonight if you want." Tanner owned a small, older home on the sound side of the island at the end of Nixon Avenue.

Surrounded by water and trees, it was the perfect setting.

Matt raised his eyebrows. "Brittany?" he questioned. "You don't usually date the grad students."

"Date? Jesus, Pops, how old are you? People can just go out to dinner."

"I seriously doubt that's how Brittany is looking at it, but what do I know?" Matt knew because he saw how Brittany acted around Tanner. It didn't take a super detective to figure it out. "But yes, you can use my place, let me get the keys for you."

Tanner started laughing. "I made duplicate keys when I was still in school, old man. It was my go-to place when you weren't home. For a smart guy, you can be clueless."

Indeed, Matt thought. "By the way, I spoke to Sedona last night. She wants us to come to Montana for Thanksgiving. You in?"

"Sounds great."

"Can you give her a call and let her know? I'm sure she would love to hear from her brother."

"Yes, father," Tanner responded sarcastically.

"Maybe you can check in on how the pregnancy is going."

Tanner gave him a sheepish grin. "I guess she told you, huh?"

"Yes she did, you traitor."

"It wasn't my place to tell you, Pops. Perhaps she would have told you sooner if you weren't such a pain in the ass."

"Jaysus, when did my kids turn against me?" Matt chuckled.

Dan popped into the doorway. "Is it safe to come in?"

"Since when did you care if we're behaving?" Matt said, chuckling.

"I don't think he meant for him." It was Katie.

Matt sat there for what seemed to be an eternity. He looked back and forth between the two of them, unable to form any words. Eventually, Tanner stood up and spoke, "Hello, Ms.

Kenny. I didn't expect to see you again so soon. Please excuse my suddenly mute father."

She smiled back at Tanner. "Hi Tanner," she said. "Hello Matt."

Matt finally spoke, almost in a whisper. "Aoife" was all he could say.

Tanner looked a combination of amused and concerned. "Are you having a stroke, Pops? What's Aoife?" He pronounced it as Matt did, EE-*fa*.

"It's my name," Katie interrupted. "Aoife Kathleen Kenny. Everyone calls me Katie, except for my grandfather when he was alive and your father. The buck eejit." She turned and looked at Matt. "Can I at least get a proper greeting?"

Matt walked over to where she was still standing by the door. "Hello Aoife," he said. He didn't know whether to hug her or maybe scream at her for leaving him years ago. Instead, he just stood there. He could see the pain in her face, waiting for more from him, but there was nothing more.

Dan sighed. "Well, I don't know about y'all, but I sure could use a drink. How about you, Katie?" Without waiting for an answer, he put his hand gently on her back and led her to the bar cart. "Apparently, we have Irish whiskey or rye. I'm sure I can find some kind of mixer around here." He shot Matt a *what the fuck* look.

"Irish whiskey is fine. Neat, please."

Dan poured the drink and handed it to her, then looked at Matt again, this time with a bit of anger in his eyes. "Katie is in town to help out her cousin for a few days. I told her she can use one of the guest houses here while she's around." Matt could tell in his voice it wasn't up for discussion.

"I don't think that's a good idea," Katie said. "I'll find another place, Dan."

Dan put his hand up. "We wouldn't hear of it, would we, Matt?"

Matt looked up at Katie's face again, so many emotions running through his mind. "It's fine," he said quietly. "You can stay here."

About that time Brittany walked in looking for Tanner. She started to ask him if he was ready to go when she saw Katie standing there and froze in sheer panic. It lightened the mood of the room for the moment.

"It's alright, darling, I won't bite. Probably," Katie said as she started to laugh.

God, she's beautiful when she smiles, Matt thought.

As Tanner and Brittany left, Matt spoke up. "It's time for our sunset viewing. You can join us if you want to, Aoife."

"How can a girl pass up an offer like that?"

It was another spectacular sunset. As the sun reached the horizon, it was as if the sound caught fire, the bright orange sky meeting the blue-green waters. Matt, Dan, and Katie sat silently as they watched the sunset, nothing but the sound of Norah Jones playing softly in the background.

Afterwards, the conversation was polite but forced. They talked about the weather, current events, basically white noise. Most of the conversation was between Dan and Katie, with Matt only adding a word or two here and there. Katie tried, even asking Matt about his brothers, but his responses were as brief as possible. It was like sitting through a deposition. "The weather is nice," "My brothers are fine," "Glad tourist season is over," was about the most Matt had to offer.

The sun had been down for about an hour when Katie got up.

"Well, this has been riveting, but it's getting a little chilly out here, temperature-wise I mean," she said. "I've got an early day with my cousin, so I best be on my way. Thanks for the drink and the sunset."

"Let me walk you to the guest house," Dan said.

"I'll do it," Matt offered. "I'm staying at Tanner's place tonight, so I have to head that way to my car."

Katie and Dan exchanged glances, surprised by the offer.

They walked down the path to the guest house in silence. When they got to the front door, Katie turned to Matt. "Well, thanks for ahh…" she searched for the right words, "…well, just thanks."

"Why are you here, Aoife?"

She tilted her head. "Did you miss the part about me helping my cousin?"

"That's not what I mean. Why are you here, and not at some hotel?"

"Dan offered me…"

"Stop it, Aoife, just," Matt paused to catch himself, "stop. I want to know why you came back into my life all of a sudden."

"Back into your life? Jaysus, Matt, I was in the area and thought it might be nice to say hello."

"Oh, I see now. To say hello after, what, thirty years?"

"You can be such an arse, Matt Sheehan."

Matt shook his head slowly. "You broke my heart, Aoife. All of a sudden, you were gone."

Katie bit her lower lip to keep it from quivering. "It wasn't easy for me, you know, I was only twenty-one."

"Walking out, without so much as a note? 'Dear Matt, it's been fun, but it's time to move on.' Yeah, pretty damn hard for you, I'm sure."

The sarcasm stung. Katie took a moment to collect herself, not wanting to break down right there. "Well, apparently you did move on, Matthew Sheehan, and from what I can tell, you had a pretty fucking good life."

She opened the door to the guest house, her back to Matt. "Dear Matt, it's been fun."

She closed the door behind her.

Tuesday, October 11

THE NEXT MORNING, Matt got up and headed for the shower. As he looked into the mirror, he noticed the sadness in his eyes. It's funny how sometimes it takes your own reflection to realize how miserable you really feel, Matt thought. He was just finding that out.

"What the fuck were you thinking," he said to his reflection. "Did you have to be such a dicksmack!"

Matt thought back to when he and Katie were together. They were young, full of themselves, believing it would be like that forever. Like everyone that age. They were inseparable for a while; Matt, Katie, and Dan were the Three Amigos. Matt calling her Aoife as if he was the only one that could truly occupy her heart. And then she was gone. No warning, no tearful goodbye, just gone.

In fairness to her, Matt knew he wasn't the most ambitious person when it came to considering a real career, happy enough just getting by and running the occasional confidence game. Sure, he and Aoife talked about the future, even argued about it, but Matt was sure they would figure it out.

He should have seen it coming.

But he didn't.

Matt went to town hall determined to settle the matters at hand, most notably the lost FEMA funds and the proposed dredging legislation. He had already decided to move on from Holt Bratton's death, that was a police matter. He called the mayor, asking him to come by town hall. He needed to give him a heads-up on some of what was going on, knowing he would be anxious to take action of any kind. Matt wanted to meet the mayor in person, better to control the narrative.

Before the mayor arrived, Matt got a call from the police chief.

"Hey Boss, how are you this morning?"

"I'm good, Chief, just keepin' it above the waterline."

"I hear ya." He chuckled. The chief was the most even-keel person Matt knew. "I just wanted to let you know that I heard from the medical examiner this morning. He said they were ruling Holt's death an accidental drowning."

"I appreciate the heads-up." Well, at least there's nothing sinister going on, Matt thought. One less thing on his plate.

"I thought you would like to know," the chief responded, but Matt knew that tone. He could tell the chief had more on his mind.

The voice in Matt's head screamed *let it go*, but his mouth kept moving. "Is there something more, Chief?"

"I'm sure not, I mean I'm no medical expert." He paused. "But when the M.E. came on site to pick up the body, he mentioned that Holt had a significant contusion on the side of his head, one he felt would come from a blow from behind. When

I asked him about that this morning, he got a bit defensive, which is not like him. Said it probably came from the fall, was no big deal, and then abruptly hung up. He's probably right, it just seemed strange."

Goddammit, Matt thought.

The chief noticed Matt's hesitation. "I don't want to create any bad feelings between us and the county, you got enough on your plate as it is, Boss. Maybe we just let this go."

Matt knew him better than that. "Rob, don't worry about the county, I got that covered. What steps would you like to take?"

"Maybe just get a hold of the autopsy report, talk to Ms. Bratton about what Holt may have been up to, that kind of stuff. I'm sure the examiner is right, but I'd feel more comfortable if we followed up just to confirm. But I don't want to cause you problems."

"Do what you gotta do, Chief. As big an arse as Holt was, we owe it to him to know the truth."

The chief laughed. "'Arse'? I haven't heard that one from you. You never seem to surprise me."

If only he knew.

Shortly after Matt hung up, the mayor came into the office. He gave him a quick update on the situation with Holt Bratton.

"The county's medical examiner has ruled Holt's death an accidental drowning," he told the mayor. "But Rob has his doubts."

"Doubts?"

"More like a few unanswered questions. He's going to do some follow-up, just to make sure."

"Do I need to run interference with the county?" Mayor Davenport asked.

"It's an active case. I think it best if you and I stay clear unless any county representatives call on us." Matt knew the mayor would be itching to get involved, but to his credit he agreed not to discuss anything publicly. Of course the mayor would go straight to the chief after he left Matt's office.

Matt explained the email they received from FEMA regarding denial of their disaster assistance request. The mayor sat patiently and listened as Matt went through what he knew.

"Do you want me to reach out to our congressman?" Davenport asked.

"Not yet, let's wait until we get the formal notification. You, Chris, and I can discuss next steps then. It is probably wise to let the board know at tomorrow night's commissioners meeting. Just short and to the point. We can do it as part of a closed session since it will likely become a legal issue. There is no need to get the public in an uproar until we know more."

"I can take the lead on that," the mayor responded as he got up to leave.

Matt texted the chief to warn him that the mayor was likely coming by. It was the best he could do.

ALEX SPENCER WASN'T SURE if the paranoia he felt was real or simply due to drugs. He was pacing in Willie's living room, trying to figure out how to tell him that his brother-in-law wanted him out. When he went to Willie's house, he had every intention of telling him immediately, but Willie offered him a joint and the next thing he knew, he was high. *I bet Willie laced this with something,* he thought. His mind continued to bounce back and forth between Willie, Jack Fleming, and Holt Bratton. He started to tremble.

"Sit the fuck down, Alex," Willie barked. "You're driving me nuts. Take another hit."

"We killed a guy, Willie. I think we need to drop this treasure hunt stuff and lay low for a while, you know."

"Hell no, we're getting close. I can practically taste that gold."

"Close?" Alex cried. "All we've done is harass some fish farmers into selling leases to us, something my brother-in-law wanted. We don't have any idea where the treasure is."

"I've been thinking about that. Maybe that gold is at one of these leases, and your brother-in-law knows which one, but he's covering his tracks having us buy up a bunch of them." Willie's eyebrows furrowed into a scowl. "You don't think he's playin' us, do you? Like maybe he's gonna get the treasure after we do all the work?"

"Nah, it's not like that. I just think we need to hold off for a few weeks, make sure nothing comes from this Bratton thing."

"Nuh-uh. We keep at it."

"But Willie..."

Willie stared at Alex, eyes narrowed. "I said we keep going. Ain't you or your brother-in-law takin' this away from me."

AT LUNCHTIME, Matt went back to the Slaggers compound. He wanted to take a walk around the point, figuring it might clear his head. He knew Aoife was planning on meeting her cousin that morning, so she would likely be gone.

What was it about her that had him twisted up? He kept thinking about her smile, her eyes, her laugh, her irreverent attitude. All the things he loved about her all those years before. And then he thought about how it ended. Was he really still angry at her, or was he afraid of the feelings she stirred in him? Whatever it was, he needed to get past it and deal with the other matters at hand.

Matt walked out to the outer edge of the property, which was public trust land. It may have been the most popular spot on the island, loved by fishermen, sunbathers and seashell hunters. The mini-maze of dunes allowed the occasional topless sunbather to relax in relative privacy. The violent collision between the ocean and the sound at New Topsail Inlet made for dangerous swimming conditions but amazing views.

Matt loved the water's edge. The sand was soft and fine, with very little broken shell material, easy to walk in bare feet. It was another gorgeous October day, and he had gone back to the house first to change into shorts for his walk. This time he started on the sound side where a few people were enjoying the afternoon as well, mostly fishermen, with a few people enjoying a lunch break. There were a few boats out in Banks Channel, but for the most part it was a quiet Tuesday. As Matt rounded the corner and headed towards the inlet's edge, he saw a man sitting in the sand looking out into the water.

Matt sat down beside the man and stared out at that same water. They sat in silence for a moment before Matt spoke. "Shouldn't you be doing something productive, at least once in a while?"

"Babysittin' your ass seems to be a full-time job these days," Dan responded.

"Meaning?"

"Nothin." He waved his hand dismissively.

"Take the marbles out of your mouth if you got something to say, partner."

Dan looked down at the sand for a moment and then back up at the water. "What's your problem with Katie?"

Matt frowned. "You of all people should know what I've been through."

"What twenty-five, thirty years ago? You can't let it go?"

"My whole life I..."

"Spare me your sad story," Dan interrupted. "You've had a lot of bad shit happen; I get it. But you have a lot to be thankful for too. You have family and friends. Hannah's been gone for a while now, it's time to stop living safe and just start living."

Matt could feel the heat in his cheeks as his face reddened. "How dare you go there. And what does any of this have to do with Aoife?"

Dan shook his head. "She goes by Katie, and do you know how many people would kill just to feel the depth of love you've felt for a person, just once? You've had it twice and are willing to throw it away."

Matt got up. "I've heard enough."

Dan looked at him for the first time. "I'm not finished yet. You wanted me to take the marbles out of my mouth, partner, well here it is. Since Hannah died you've done nothing but play it safe. Except for the game we ran on the Sampsons, you've been a shell of your former self. You conned your way into a town manager job for a small town where the biggest issue is whether or not it will rain for the big festival. That's your life now."

"Maybe I like it that way."

"Really? Sleepwalking through life is your thing now? When

was the last time you had a real conversation with Sedona or Tanner? You may be surprised at what you find out."

Matt was getting hot now. "Don't cross that line, Trek."

Dan shook his head. "That's the problem, you were never afraid to cross the line when needed. I hear you got some legislative issue going on, and you want Tanner to research it. The Matt Sheehan I once knew would have been planning to burn Raleigh to the ground by now."

"Yeah, well that guy doesn't exist anymore, and I'm not about to drag Tanner into my old way of doing things."

"Why don't you let him decide? And while you're at it, how about giving Katie a break, starting with calling her Katie!"

Matt turned to walk away. "Screw you, Dan," he said in a quiet monotone voice.

Dan called back, "You're my brother, Matt, and I love you. But for the love of God, get your head out of your ass."

Matt took the long way back around the point, giving himself time to think about what Dan said. He knew Dan wasn't wrong about some things, especially about playing it safe. But what bothered him more was what Dan said about really talking to his kids. Matt wasn't necessarily ashamed of his past, feeling he was more like the Robin Hood of confidence men. His marks were carefully selected based on the type of people they were. The cons weren't always about money, but more about justice, he convinced himself.

And Matt knew he was damn good at it too.

But did he owe it to Sedona and Tanner to tell them who he once was? After all, that part of his life died when he met Hannah, before the kids were born. The father they knew was one who made an honest living, not some hustler. What did his adult children deserve to know about their father?

Then Matt thought about being a shell of his former self, the insinuation was that he was staying in the slow lane, not willing to exceed the speed limit. It gnawed at Matt. He knew instinctively that something was rotten in Raleigh, and it started with the draft legislation. It was bigger than that, he knew it, but he didn't know exactly what was going on. So, his answer was to study it further.

He stopped in his tracks. "Shit, maybe Dan's right," Matt said out loud. "Maybe I have lost my touch."

JACK FLEMING PACED in what little room he had left in his Raleigh office. He wasn't sure who he was angrier with: that arrogant redneck, Denton, or his incompetent brother-in-law, Alex. How many times had he told Alex not to be directly involved in any negotiations for the oyster leases? He was supposed to get someone they could trust to do it under another company name.

So, who does the idiot choose? Willie Covington, small time crook and even bigger moron. As it was, he had to make up a story about lost treasure and how the oyster leases would be the secret to getting to the gold before anyone else. That was the only way he could get Alex interested in the project. He sure as hell wasn't going to let Alex know the real reason for the leases, that would be foolish. His brother-in-law was a child and needed something shiny to keep his interest long enough to get Fleming what he needed.

Fleming's father-in-law had built an impressive real estate

business. Fleming admired him because they had the same drive, the same desire for power over others. Alex Spencer II was a man to be reckoned with. Too bad his genes were wasted on Alex III.

The plan was simple enough. Fleming needed to obtain enough oyster leases to launder money that he was going to get as a result of his new legislation. All young Alex had to do was find an independent broker to funnel the deals through a shell corporation that Fleming set up, and Fleming would handle the rest. But Christ, if that ignoramus couldn't even do that right.

And then there's Denton. How dare he come to his office and talk to him that way. Denton's time was over. The man has no imagination, no clue how to seize an opportunity and squeeze everything out of it. Jack knew aquaculture, specifically oyster farming, was huge in North Carolina, almost a $100 million a year industry in the state, over $2.2 billion nationwide. Mostly rural communities, easy to launder money through. How could Denton be so blind to the opportunity?

Fleming sat down at his desk and pulled a bottle of brandy and a glass out of one of the hidden drawers of his desk. He wasn't about to share that bottle with Denton, the swine.

"That overstuffed pig farmer has no idea what a cash cow this can be," Fleming mumbled to himself. "I have vision, and I'm going make this plan work. And when I become governor, I'm going squash that fat fuck like the bug he is."

Though, he had to admit, Denton had connections all over the state. How did he know about that Bratton guy so quickly, and how did he "fix" the problem? Without Denton, the path to the governorship would be a lot harder.

Fleming looked out into the front office to make sure his

assistant was still away from her desk and then closed his office door. He called his brother-in-law.

"Alex Spencer, Coastal Property Group. How can I serve you today?"

"Cut the shit, Alex, you know it's me. You always check the number before you answer."

It was true, Alex knew it was Jack, he just didn't want to talk to him. He knew if Jack was calling him, it wasn't for a friendly chat. Alex didn't think he was up to another chewing-out, but he couldn't figure out how to avoid Jack.

"Oh, hi Jack." He tried to act surprised, but it came off nervous.

"Are you alone, where you can talk?"

"Um, sure, Jack." In fact, he was not alone; he was sitting across from Willie Covington. Willie signaled Alex to put it on speaker, but Alex played stupid, as if he didn't understand Willie's gestures. He was believable that way.

"Have you gotten rid of Covington yet?"

"Well, no, not yet, I haven't had the chance. But really, I think it will be fine."

Fleming's face flushed with anger. "No, it will not, you dumbass. He killed a man. I may be able to get us out of this one, but we can't have that liability."

"He kind of knows about the stuff."

Fleming hung his head. How did he get stuck with this lot in life? He was quiet for a few moments as he gathered his thoughts.

"You still there?" Alex asked quietly.

"Listen to me closely. There is no treasure, tell Covington that when you see him. I just wanted the oyster leases and made up the story. Can you handle that?"

Alex looked over nervously at Willie, hoping he couldn't hear the conversation. It was clear, though, that he was trying to listen in. "I, I, I I'm just not sure…"

Fleming stopped him. "Just do it, you stammering idiot. If he becomes a problem I'll handle it, as always." Fleming hung up.

Alex looked up and smiled weakly at Willie. "That was my brother-in-law."

"No shit, Sherlock, why didn't you put it on speaker?"

"Oh well, I mean, I didn't know, did you want to hear it?"

"What did that spineless weasel want?" Willie's voice was calm, yet the tone of his voice was intimidating to Alex. It was cold, along with his stare.

"He was just saying that there really isn't any treasure, he just wanted the leases. Says you probably don't want to be part of that mess."

Willie looked hard at Alex, knowing he was a coward and would spill his guts. "That's bullshit, Alex. I know it, and you know it. Them leases can't be worth that much. No, there's treasure. We're close, and he wants to cut us out."

"I'm sure that's not the case, Willie."

Willie Covington stood up and leaned into Alex, getting nose to nose. Willie's breath was rancid, and it was hard for Alex to breathe. "I'm gonna get my share, Alex, one way or the other. Your brother-in-law can kiss my ass."

"Yeah, but Willie, we don't have any idea where this treasure is, or even if it exists. Like Jack said, maybe he just wants the leases."

"Don'tcha see, he's just saying that because now we're getting close. He just wants the treasure all to hisself."

Alex shook his head. "I don't know, man, even if you're right, we don't know how to go about finding the treasure."

Willie blew out his breath, his eyes narrowed to slits. "You just let me handle that, I'll figure it out. But now we're doing it my way, just like with that other fucker on the boat. You with me?"

Alex was pretty sure he pissed his pants a little. "Yeah, of course, Willie. Whatever you say."

MATT STARTED BACK TO TOWN HALL, but thought better of it. He was not in the best frame of mind, and nothing good would come from dealing with the public at that point. Matt decided to stay at the compound, so he called Kelly to let her know he wouldn't be back that afternoon. He asked her to let him know if any of the commissioners needed him. The next night was the monthly Board of Commissioners meeting, so it was not unusual for elected officials to come by to discuss meeting topics.

Matt tried to focus on the agenda for the meeting the next evening, but his mind kept wandering to the last forty-eight hours. Holt's death, the sudden appearance of legislation that would devastate Topsail Beach's beach nourishment program, the surprising FEMA notice about recent recovery funds. He thought about his conversation with Dan and whether or not he was getting soft.

But mostly he thought about Katie. She was still Aoife to him, and seeing her clearly stirred a lot of emotion. But was it anger? He wasn't so sure.

He walked down to Dan's office and found him sitting behind his desk, working on one of his many side projects. Matt rarely knew what he was up to, but he trusted him. Matt went straight to the bar cart and poured a drink.

"Aren't you still on the clock, Mr. Manager?" Dan asked.

Matt just grunted and poured a second drink for Dan.

"What happened to me, Trek? When did I get so…" He paused for a beat, "Conservative?"

"I was a little harsh today, brother. You're fine."

"That's bullshit, Dan, and you know it. Don't get me wrong, I like being manager of Topsail Beach, and I love working this close to Tanner, but I've clearly lost my edge. All I do is play it safe."

Matt waited for his response, but it didn't come. He was hoping Dan would disagree, at least a little. He finally spoke again, "Feel free to weigh in."

"Awright, you've clearly lost your edge, and you play it safe. Wasn't that the gist of what I told you earlier? Look, you got a good thing here, I get it. I'm not saying you should go back to con games and weekend benders. But when was the last time you told that board of yours to back off and let you do your job? When was the last time you used that beautiful brain of yours to completely bewilder people, get them to do what you want and think it was their idea? You can use your powers for good, my friend, but please use them. You're kinda boring and needy right now."

Dan sure does have a way about him, Matt thought. But he knew Dan was right this time. Matt looked down at his feet. "I don't want to be this way anymore."

"It's about fuckin' time." Dan practically jumped out of his chair as he spoke. He grabbed a bottle of rye. "Get your ass up, we're heading for the dock. This time the music selection is

Kendell Marvel and maybe some Jerry Jeff Walker. We're gonna start with whatever this legislative crap is."

TANNER PULLED INTO the Slaggers Compound around five thirty that evening, having spent most of the afternoon with Chris Taylor. They were reaching out to their various connections: Tanner on the legislative side and Chris working the coastal engineers and dredging industry experts. No one seemed to be aware of the proposed legislation, or at least they weren't willing to talk about it.

He walked into the main building looking for his father, but when he couldn't find him, he went back outside. The evening air was getting a little cooler, but still quite pleasant for October. He took in a deep breath, allowing the salt air to fill his lungs. He had spent most of his life at the coast, but never took for granted the medicinal powers that the ocean air provides.

As he turned to go back to his truck, Tanner noticed a light on at the back of one of the guest houses, so he went to check it out. He found Katie sitting at the table in the lanai, thumbing through some paperwork.

"You know what they say about all work, no play," Tanner said, smiling as he walked around to greet her.

Katie looked up from her work and returned the smile. Her heart skipped a beat as she was thinking again how much Tanner looked like his father when Matt was around the same age: tall with broad shoulders, more of an athletic build than Matt had when they were together. Same facial features, though. She did notice that his hair was much lighter than Matt's, and his eyes were electric blue. That must have been from his mother.

"What could possibly be more important than enjoying an evening like this?" Tanner asked.

"Financials for my cousin Frank's business. I'm trying to figure out why anyone would want to buy it. What brings you out here?"

"Looking for my pops, I have some information to pass on and was hoping to catch him. Have you seen him by chance?"

She tilted her head and made a slight grunting noise. "No, I haven't seen him today," she said. "I'm pretty sure he doesn't want to see me."

Tanner pulled out one of the chairs at the table where Katie was sitting. "Mind if I sit?" He didn't wait for an answer. "What makes you think he doesn't want to see you?"

"You mean other than the fact he said so last night?"

"Yeah, he can be a schmuck that way sometimes."

Katie had to laugh at that one.

"Doesn't mean he doesn't want to see you."

Katie laughed again. "You're sweet, and charming. No wonder Sugartits has the hots for you. But I'm sure you're wrong on this one."

It was Tanner's turn to laugh. "You certainly left an impression on Brittany. You were all she could talk about last night. I think she has a crush on you." Tanner got serious as he looked directly at Katie. "I saw the way my dad looked at you. It was not anger in his heart."

Katie had a thin smile as she thought about it. "There may have been a time, but not anymore. There's a good bit of history that I'm sure you aren't familiar with."

"That may be, but living in the past and learning from it are two very different things. There's a lot I'm sure I don't know about my dad, but I do know your presence has affected him."

"Either way, cowboy, I'm planning on leaving tomorrow, so this story has a very quick ending."

Tanner nodded. "Well, if that's the case, at least let's not waste the night. Come on, let's take a walk down by the water. There is no greater healer of the soul than coastal waters."

So full of shit, Katie thought, just like his father.

MATT AND DAN HAD SETTLED in at the boat dock overlooking Banks Channel. They sat in two tall Adirondack chairs with a table between for drinks. Matt told Dan everything he knew about Holt Bratton's death, the proposed legislation, FEMA's denial of the town's damage mitigation request, and the Army Corps' recent behavior. Matt couldn't find a common thread between any of the recent events, but he couldn't shake the feeling they were somehow intertwined.

Dan sat and listened closely, only interrupting a few times for some questions. "I'm not following, why would the Corps look to limit FEMA funding? Wouldn't that blow back on them as well?" he asked.

"Good question."

"And for that matter," Dan continued, "why would the elected officials create legislation that would reduce the amount of money that would come into the state?"

Matt rubbed his chin, his brow furrowing. "They wouldn't." He paused before he spoke again. "Unless it was a way to manipulate the federal funds to go to the state agencies instead of the local municipalities."

"That seems counterproductive to me."

That's when it hit Matt. "Goddammit, the fucking Corps."

"Help me out here, partner."

"FEMA lowered our recovery funds based on the Corps calculations and threw out ours. If the legislation is passed and the state controls who does the projects, they would rely heavily on the Corps calculations."

"You think the Army Corps of Engineers is manipulating data to land more money in their coffers?"

"No no, the Corps isn't crooked. But I do think the Corps would love to control the narrative."

"You lost me."

"We know the Corps calculations are based on twenty-year-old data," Matt explained. "They hated that our program was successful using our own data and that other communities were beginning to look at Topsail Beach as the model. I think they might like it better if their way was deemed the official process to qualify for FEMA money."

"If this shit is true," Dan responded, "it goes beyond some yahoo congressman looking to make a name for himself." He paused. "You're not going to get to the bottom of this the conventional way. Maybe it's time you got Tanner more involved in this."

"Absolutely not. You're right that whatever I do will likely involve some shady action. If we do end up making a play, I won't expose Tanner to it. Better he doesn't know how we did things before."

Dan set down his drink and let out a long, hard laugh. "Are you serious? What makes you think he doesn't know?"

"How would he, unless someone's been talking?"

"Oh, I don't know, maybe it's the fact that all of a sudden you had a multi-million-dollar corporation at your command. Tanner isn't stupid."

"You told him, didn't you?"

Dan shook his head. "Of course not, that's not my place. But he has questions, and I can't and won't lie to him. He's gonna figure it out, if he hasn't already." He paused for a second. "Be mad at me if you want, but he deserves to know, and it's best if he hears it from you. Just talk to him, and let him decide."

"Sedona?" Matt asked.

"Oh please, she saw you in action, you were just too drunk to realize it. You'd be running some half-assed con on some poor slob when she came to drag you out of the bar."

Matt dropped his head. "Do they know about the Sampsons?"

"I don't think so, but I imagine they have some suspicions. After all, Sedona won't have anything to do with Slaggers."

They sat quietly as sunset approached, following their rule of no talking during sunset, just music in the background.

After the sun was lost behind the horizon, Matt turned to Dan. "Why do you think Aoife came here?"

Dan sighed. "*Katie,*" he emphasized, "is here to meet with her cousin. Something about the sale of his oyster lease. Although I think she may be here for other reasons." He winked at Matt.

Matt waved him off. But his mention of her cousin's oyster lease got him thinking. He spun his drink in his hand, the rye twisting like a vortex in the tumbler, as he stared at the calm sound waters.

"Am I missing something?" Dan asked, breaking the momentary silence.

"Holt Bratton died out in the marshes. I'm pretty sure he had an oyster lease in that area."

"You think there is a connection?"

"I don't know, but it's not nothing."

"Well, I believe we may need nature's help about now." Dan pulled out several joints from his shirt pocket. "I only smoke on special occasions, and you not being a dork anymore is a good one."

"Jaysus, Mary, and Joseph, I can't remember the last time I smoked weed."

Dan lit one up. "You gonna call the cops, Mr. Manager?"

Matt smiled. "Don't bogart that joint, my friend."

It wasn't long before the conversation changed to laughter and old stories. It had been a long time since Matt got stoned, but it was a lot like he remembered. Both he and Dan were happy when they were drunk or stoned, never angry or paranoid. As the saying goes, ain't nobody got time for that shit.

Katie and Tanner heard the laughter as they got closer to the docks.

"Sounds like a party," Tanner said.

"Smells like one too," Katie replied.

"What do you say we crash it?" he said, a wry smile crossing his face.

Matt and Dan heard footsteps approach from the dock.

Dan didn't even look back. "If you don't have any Taco Bell with you just turn your ass around." He and Matt laughed hysterically like fools.

Matt turned around and saw Tanner and Katie standing there. "Busted," he said, and they started laughing again.

"Are you stoned, Pops?" Tanner asked with mock surprise.

Matt did his best to look serious. "No, no, no." He paused and then snickered. "Well maybe. Ok, yes, but it's Trek's fault."

"What kind of example does this set for our grad students?" Tanner said with feigned indignity. Matt knew Tanner was having fun now.

"Where do you think I got this shit?" Dan replied, and the laughter started again. "Speaking of which, can you get one of your girlfriends to bring us some food? And another bottle of rye. We seem to be out, and I'm sure you and Katie want to join us."

"Katie," Matt stumbled with his words. "Trek says I have to call you Katie, Aoife, not Aoife anymore."

Dan snickered. "Not Katie Aoife, just Katie, you fool."

"That's what I said, I think."

Katie smirked as she looked over at Tanner. "I think we should stay; this could be fun. Plus, I'm not sure your dad or Dan will be able to find their way home."

Wednesday, October 12

MATT WENT INTO TOWN HALL early Wednesday morning. The booze and weed had taken its toll, and he felt like some medieval torture device was lodged in his skull. But the Board of Commissioners meeting was that night, and he had to be there. He hoped to go straight to his office without being noticed. Best laid plans and all that.

Matt closed his door in hopes that no one would bother him, but a closed door is just an invitation to knock, loudly. First it was the Public Works Director wanting to know if the commissioners were going to make him keep the public bathrooms open all winter. Matt got to hear about how they weren't designed to stay open, and they should be winterized, but the "Pickleball Nazis" were going to demand otherwise. The director wasn't wrong, but Matt just didn't have it in him to go through that battle. Of course, the bathrooms were going to stay open, these are voters in a small town where twenty votes easily make a difference.

Once he finally left Matt's office, the police chief was next in line.

"You alright, Boss?" he asked. "You look like last night got the better of you."

No, I'm not alright, not even close, Matt thought. "I'll live," was all he could come up with.

"We did get a report that there was possible partying down around the Point. You wouldn't know anything about that I assume." He said it with a grin.

"I'm sure it was the grad students," Matt lied. "Hopefully, it wasn't a problem."

"My officers didn't even bother following up. It didn't seem serious."

This is exactly why Matt loved the chief. "I'm sure you're not here to check on my health. What's up?"

"Just checking in to see if you needed me to cover anything specifically for the meeting tonight. I know paid parking is on the agenda. I'm happy to give my two cents on the problems that will cause my officers."

He was right, one of the commissioners wanted to open up discussion on paid parking. Most of the other beach communities had already moved in that direction, but Matt was doing his best to fight it for many reasons. He figured he would eventually lose the battle, but not without a fight. "Let's see how the flow of the meeting goes tonight. I'm hoping I can push the topic off to a later date."

"Works for me," the chief said. "I also wanted you to know I spoke with Holt's wife, Jennie, yesterday. She's a piece of work, just like he was. Apparently, his death is somehow the town's fault, and she's threatening to sue."

"Again? How many times is this now, three or four?"

"Counting the 'handcuffs were too tight lawsuit,' I think it's five." He rolled his eyes.

"Did she have anything of value to say?"

"Nothing much, although she did say Holt was drunk the night before he died and was complaining that some asshole kept pestering him to buy off his oyster lease."

Matt raised his eyebrows. "She didn't happen to have a name, did she?"

The chief looked at Matt as if he had asked a strange question. "She was pretty unclear about it, but she said it was something like Coppertone. I'm pretty sure she was wasted when I spoke to her. Why do you want to know?"

He doesn't miss much, Matt thought. "Just curious," he said, hoping that would be enough to satisfy the chief.

Once the chief left, it was Kelly's turn. She was much more in tune to Matt's situation.

"The mayor wants to meet with you before tonight's meeting, so does Commissioner Phelps. I'm sure he wants to push paid parking. I told both of them you were tied up until two o'clock. That should give you enough time to go get a nap and a shower before you return."

"What, I showered this morning."

"Well, you still smell like a distillery and marijuana. Try again, you'll thank me." She was practically laughing. "Honestly, I had no idea you had it in you."

"My party days are few and far between. That said, I think I'll take your advice."

"You may want to try some eye drops while you're at it," she said as she walked out of his office.

Matt went back to the Slaggers Compound and looked for Katie's car. Despite the fact that he was doing his very best to keep his distance physically and emotionally, he was disappointed that she wasn't there. Seeing her again after so much time had passed was having an effect on him, no matter how hard he tried to convince himself otherwise.

Matt went in and took a nice, long nap. Afterwards, he showered, got dressed, and stepped out onto the front balcony. He watched a lone brown pelican skim across the water. He couldn't help smiling as he watched this large bird with its comically oversized bill and long neck glide effortlessly just above the surf. As elegant as they are in flight, they are quite awkward on land. And even though they are excellent hunters, they are not above stealing food.

"You and me, buddy," Matt said to no one in particular. "We keep'em guessing."

"Talking to yourself, partner?" Dan asked as he came out on the balcony. He was unshaven and more than a little disheveled. "How ya feeling?" He had a wry smile on his face.

"Better than you look, brother."

"Recovery day. Remember I don't have that 9–5 job like you, sucker. Based on the way you're dressed I assume you are going back."

Matt grunted. "Meeting night."

Dan looked out at the ocean, watching that same pelican as he spoke. "Not sure how much you remember from last night, but the old Matt Sheehan seemed to return."

"I remember, sort of. A lot of talk about ways to deal with legislators and proposed laws. Lots of lip service, little substance. But then again, we were not exactly in our right minds. There's more to it than a drunk night. We would need a plan."

"Isn't that your specialty?"

"Uh huh. By the way, where's Aoife—I mean Katie?"

"She went to see her cousin again. Don't worry, based on your behavior last night, I'm sure she will leave either today or tomorrow."

"What the hell is that supposed to mean? I wasn't ugly last night."

Dan laughed and shook his head. "No, you weren't. You just barely acknowledged her the whole night. I thought for sure you would loosen up. But I guess you lost all heart and passion."

"Not now, Trek."

"If not now, when? When was the last time you spent any significant time with a woman, any woman that wasn't your wife? And now Katie of all people walks back into your life, and you can't even get out of your own mopey way."

"Leave Hannah out of this." Matt's eyes narrowed as his voice trembled. "You don't have a fucking clue what I've been through."

Dan violently shook his head, his lips tightening as he spoke. "Really? I don't have a clue? I was at your fucking side when Katie left, and when Hannah died." He paused to catch his breath. His voice got quieter as his facial expression softened. "I don't claim to have experienced the level of pain you suffered, but don't tell me I haven't a clue."

Dan walked over to Matt and put his hand on his shoulder. "What I know is that you found a soulmate twice in your life when a lot of people don't ever find one. You are just damned determined to throw it away. And I just can't fathom why."

Matt turned to leave. "I don't have time for this, Dan. My life is what it is now. See if you can get Tanner to hang around tonight, so we can meet after I'm done with the board."

Dan closed his eyes, trying to hide the sadness he knew was in his soul. "Get your shit together, Matt. Playing the martyr doesn't suit you."

THAT AFTERNOON Alex Spencer III called Jack Fleming to tell him about his conversation with Willie Covington. They both scared him, just in different ways. He must have picked up his phone four or five times, but would hang up before it rang. The more he thought about it, the more confused he got. Was there treasure, or did Jack make that up? And if so, why not just tell him the real purpose for buying these leases?

Alex knew Jack was no fisherman, in fact, Jack despised anything related to the fishing industry that didn't come on a plate at a restaurant. So maybe Willie was right, maybe he was trying to cut them out. But Willie was also a psycho. After all, he's the one that really killed that guy on the boat like it was nothing. Sure, Alex hit the guy, but Willie was the one to drown him.

Alex was getting tired of being used. It was time he looked after himself. He finally made the call.

Jack answered after the first ring. "What do you want, I have a committee meeting in five minutes." Abrupt, as usual.

"I spoke to Willie last night. He doesn't believe you, thinks you want the treasure for yourself." Alex spoke to Jack without a stammer, which may have been a first with his brother-in-law.

"I don't care what that bucket of shit believes. Did you make it clear he's out?"

"He killed a man, Jack, do you think he's just gonna lie down on this?" Alex tried to sound forceful. "Is it true, Jack, is there treasure or not? 'Cause I'm telling you, none of this makes sense to me. Why would you lie to me?"

Jack's voice got real quiet: "We'll talk about this later. In the meantime, do whatever it takes to get Covington out of this. Pay him off, I don't care, just get rid of him." Once again, Jack hung up on Alex.

Alex sat there for a moment staring at the phone. Fuck Jack and Willie, he thought. He decided he was going to do things his way moving forward. He just didn't know how.

IT WAS EIGHT O'CLOCK when Matt walked out of town hall. The meeting was over and the commissioners and handful of citizens that came to the meeting had finally left. Matt looked up into the cloudless sky, the stars out in force, the moon full. Thanks to the sea breeze, the evenings were getting a little cooler. Although, low sixties at night is not bad for October. Fall evenings accentuate the smells of the ocean, and the salt air fills the lungs. Matt loved the sensation, soaking it in whenever he could.

When Matt got back to the compound, he found a note from Dan saying that he and Tanner would be down on the dock waiting for him. Matt changed his clothes, grabbed a beer and half a left-over sandwich, and walked down to the dock. He could see the Slaggers company boat up on the lift and Dan's skiff in the opposite slip. As he got closer to the dock, he saw three figures chatting: Dan, Tanner, and Katie. He took a deep breath but kept going.

"Evening, Pops," Tanner said with his usual smile. He looked at the beer in Matt's hand. "Rough one tonight?"

"Not really," he said and looked at the cooler sitting on the dock. "Looks like y'all had the same idea."

"Gradual recovery from last night," Dan said. "Felt like cold turkey wouldn't work."

Katie got up. "I should go and pack. I want to get an early start tomorrow, and I'm sure you have things to discuss."

Matt walked over to where she had been sitting. My God, he thought, she smells incredible. "Why don't you stay for a little bit? You're not going to get these views in Charlotte."

"It's probably better that I go. I think it's pretty clear that I've overstayed my welcome."

Matt stole a glance at Dan, who had his eyebrows raised. "I'm asking Katie, please stay, just for a little while."

"So, it truly is Katie now." She smiled. "I didn't think you would remember from last night."

"I just hope your grandfather will forgive me," Matt said, smiling back at her.

Matt sat down in the chair beside her and finished his sandwich. He was sipping his beer when Dan spoke up. "You called this meeting, partner."

"Gents, and lady, it has been brought to my attention that my approach to problems recently has been more timid than in the past. That said, life and responsibilities change, and the old ways aren't always appropriate."

Dan sighed in disappointment.

"Look I can't run a con on governmental officials over legislation. It doesn't work that way." Matt looked at Tanner who was oddly stoic. It was the first time Matt ever hinted about his past with Tanner around.

"No one is suggesting you scam these guys," Dan said. "What

I am suggesting is for you to be more creative in the way you approach the problem. You sit here and grumble about some legislation, or recovery monies being withheld, or some other crap and how to work through the system to get it fixed. How's that working out?"

"It's not that easy."

"So, when we were consultants getting funding for those communities or non-profits, was that always by the book?"

Tanner jumped in, "This legislation—and the Hurricane Isaias money—if we don't get this resolved, it will set Topsail Beach way back in our program. If there is a way to tilt things in our favor, we need to do it."

Matt had nothing. That's when he realized what was really pissing him off. He had nothing. He always had the answer before, without fail. But now, he was getting beat.

They sat in silence until Dan finally spoke, "How did your visit with your cousin go, Katie?"

"OK, I guess. I'm not sure what to make of his oyster farm. It's a nice set-up, I suppose, and he loves doing it. But financially, it's not exactly a goldmine. It's fine for Frank, but it's not big enough to make real money, at least from what I can tell."

"So, what's the issue?" Tanner asked.

"The issue is some guy is offering him at least twice what it's worth. But Frank doesn't want to sell. He says the guy was pretty aggressive and not very professional. He's supposed to meet with the guy and his partner again tomorrow."

Matt looked at Katie, thinking something was off. "Was this some company trying to buy his lease?"

"I'm not sure. He just mentioned the guy's name, a Willie Covington."

Fuck, Matt thought. Jenny Bratton told the chief that Holt

was meeting someone named Coppertone. Being the addict she is, could she have meant Covington?

"Call your cousin as soon as possible, Aoife," Matt said. "Tell him not to meet with this guy."

Katie tilted her head and looked at Matt with a frown. But it was Dan who leaned forward in his chair. "What is it, Matt?" he asked.

"I'm not sure, but that may be the same guy who met with our floater recently, also an oyster farmer. It may be nothing, but no need to take chances." Matt looked at Dan. "We need to find out more about this Covington guy. We also need to find out if any other oyster leases have changed hands recently."

"Maybe your police chief can get some information on this guy," Dan replied.

"We can't involve him, not yet. He's still investigating Holt's death, and we need some time to figure things out." Matt felt guilty withholding information from the chief. He is a good policeman, but they needed to keep him out of this for the moment.

Tanner chimed in, "There must be a number of Willie Covingtons in the Wilmington area. Where do we start?"

Dan thought for a moment. "The police chief in Elizabethtown may be able to help. He still likes us from when we got him the assault vehicle."

"Why in the name of God does Elizabethtown need an assault vehicle?" Katie asked.

"We didn't often question our clients; we just got them what they wanted."

"Can we just focus, people?" Matt asked, slightly exasperated.

Dan chuckled. "Just like old times. Tanner and I are on Willie and the oyster leases."

"No, not Tanner."

"Yes, Pops."

"What are you thinking, Matt?" Katie interrupted before Matt could respond to Dan and Tanner.

Oyster leases, dredge legislation, spoils islands limitations, funding delays. Matt had pieces, but no answers yet. "I don't know," he answered. "But we may finally have a connection."

A NONDESCRIPT WHITE VAN was parked at a lot near a house under construction. The lot was along one of the many creeks that flowed to the Intracoastal Waterway. Willie sat at the wheel with Alex in the passenger seat. Willie was watching the creek, waiting for a boat to come by.

They sat in silence for some time before Alex finally spoke, "Let's just offer the guy more money, Willie, I'm sure he'll sell."

Willie was amped. Alex wasn't sure what he was on, but he didn't like where all this was going. The two had met earlier in the day when Alex decided he was going to tell Willie that they were going to do things his way, not Willie's. It didn't go as well as Alex hoped. Willie punched him so hard in the gut that Alex was sure something ruptured. When Alex fell to the ground whimpering, Willie kicked him in the ribs. Alex knew Willie as a small-time dealer and thief, but he never seemed this violent before.

Now Alex was scared. He knew he had miscalculated his position of authority. He should have listened to his brother-in-law.

"Nah, he ain't sellin' on his own." Willie's leg bounced up and down. "We're gonna have to convince him it's in his best interest."

"We don't need another body, Willie," Alex whined.

"I told you that wasn't my fault, that first one is on you." Willie was agitated, and his voice got louder as he spoke. "Obviously, I ain't gonna kill this guy, we need him to sign the lease. I'm just gonna scare him a bit, so he comes to you tomorrow to sign over the place." Willie looked up and saw a boat pulling into a dock two doors down. "There he is now. You stay here, I'll be right back."

"Just let me pay him tomorrow, Willie."

"Stay in the car, and shut the fuck up."

Willie moved carefully toward the dock, avoiding any lights wherever he could. He waited in the dark behind a stand of river birches as Frank Kenny came off the dock. Willie followed close behind, hitting the man in the back, knocking him to the ground. Willie jumped on him, rolling him over and covering his mouth with his gloved hand.

It took Frank a few seconds to get his bearings before he realized what happened and who was on top of him. He had gotten a message from his cousin to cancel his meeting tomorrow with this guy Covington and his partner, but he didn't get a chance to call back and ask why.

Willie looked down on the man and whispered to him, inches from his face. "I'm gonna move my hand, but if you scream, I'll kill you. Got it?" Frank nodded. Willie removed his hand, and then yanked Frank up by his collar. He spied a picnic table under some trees where it was nice and dark and dragged Frank to it.

"Tomorrow you're gonna see my friend, and you're gonna sign that lease over to us, at half the price we originally offered.

That's because you caused me all this trouble. If you don't, I'm gonna be very unhappy." It was clear Willie watched too much TV. "Now, put your hands on the table."

"Why? What are you going to do?" Frank asked in a panic. "I'll sign whatever you want, just don't hurt me."

Alex ran up to the table when he saw what was going on. "What the hell are you doing?"

"Shut up." Willie looked at Frank. "What hand do you write with?"

"I'm right-handed, but really, I'll do whatever you want."

Willie slipped on a set of brass knuckles and punched Frank in the temple, knocking him out cold. He fell back onto the ground.

"Jesus Christ, Willie, whatcha do that for?"

"Shut up and pick him back up."

Alex struggled to get him back up to the picnic table. Willie took Frank's right hand and proceeded to smash it. Even though Frank was out cold, his body jerked on impact. But he never made a sound.

The sound of the shattered bones nearly made Alex puke.

"Now he'll know we weren't fuckin around," Willie sneered.

"He said he was right-handed, Willie, why'd you bust his right hand? How's he going to sign anything now?"

"That ain't his right hand, it's his left. See this is my right hand." Willie wiggled the fingers of his right hand in the brass knuckles.

"It's like a mirror image, Willie, it's the opposite. You were supposed to hit the other hand."

Willie looked confused, holding up his right hand, staring into a non-existent mirror, trying to make sense of what Alex was saying.

"You crushed the wrong hand," Alex said, resignation in his voice.

"Well fuck, I guess I need to bust the other hand too."

Alex lifted his palms in the air. "Why?"

"Because I have to, you fucktard." Willie's eyes were wide, his smile crooked when he looked at Alex. "You better turn away, pussy boy, I don't want you spraying chunks everywhere."

MATT AND THE GANG finished up around eleven, and everyone started to go their separate ways. The night air had gotten cooler, but the sky was still lit up by the moon. Matt marveled at the wonders of nature that the human race hadn't completely fucked up yet. He and Tanner were walking back towards the main house when Tanner stopped and grabbed Matt by arm.

"Pops, whatever reasons you have for trying to exclude me, it's not enough. I know you and Dan are good people. Whatever the two of you did in the past is just that, the past. We have a real issue now, and I am part of this team. Don't shut me out."

Matt looked at Tanner, seeing him for the man he was. Perhaps truly for the first time. "I make no apologies for what I've done, Tanner, but it wasn't always legal. I could justify it in my mind, but there's always a risk with the law. I don't want to drag you into that. Your mother would never forgive me."

Tanner smiled. "From what Dan's told me, you and Mom weren't that different. She was just smarter about how to get things done without the risk. I'll be fine, Pops; I believe I got the best of both of you."

Matt let out a big sigh. "Don't listen to Dan anymore."

"Does that include what he's told me about you and Katie?"

Fucking Trekor just can't mind his own business, Matt thought. "It's complicated," Matt said.

"He said that's what you would say. For what it's worth, I like her." He switched subjects, "Do you still have the keys to my place? You're welcome to stay there tonight."

Matt figured Tanner was trying to save him the long drive. "I'm gonna go back to the condo tonight, but thanks."

"Yeah, about that. Brittany and I are going there tonight, soooo…"

Matt shook his head.

"Thanks, Pops," he said with a wink. "See you in the morning."

Tanner took off towards the lab building where Brittany was waiting. Matt stood outside for a bit before realizing that he was staring at the guest house that Katie was using. It was just like when he first saw her in college, trying to build up the courage to talk to her. He was twenty all over again, feeling foolish, standing there staring. Matt started walking towards his truck but stopped. The next thing he knew, he was at her door. He stood there for another few minutes, debating whether to knock or not. "Jayus, you're not a kid anymore," he said out loud and knocked on the door.

When she opened the door, Matt stood there, slack-jawed, unable to speak. She had just finished showering and was wearing one of the Topsail Beach fishing shirts that Matt usually wore to work. It went down to just above her knees, and while it was loose fitting, he could still see the curves of her body. Her hair was wet and pulled back, opening her face more than usual. And those eyes. He was already lost.

She stood there, biting her lower lip. When it was clear Matt wasn't talking, she spoke first, "I wanted to get that last outdoor shower in, ya know. It's a little chilly, but worth it."

I'll say, Matt thought. He nodded, lingering just a tick too long.

She went on, "I found this shirt inside the closet; I hope you don't mind."

Matt finally found his voice, however meekly. "Ah, no, no, it's fine." It took another moment, but he finally spoke again: "Katie, I just want to say..." He didn't finish. She took his hand in hers.

"Tonight, you can call me Aoife," she said as she led him inside.

II

It's Not a Con, It's a Stratagem

Thursday, October 13

THE MORNING SUN hadn't made its way over the horizon when Matt woke up. He could feel Katie stir by his side, hearing a gentle sigh as she shifted her body. He looked at her and smiled, the memory of the night still fresh in his mind. It was the best he felt in a very long time.

That happiness quickly changed to doubt. After all, he thought, one night of passion doesn't erase the past. She left him once, why would he expect things to be different this time? Matt knew he had to shut down the emotional connection he was feeling. His life's greatest pains were a result of his emotional investments. But damn, she made it really hard for him.

Matt quietly got up, trying his best not to disturb Katie. He went downstairs to the lanai, where he could focus on recent discoveries, try to make sense of everything.

Her voice startled him. He hadn't heard it in years.

"Well, well, someone had himself quite the night."

Matt looked up at the lady standing in front of him. "Hannah."

"Surprise."

Matt shook his head. "This isn't real. Whatever Dan had us smoke must be having residual effects."

"Nice try, Chachi, but you know better. It's not like this is the first time."

"It's the first time in years, and don't call me Chachi." Guilt suddenly struck Matt. "Are you here because I slept with Aoife?"

Hannah laughed. "Really? I forgot how self-absorbed you could be, but I love you anyway. No, Casanova, I'm not here to haunt you over sleeping with someone else."

"Hmm, I guess that makes sense. You haven't come back any other time I slept with someone since you died."

"You mean the two other times?"

Even Matt had to laugh. "OK, so you've been irreplaceable." Matt's smile faded. "I miss you so badly, Hannah."

Her smile was gentle, leaving a warm feeling. "I know, baby, but it's been a while. This one is different, isn't she? And that's OK. That's not why I'm here. Do you remember the last time we spoke?"

Matt nodded his head. "Yep. You wanted to make sure that I knew if I didn't make things right with Sedona, you were going to haunt me throughout eternity."

"That's right. Now pay close attention. You and Dan are about to do something you haven't done in a long time, and you're going to include my son."

"Hold on, Hannah, nothing has been decided."

"Matthew Patrick Sheehan, I don't think even you believe that. I'm just here to tell you to take care of my boy. Do not screw this up."

Matt scratched his head. "Wait, you're OK with it?"

Hannah looked up to the heavens. "No, you idiot, I'm not OK with it. But I know you, and I know Tanner, and I know I can't stop it. It's just who you are. Plus, you're doing it for the right reasons."

"Doing what? I don't even know what's going on."

Hannah smiled at him one more time. "I love you, Matthew. I don't want to haunt you for eternity. Take care of our boy."

And she was gone.

Matt watched as the sun rose in the horizon, but his mind was elsewhere. He felt her presence before he felt her actual touch. Katie stood behind him, hands on his shoulders, before leaning in closer to his ear.

"You didn't sit in the bedroom and watch me sleep, which is good 'cause I always thought that's kinda creepy. You also didn't make me coffee."

He looked up at her and smiled. She was wearing that shirt again, and nothing else. "Sorry, Aoife, I don't drink coffee, remember. And besides, it's a coffee pod thingy, how much time can it possibly take?"

"The romance is over." She feigned dramatic, putting the back of her hand on her forehead. She walked over to the corner to make herself a cup of coffee.

"Are you still planning on leaving today?" He knew immediately that question was a little too abrupt.

She didn't look back, her tone changing, as she spoke, "Probably. I'm just waiting to hear back from my cousin, then I'm gone."

"I see."

"Do you?"

Matt knew she meant what happened between them, but he didn't want to get into it. He shifted the conversation. "I'm lost, Aoife. I have all this crap going on, and I can't put it together. I'm not used to this; I feel like I'm the mark."

She sat down across from him, coffee in hand. "As far as all this *crap* goes, maybe you need to stop thinking like a town manager and start thinking like the hustler you used to be."

"I don't think you understand what I mean."

She ran her hand through her hair, shaking it free. "What I think is that you are afraid to do what you do best. You know what's going on reeks of underhanded bullshit, you just don't want to think like they do, whoever they are. What are you afraid of, that you are no better than them? *That* is bullshit."

When he didn't respond after a few moments she got up to walk away. "Last night was nice, we should do it again sometime."

Matt got up to leave. "I'm heading to the main house to call the office and tell them I'm taking a few days off. It would be great if you did the same, at least until we figure this out."

"Another of your hard-to-resist offers," she said as she headed back to the bedroom. "I'll let you know."

Matt walked out the door and ran into Brittany. She had a box of equipment she was taking to the university's boat out on the dock. "Good morning, Mr. Sheehan," she said with a big smile.

"Good morning, Brittany," he replied. Then he felt Katie coming up behind him.

"You forgot something, Sheehan." She was still wearing just the shirt as she grabbed Matt's face with both hands and gave him a long kiss. Then she grabbed his ass.

She looked over at Brittany. "Morning, Sugartits." She smiled and turned and went back into the house.

Brittany just stood there for a second before turning to Matt. "Oh my God, she's so terrifying and so hot."

Matt smiled. "That she is Brittany, that she is."

ALEX SAT IN HIS OFFICE, staring into his coffee cup, lost in a daze. He was trying to figure out how things went so badly. The previous night was a disaster. They left that poor man on the ground and took off, not sure if he was dead or alive. Willie kept telling him to be cool, that everything was fine. He said that they were going to get that lease, and then they could figure out where to start looking for the treasure. But Alex knew they didn't have a clue about how to treasure hunt. Hell, they didn't even know what the oyster leases had to do with the treasure, other than it was somewhere close. These stupid oyster farms weren't even next to each other, they just happened to be around Topsail Island.

Alex had always heard the story about the Gold Hole in Topsail Beach, how back in the 1940's a group of men dug up an area they thought for sure was where Blackbeard buried his treasure. They got some of the locals to invest in the project, dug a great big hole, and then one day just disappeared. No one knew if they found the treasure or if the whole thing was a scam. Jack told him the gold was real, those people just didn't know where to dig. Something about water shifting in the marshes. Alex never did understand, he just wanted to hunt treasure.

Now there was a dead man, another who might be dead, and Jack pissed off at Alex for bringing Willie on board. In retrospect, maybe that was a bad idea, but he was high at the time.

It all seemed so exciting at first. Now he couldn't get rid of psycho Willie, and he was afraid to tell Jack about what happened. Alex started to sob.

JACK FLEMING'S CELL PHONE RANG. He sighed, stuck his head out of his office and told his assistant to hold all calls. He closed his door and answered the phone.

"Good morning, Senator," he said as cheerily as he could muster.

"I was just wonderin'," said the voice on the other end of the line, "if sometimes I think I said something, but I really didn't. You know, like if you think you ordered grits but you got hash browns. Which did I really ask for? It starts to make you wonder."

Riddles, Jack thought. I don't have time for this bumpkin. "I gotta say, Senator Denton, I'm not sure I follow."

"Well, it's like when I thought I said drop this shellfish lease bullshit, but then I get a call from friends in Pender County telling me some ole boy was found layin' on the ground left for dead last night, a busted skull and, oddly enough, two busted hands. Boy happened to be an oyster farmer. Quite a coincidence I'd say."

Fleming started to rub his forehead. Goddammit, Alex, he thought. "Senator… I, uh, I don't know anything about that."

"Here's the thing, son, you're either lyin' to me, or you've lost control of what was once a simple plan. Either way, that's not ideal, wouldn't you agree?"

"Senator, I assure you—"

"This is my last phone call, understand, son," Denton interrupted. "All I wanted was some simple legislation passed. Clean up this clusterfuck quickly, or I'll make sure your political career goes the way of the giant turd I left in the commode this morning."

As soon as Denton hung up Jack dialed Alex, but got his voicemail. "Call me back, Alex, as soon as possible." Fuckin' imbecile, Jack thought, his hands clenched so hard they were turning white.

MATT WENT BACK to the main house and called town hall to let them know he was taking a few days off for some much-needed rest and relaxation. Kelly agreed it would be a good thing since he was acting a little strange.

Matt wanted a shower and to gather his thoughts before everyone showed up at the compound. The problem for Matt was, despite everything else going on, he could not get Katie out of his head. Was she staying or leaving? What did last night mean? For that matter, what did this morning mean? And did Hannah give her blessing? The cruel side of his conscience chided, *why don't you send her a note, you nerd, do you like me, check one, yes or no.* God, I could be a dick even to myself, he thought.

Once he was cleaned-up, he went downstairs to the conference room to find Tanner standing by the table with a map of the island and the surrounding waterways splayed out. He was making some marks on the map as Matt walked in.

Tanner spoke without looking up, "My house seemed awfully empty this morning when I came home."

"I stayed here at the compound," Matt replied. It wasn't a lie, he was at the compound, just not necessarily in this particular building.

"Uh huh. I hope the guest house had everything you needed."

Matt ignored the comment and asked, "What are you doing?"

Tanner sat down at the table and leaned back, still looking at the map. "I called a friend at the Division of Marine Fisheries early this morning and asked about recent shellfish lease activity. At first, she was reluctant to talk, but I finally assured her that the conversation wouldn't go beyond us. As we talked, she told me more than I'm sure she planned to."

He waved Matt over to the map and continued, "At first I just asked her if there had been any lease transfers in the past six months or so. She said there were a few, mostly among family members, but she did say that there were two that were transferred to a company called Majestic Oysters, Inc."

"OK," Matt said, "is that unusual?"

"Most of these leases are more or less family or individually owned. Companies are more likely to have franchises."

"What's the difference?"

"Shellfish leases are on public trust waters where the lease-holder is charged a yearly fee by the state, with renewable contracts. A franchise is more of a commercial shellfish aquaculture operation located on a recognized submerged land claim."

"Private property in the water," Matt said, rubbing his chin.

"Exactly. Because franchises have deed rights, some of the rules are a little different. But all shellfish leasing is for commercial production, so even the mom & pop jobs must be sold to a licensed dealer. Franchise owners tend to cut out the middleman."

"I'm not following, why is this important to us?"

"I'm not sure yet, but I am seeing some red flags. Not only have they picked up two transfers, they've also applied for two new sites. That's why I started working on this map. I've marked in red the two sites that they had transferred, and in yellow, the two new sites." Tanner pointed at the map. "See a pattern?"

Matt noticed that they were located in the marshes close to the federal portion of Banks Channel, within Topsail Beach's town limits. He looked up at Tanner and asked, "Do you know where Holt Bratton's and Frank Kenny's leases are located?"

"Marked in green. Pops, we're scheduled to have our dredge project next January that includes dredging Banks Channel. Between these leases and the fisheries designations of primary nursery areas, we could have significant permit issues. The new legislation coming down the pipe allows for businesses whose primary income is derived by shellfish farming to have input in the permit process."

"Businesses like Majestic Oysters, Inc."

"Exactly. At a minimum, this will prolong an already difficult process. It will make it significantly harder, and more expensive."

"None of these sites are particularly large, especially if you're a commercial operation," Matt noted. "So why would they be interested?"

"I wondered about that myself."

"Anything else?"

"Yeah, transfer of existing leases and any new ones require a public hearing. In all cases, these requirements were waived for Majestic Oysters."

Matt's body tensed up, and his head turned sharply towards

Tanner. "What do you mean, requirements were waived? How the fuck did that happen?"

"Don't know yet. I'm not sure if my contact didn't know or didn't want to say. I didn't want to push too hard for fear she would shut down completely. Dad, this connects the recent shellfish attacks to the legislation."

"Maybe. There's definitely some shenanigans going on."

For the first time in years, Matt began to feel the thrill of a confidence game, the beginnings of a plan underway. He started thinking that the waiving of the public hearings had to come from a legislator, could it be the same one behind the proposed dredging legislation? He wasn't sure how it fit, but he knew they were finally getting a break.

Dan walked into the room. "Mornin', boys," he said in his usual jovial way. "How's it hanging?" The smile on his face turned more quizzical as he looked first at Tanner and then back at Matt. He paused, tilting his head, eyebrows furrowed as he looked back at Tanner. Then he walked towards Matt, staring into his eyes. "You sons of bitches got laid last night."

He looked again at Tanner, who shrugged and then came back to Matt "Holy shit, you slept with Katie."

"You don't know what you're talking about, Trek."

"Don't feed me that shit, I can see it in your eyes. I've only seen that look when you were with her or Hannah."

"Easy brother, don't cross that line."

He held his hands up in a sign of surrender. "Just happy for you, partner." He looked over at Tanner. "Maybe he'll get his head out his ass now."

"Any chance you're here for a reason other than to piss me off?"

Although truth be known, Matt was kind of glad it was out.

He was just surprised it wasn't Katie announcing it as a way to make him even more uncomfortable.

"As a matter of fact, Kemosabe, there is. I spoke with the chief in Elizabethtown, and he was more than happy to help out. He found several William Covingtons in the area, but I think we were able to narrow the field." He said the last sentence with his personal flair for the dramatic. He waited for Matt to ask, his favorite game. Always did, just to annoy him.

"Would you be willing to explain?"

"Why, yes I would. Out of all the William Covingtons we found, one is a podiatrist, one is over the age of seventy, and another disabled. We ruled these gentlemen out. That left two other possible suspects."

Matt closed his eyes and leaned back in his chair; face turned up to the ceiling. "And?"

"And, William James Covington lives in Burgaw, but is five-foot-three. William Randolph Covington is six-foot-two, more likely to be the physical type."

"That's not conclusive, though," Tanner interjected.

Wait for it, Matt thought.

Dan smiled at Tanner. "Did I forget to mention that Willie R. has a rap sheet? Drug trafficking and assault."

I swear to God, he takes joy in trying my patience, Matt thought. "Thank you, Dan, for that riveting, although completely unnecessary, trip through the Covingtons of eastern North Carolina. Do we have an address for Willie R.?"

"Last known. I figured young Tanner and I can stake him out, maybe get a feel if this guy is our mysterious Mr. Coppertone." Dan's smile faded. "Guy has a rap sheet, Matt. We may need some help here."

"Yeah," Matt replied. "See if you can locate this guy, find out whatever you can. In the meantime, I'll give Shay a call."

Tanner, who up to this point had been enjoying the back-and-forth banter between Matt and Dan, suddenly sat up straight, eyes wide. "Uncle Shay? Holy fuck."

After Dan and Tanner left, Matt continued to look at the map that Tanner put together. If there was some scam going on, it certainly was well planned. The pieces didn't seem to go together, but he knew, somehow, they did. It was just a matter of time before he figured it out, then he could counter with a plan of his own. They needed to make a connection between Willie Covington and the shellfish leases. Then Tanner could connect the shellfish leases to the proposed legislation.

And then a leprechaun can take me to a pot of gold, he thought. He hated being on this side of a con. He was used to being the one in control.

Matt stepped out onto the porch to feel the October sun and the sea breeze. He could never understand why some people hated the salt air. It is the best medicine for the soul, the more it sticks to your skin the better. This day was exceptionally grand as the wind blew in from the southwest bringing a comforting warmth with the sun's rays. Banks Channel was a beautiful blue, and he could see the direction of the tide's flow. The waterway was quiet. Most of the recreational fishermen had already returned from their early morning excursions, and the weekenders hadn't arrived yet. Matt wouldn't trade these moments for that leprechaun's gold.

He stood there watching the sea oats sway back and forth on the dunes, almost feeling guilty that the Slaggers Compound was built in the middle of this beauty. He and Dan bought it in part to make sure the rest of the point remained undisturbed for perpetuity. The relationship with the university was a bonus.

Like always, Matt could feel her presence before he saw her. He could get a faint whiff of her perfume, Quartz, which was always so damn hard to find. She stood behind him, and he turned around, excited to know she was still here. But that excitement turned quickly to concern when he saw her face.

"Matt, my uncle called. My cousin Frank is in the ICU." There was a vulnerable side she rarely showed.

Matt was stunned. "What?"

"Someone attacked him last night and left him for dead." She looked at Matt with a combination of hurt and anger. "My uncle was so upset. He was all over the place, wanting to know why. What the fuck is going on, Matt?" she pleaded.

"I wish I knew." He grabbed her and pulled her in close. It was an embrace meant to comfort, but somehow it felt like more.

"Where is he now, did your uncle say?"

"New Hanover Regional Medical Center."

"OK, let's go. I'll take you there."

TANNER TOOK A FEW MINUTES of down time to give his sister a call. She answered on the fourth ring, sounding groggy as she spoke.

"TJ, why are you calling in the middle of the day, is something wrong?" She knew he hated being called TJ, and she was the only one who could get away with it.

"Did I wake you, Sleeping Beauty?"

"When you're three months pregnant, you can talk shit. Until then, screw you." They both laughed before Sedona continued, "Again, why are you calling me in the middle of a weekday?"

"Pops said you wanted to know if we would come for Thanksgiving. I'm calling with my RSVP. Does the invite come with a plus one?"

"Only one, Romeo?"

"That hurts. You know I'm a one-woman kinda guy."

"One at a time, maybe. And I'll think about the plus one." Sedona changed to a more serious tone. "What's this call really about?"

"Thanksgiving."

"Bullshit. You could have texted me you were coming, and that's what you would normally do. You don't like talking on the phone."

"I just wanted to hear my grumpy, tired, big sister's voice."

"OK, we'll play this game. But I will find out TJ, I always do."

"That's why I love you, Sedona."

MATT AND KATIE had been at the hospital for a couple of hours trying to find out what they could. Frank was still unconscious with a fractured skull and bleeding around the brain. Doctors were concerned that fragments from his skull had nicked the brain, causing swelling and pressure. They were performing emergency surgery to minimize additional damage to brain tissues.

As Katie sat with her aunt and uncle, Matt stepped outside to make a few phone calls. The first was to Shay. Shay was Matt's big brother, literally, standing six-foot-seven. He was boisterous and charming, always the life of the party. It was a cliché, but with him it was true: men wanted to be him, and women wanted to be with him. He could be the warmest, kindest person you would ever meet.

He could also be the most intimidating. If you didn't have beef with him, he was the greatest person you knew, but if you did, God help you.

Shay played a big role in Matt's con on the hog farmers. He took his share of the Slaggers money, as they fondly called it, and purchased a minor league baseball club. He somehow convinced his beloved New York Mets to make his team an affiliate and promptly located it in Charlotte just to piss off Atlanta Braves fans. He turned the team into a profit maker and holds court at every home game. He got developers to help build the stadium and several venues around it. All done without taxpayer dollars. He was a freaking hero to the entire city. Everything Slaggers touches turns to gold.

Shay answered on the first ring. "Matty-Boy, how's the short knocker hangin'?"

"Still to the right, brother," Matt answered. "You keepin' it between the lines?"

"Fuck that noise, sainthood ain't in my future anyway." He chuckled before he spoke again, "Social calls don't usually happen in the middle of the week. I suspect you're calling me for a reason. Is something sour in paradise?"

Matt explained what was going on, as much as he knew anyway: the murder of Holt Bratton, the strange new legislation, and the shifting of shellfish leases. He told Shay about Willie

Covington and how Dan found a possible connection. Shay soaked it all in, as he always does, before he made any comment.

"No doubt, some squirrelly shit is going on, but I don't see the connection."

"I know it's there, and it starts with Willie Covington. I just need to put the pieces together."

"And then what?" Shay asked.

Matt didn't answer him directly. "Can you come down here? I think we're gonna need your help."

"Godammit, Matty, I thought you were done with hustling. From what I'm hearing, none of this affects your life as small-town babysitter, or whatever the fuck it is you do. Why do you want to go down this path?"

Matt blew out a lung full of air. "I need your help, Shay, you coming or not?"

There was resignation in his voice when he spoke. "I'll be there as soon as I can. Let me get a few things off my calendar."

Matt's next call was to Dan. "Did you find our guy?"

"Yeah, we found him and the shithole he lives in. Tanner and I sat on it until he showed up with some tweaked hooker. They haven't left the house for a few hours now. Where are you?"

"I'm at the hospital. Aoife's cousin was busted up pretty bad."

"Fuck, how bad?"

"Bad," he said. "Severe head trauma. Someone did a number on him, and I think we may have a candidate." Matt took a beat before he spoke again. "Dan, if this is the guy that killed Holt Bratton and put Aoife's cousin in ICU, we're dealing with a psychopath."

"Yep."

"You be careful, and make damn sure Tanner never leaves your sight, read me partner?"

"Loud and clear." Matt knew Dan was already ahead of him when he spoke. "Any word on Shay?"

"He's on his way."

"Buckle in, brother," Dan said. "It's time to get this party started."

As Matt hung up the phone, an older couple was walking towards him. It had been a while, but he recognized them almost immediately. The man moved slowly, but he still stood straight, with a determined look on his face. The woman had a much gentler air to her as she tried to keep up with his stride. It was with her that Matt made eye contact. She slowed to a stop, looking directly into Matt's face.

"Matthew Sheehan, is that you?" she said, her voice warm and genuine, just like he remembered.

"Yes ma'am," he said to Mrs. Kenny.

She walked up to him and gave him a hug. "What are you doing here? I hope everything is OK."

"Actually, I brought Aoife here to see her cousin. I'm so sorry about what happened."

She shook her head slowly. "I'm saying a rosary for him, Matthew. I hope you will too."

"Yes ma'am."

"Let's go, Mary." The voice was gruff, and impatient.

"I'm coming, Jim." She turned back to Matt. "Thank you for bringing Aoife here. You are a sweet man."

She left him to catch up with her husband, who was glaring at Matt.

Matt watched them walk into the building, waiting before he walked in himself. He had no desire to meet up with Mr. Kenny. The man was never a fan of Matt's, and he certainly didn't approve of him dating his daughter back in the day. As Matt walked into the building, he overheard the older couple talking.

"Just stop it, Jim, it was a long time ago. We're here to see about Frank."

"I don't care how long ago it was, I don't want him anywhere near our daughter. What the hell is she doing here with him anyway?"

"It's none of your business who she's with, you old fool. She's not twenty anymore."

"Maybe not, but I stopped it back then, I sure as hell ain't letting it happen now. He's no good."

"You need to stay out of it. I swear you're gonna be the death of me, James Kenny."

Matt stood in the hallway, trying to wrap his head around what he just heard. He knew that Jim Kenny never liked him or his family. As far as Jim was concerned, it was people like the Sheehans that played into the stereotypically Irish family: drinking, fighting, dirty. But would he have gone as far as breaking up his daughter's relationship?

JACK FLEMING SAT BEHIND his huge desk, fuming. He had been trying to call his brother-in-law all day, but the little shit wouldn't answer or return his messages. Maybe it's possible that Covington killed him, but Fleming thought he wasn't that lucky. If those two were involved in the second incident, then they've gone rogue, Fleming thought. If that was the case, he no longer controlled the situation, and if they got caught, they would surely implicate him. He couldn't have that. The two of them would have to disappear, whether short term or forever.

Fleming decided that if he didn't hear from Alex by the end of the day, he would need a new plan. He was determined not to lose access to the shellfish leases. In his heart he knew it was a good plan. He wasn't about to let a bloated ex-senator and two bumbling idiots ruin this for him. He wondered if he could pull off looking sad at his brother-in-law's funeral.

KATIE AND MATT LEFT THE HOSPITAL around six o'clock with no new information about her cousin's condition. The sun was beginning its descent, and the air was turning crisp. Matt expected they would need a little warmer clothing as the evening got later, so when they got to his truck, he retrieved a lightweight fleece jacket with the Topsail Beach insignia on it and handed it to her. Underneath the insignia were the words *Town Manager*. She looked at it and smiled.

"Do you own any clothes without *Topsail Beach* written all over it?" She laughed.

"I like to represent," he replied, trying but failing miserably to sound cool.

She put on the jacket, but Matt could tell her mood had changed. "I should have warned him in my message."

Matt grabbed her hand and squeezed it. "You couldn't have known what was going to happen."

She had the heat of anger as she spoke. "Bullshit. We had already figured there was a threat, which is why I called in the first place." She wiped away a tear from her cheek.

"This is not on you, Aoife, and you know it."

She was looking down at the jacket she had just put on. "I didn't plan on staying this long, I'm running out of clean clothes."

"We'll go shopping tomorrow. In the meantime, you can wear another one of my shirts," he said with a wry smile.

"I suppose you have *Topsail Beach* monogrammed bra and panties for me too?"

"Let's go downtown for dinner. Afterwards, I know a great place for drinks. We can spend the night at my condo, assuming my son hasn't claimed it."

"Well now, it looks like this shanty Irish girl has found herself a sugar daddy. What would me Da say?"

"My guess would be a not-so-polite *no*."

She looked deep into Matt's eyes and spoke quietly. "I'm sorry, Matt, I know you weren't thrilled to see me show up. I deserve that. I don't want you to feel like you owe me anything, and you certainly don't need to treat me like nothing happened. I know I can't replace Hannah, or pretend like time hasn't passed. Last night was nice, but you don't need to—"

"Aoife, I don't have a clue where my head is right now. I know I loved you once, and clearly there are still feelings. Last night made my heart explode and my head panic. Maybe tonight we just enjoy the evening. I can sleep in the second bedroom, and tomorrow we will figure out next steps in both our mystery case and our lives. Fair?"

"Fair," she said, "except for the second bedroom part. I'm going rock your world tonight."

"Oh, thank God."

They stopped at Matt's condo to park the truck. The place was located along the southern end of the Wilmington Riverwalk. From his balcony, he could see the Cape Fear Memorial Bridge and the USS North Carolina. The city had recently renovated the boardwalk. Matt loved downtown Wilmington.

They went inside for Matt to change. He needed something warmer for their evening stroll, plus it gave him a chance to grab his Stetson Pawnee. The hat was chocolate brown with a medium curved, brim-down design and a pinched crown. Cowboy hats are not exactly commonplace in Wilmington, but Matt didn't care. He loved his Stetson.

"Jaysus, would you look at this," Katie said as Matt walked into the living room.

"What?" he asked innocently.

She came closer and looked at him from head to toe, noticing the boots as well. She smiled and shook her head. "It's not bad, I suppose, especially with your beard. By the way, there seems to be a good bit of gray mixed in there."

"You don't like the beard?"

"I didn't say that. It gives you that rugged, yet still distinguished look. Plus, it tickles." She fluttered her eyelashes at him.

"Well, now you're just making fun of me."

She put her arms around his neck, pulling him closer to kiss him on the lips. "Never. Now, take me to dinner, my coastal cowboy."

They avoided the tourist-trap restaurants. He took her for tapas, knowing she would eat off his plate anyway. Matt kept the conversation light, and she talked about her daughter. As Katie described their relationship, Matt couldn't help but see there were more similarities than differences between mother and daughter. When the conversation moved to Sedona, Matt became a little more uncomfortable.

"Sedona and I have had our struggles," Matt responded when Katie asked about her. "All because of me."

"Dan says you talk to her a lot, though."

"It's Dan who talks too much," Matt grumbled. "But it's true, I try to talk to her as often as I can. Sedona is a lot like her mother, very strong in her convictions. And very protective of her family. When Hannah died and I lost my shit, it was Sedona who fought to keep us all together. There was a lot of resentment that I wasn't there for her when she needed it most."

"But it's better now, right?"

Matt shrugged. "Sure, but I can never replace the lost hugs, or wipe away the tears from her grief over losing her mother. I can't go back and give her the comfort she needed at the time. That's opportunity lost, a void I created and can't go back and repair."

"You're her father, Matt, that doesn't change. She will always need you, no matter how independent she is. Be there moving forward. Be there for her and your grandchild."

Afterwards, they walked down the Riverwalk, then Front Street. He took her down a short alley to The Blind Elephant. It had an old speakeasy feel. They walked in and were greeted by a gentleman sitting at a table watching the door.

"Good evening, Mr. Sheehan, I see you have someone other than Mr. Trekor joining you tonight. It's not my place, but this is a pleasant surprise."

"Thanks, Billy. What's the haps?"

"Same old, same old. Things are starting to die down a bit. If you want to grab you a table, I'll have Mary bring your usual." He looked at Katie. "Ma'am, is there something we can get you?"

"Mary makes a great Old Fashioned," Matt told Katie. "By the way, Billy, this is Katie Kenny, a close friend of mine."

She smiled. "I'll try the highly recommended Old Fashioned."

"It would be our pleasure, Miss Kenny."

They grabbed a table in the corner as Billy went to the bar to place the order. The room was dark, with two TVs located over the bar, both playing an old black and white movie with Clark Gable. There were lights around the old 1920's-style bar, and the walls were all exposed brick.

They sat down, and Matt placed his hat on the table, crown down.

"I see you introduced me as Katie," she said.

"I kinda like being the only one to call you 'Aoife.' Makes me feel special."

"I see. And you have a 'usual' here?"

"It's mostly a bourbon bar, but they keep a bottle of Slane Irish Whiskey on hand for me."

"Oh god, you're one of those."

He looked at her meekly. "But in a good way."

They sat there for over an hour, drinking, laughing, remembering. Matt thought about how he hadn't felt anywhere close to that good since Hannah died. He wanted it to last forever, but he knew tomorrow was another day. He was determined to savor the moment.

They finally hit one of those silent pauses which could be uncomfortable, but not in this case. Matt gazed into her big emerald eyes, lost in a memory.

"Pay the tab, sugar daddy. It's time to take me home."

Friday, October 14

SEAMUS "SHAY" SHEEHAN was up before dawn, packing for his trip to Wilmington. He stared at the suitcase, trying to figure out exactly what he needed. Matt didn't tell him much on the phone, just that he needed his help. To Shay that meant only one thing; Matt was planning something that wasn't on the up-and-up. He tossed in the usual, of course, but he wasn't sure what role he was going to play. Maybe he was going to be some random tourist-type: Hawaiian shirt, cargo shorts, sandals kind of guy. Or maybe he was going to play someone more menacing, a body guard type. Tight shirts, porkpie hat, slacks, dress shoes. Hell, maybe a businessman, full suit and tie. He would probably be providing the muscle, but he grabbed his garment bag just in case.

It was the way it had always been. Matt or one of his other brothers would find a way to get into some trouble, and Shay would be there to clean up the mess. In fairness, Shay was usually in the middle of the mess as well.

There were five Sheehan boys, Shay being the true middle child. Growing up, they were a savvy, mischievous bunch that constantly befuddled the nuns at school. Whether selling contraband, running numbers on high school sports, or skipping class to get laid, they were constantly in trouble with the monsignor. But it was Shay who was in and out of trouble the most. He was the enforcer, even at a young age. His size and menacing scowl scared even the toughest kids. If a kid showed up with a black eye or bloody nose, Shay was the first one to be questioned. He took the heat for the Sheehan boys every time.

As an adult, Shay lived on the edge of the criminal element. He had connections with local gang leaders, mobsters, and white-collar criminals. He also had ties with civic and political leaders. He made it his business to know what was going on, even if he wasn't directly involved. This knowledge gave him leverage, and while he never used it for criminal activity, he did use it to his advantage. Many a deal was brokered under his facilitation, usually at his ballpark.

As Shay packed his suitcase, he wondered why Matt needed him. Since his marriage to Hannah, Matt steered clear of trouble, content to live the domestic life. Even after Hannah's death, Matt played it straight. Except for the Sampson con, but that was revenge. Shay felt an uneasiness settling in, a premonition of violence he didn't like. He sat on the edge of his bed, debating what he should do. He took a deep breath, letting it out in an audible sigh.

He went to his large walk-in closet where he kept his gun safe. He thought about what to bring, but since Matt didn't say what they were doing, he wasn't sure what he would need. He eventually pulled out his Glock and Sig Sauer. He put the Sig Sauer in his suitcase, but decided to wear the Glock. Shay was partial to the shoulder holster. It was easy and offered rapid access, allowing for a quick draw whether sitting or standing. Plus, it was more comfortable than a belt-mounted holster. It also was old school, just like Shay.

He went into the bathroom to collect his toiletries when he caught a glance of himself in the mirror, noticing how tired he looked.

"We're getting too old for this shit."

MATT WOKE UP EARLY and went outside to the deck overlooking the river. The morning air was cool, fog rolling over the still-warm water. The river was calm, no boats to create a wake. The stillness of the water and crispness of the air made Matt melancholy. Winter was coming soon.

Matt thought about Sedona and the bitter Montana winter in store for her and her husband. He hated when they were out there, convinced that the outfitters and guide service they ran was dangerous. Her pregnancy only made him worry more.

He was much happier when they were back in Wilmington, running their farmers' market, selling local produce and seafood. They also sold local craft beers. On the weekends they brought in a food truck and had live music. It went beyond just a farmers' market. It was a social gathering point, and an extremely popular one. Why can't that be year-round, Matt wondered.

Though it had taken a while for Matt to make it right with Sedona, he thought maybe they were finally there. They talked frequently, although it was harder when she was out west. "I fucking hate winter," he whispered to the birds flying low over the river.

Katie came out to join him. Matt looked to her and realized that any resentment he felt from her leaving him years ago was gone. It wasn't that he missed Hannah any less, but maybe Dan was right, maybe he was fortunate enough to have had two soulmates in one lifetime.

"Mornin', cowboy." She held the coffee up close to her face, wrapping her hands around the cup for warmth. "This is the second time you left me alone in bed, are you trying to tell me something?"

"I was actually thinking how nice it would be just to stay in bed with you all winter, Aoife, but sadly, we have work to do. At the moment, I'm having trouble putting it all together."

"Alright, so talk it out with me, like we used to."

Matt looked at her sitting in the chair, long legs curled underneath her, hair pulled back away from her face. It was like a flashback from when they were just kids, planning their next hustle. She caught him staring and smiled.

"Focus, perv, quit staring at me. What do we know?"

Matt thought about it for a moment, thinking he needed to break it down into key groups first and then find the connection if there was one.

"OK, first, there is the business of shellfish aquaculture and state leases. All of a sudden, leases are changing hands, and there's at least one oyster fisherman, Holt Bratton, dead."

"And Frank's been badly beaten."

"Right. And a new company, Majestic Oysters, suddenly appears out of nowhere, buying leases without having to follow standard procedure.

"Next," Matt continued, "new legislation is being drafted that would greatly impact access to both state and federal funds used to dredge waterways and how the spoil sands could be used for beach nourishment. It would require communities to use the new state-owned dredge if it wanted to be eligible for the funds."

"How do these two things connect?"

"Not sure yet, but I do know that shellfish lease owners may have a say in the permit process. It's thin, but there might be a connection."

"C'mon Matt, what else?"

Matt sighed and shook his head. "I don't know, maybe there is something in the fact that spoil sites in the state are largely controlled by either the state or the US Army Corps of Engineers."

"I don't see what that has to do with shellfish leases," Katie said.

Matt leaned back in his chair, tilting his head in thought. "It's like a jigsaw puzzle. I have the pieces; I just can't make them fit. There's state regulations and federal agencies involved, but there has to be a connecting piece."

"So, if I have this right," Katie said, "state money can only be used to purchase and develop new spoils sites in the Intracoastal Waterway, which happens to be dredged solely by the Corps, a federal agency."

"Yep," Matt replied. "And now, all FEMA recovery funds, which go through the state, would have to meet the same requirements proposed in the new legislation."

"You think federal agencies are scamming towns?"

"No, I don't believe the Army Corps of Engineers would develop a plan to steal from the towns. I believe their thought process is often outdated, but they aren't purposely doing harm. They would take full advantage of any new law that benefits them, however. I definitely know FEMA isn't involved. While their processes are a giant pain in the ass, their goal is to get money where it is needed."

"Where does that leave us then?"

Matt rubbed his chin. "The money trail leads to the general assembly, our elected leaders. That's where everything is being manipulated. There's a snake or two in the woodpile. That's where I need to focus."

"Maybe that's where the shellfish leases come in," Katie offered.

"I don't follow."

"Well, you said the money trail leads to elected officials, maybe the shellfish leases are a way to launder all that money coming in."

"Launder money?" Matt started to laugh. "It's not dirty money coming in from the feds."

Katie shrugged. "It's just a thought."

Matt knew better. Katie didn't just spout things out without some consideration. "OK, Aoife, for shits and giggles, how and why?"

"It's just a theory," she said. "We would need more confirmation to be sure. If they have a cash flow problem from excess federal funds, they would need to wash the money through a legitimate business. Enter Majestic Oysters. Whoever is heading this up would gradually deposit funds into a bank through the company and the company would exaggerate its costs and sales. For example, if they sold $5,000 worth of oysters, they may actually report $10,000. That money is then deposited in a legitimate bank account and appears as an ordinary deposit of oyster proceeds. Think about it, what better way to funnel money in the coastal area than through the rapidly growing oyster industry?"

"Wouldn't that add up too quickly over time?" Matt asked.

"Very likely," she said, "which is why if they're smart, they will layer the money." She saw the confusion in Matt's face. "I thought you were the smart one here." She laughed. "To avoid having too much revenue and becoming a bigger tax liability, Majestic Oysters would look to invest in another legitimate business."

Matt's eyes went wide as he made the connection. "The new fucking dredge is the key. They will force the use of the dredge for major projects, funneling all federal and state monies through the dredge."

They sat in silence taking in the morning sights and smells. Matt was feeling pretty smug, knowing fortunes were changing. He didn't have a plan yet, but he knew he was starting to figure things out.

Katie broke the silence. "I need to go back to the hospital."

"Absolutely. I can take you."

"No, you have other things to do. Just take me back to the compound, and I'll get my car."

Matt tilted his head as he looked back at her, thinking ahead. "OK, but I need you to stay for a few more days."

She looked at him with those emerald eyes and surprised him with what she said next: "Look, Matt, you don't owe me anything. We've had fun, no doubt, but I don't want to overstay my welcome."

Matt stood up and held his hand out to her. She looked up, her eyes even bigger and deeper than normal. She didn't say a word, just took his hand and stood up beside him. David

Gray's "Be Mine" was playing in the background, and Matt sang softly in her ear as he pulled her closer to him, swaying slowly to the music.

"I want you to stay," he whispered to her. "Besides, I need your help with this job. We are going to make those responsible for your cousin pay."

She pushed away from him. "Are you serious?"

"About which part?"

"The job, you eejit," she said as she punched his chest

"I'll take you back to the compound. Go see your cousin, and then go shopping. You'll need something that looks business casual, plus whatever else you need for the next few days. I'll give you the Slaggers credit card."

"I don't need your money, I'm not a whore," she joked.

Matt laughed. "You know I didn't mean that, but you are working for the company, and we cover that tab."

She looked at him for a minute. "You got a plan?"

"Starting to come together."

She smiled. "I guess I need to go shower then."

"Not without me."

WILLIE AWOKE TO WHAT SOUNDED like jackhammers outside his bedroom window. It was actually the snoring of the woman next to him. Goddamn, how can such a skinny bitch make as much noise as a fuckin' bear, he thought. He took his elbow and gave her a hard shot to the ribs.

"Ow," she cried out. "What the fuck was that for, Willie?" She was still groggy.

Willie sat up on the edge of the bed, his back to the woman. "I don't know why I let you stay here, Nikki. You're a useless piece of shit, and a noisy one at that."

"Don't be that way, baby. C'mon and lay back down, and I'll show you I ain't useless."

She did give good head, he thought, but he had things to do. Plus, he knew she was only there to get free smack from him. "Just get your lazy ass out of my bed. Christ, you need a shower, you reek. But make me breakfast first."

She got out of bed and stood there naked, looking around the cluttered floor for her underwear. "You don't exactly smell like roses, Willie. And you ain't got nothin' in this dump for breakfast."

Willie got up, ready to give her a good beating. But he realized he too was naked and was suddenly embarrassed. Instead, he turned away and headed towards the bathroom.

"I'm gonna take a piss. You better change your attitude if you know what's good for you. Otherwise, get your skank ass outta here."

Willie found some ripped jeans and a dirty shirt on the floor. His head hurt from the night before, so he popped a few aspirins, washing them down with a half empty can of beer he found in the kitchen. He ran his fingers through his hair and splashed some water on his face.

Nikki sat at the kitchen table, lit cigarette in hand.

"I was gonna make you breakfast, Willie, but there ain't nothing clean in this place."

The sink was full of dirty dishes, the trash can was overflowing, even the walls were stained where plates of food had been thrown. Willie noticed a roach hustling around the countertop, climbing into an old Styrofoam coffee cup. He looked over to Nikki, with her matted hair, droopy eyes, smeared make-up.

Was this really his life?

Willie thought about the money Alex had promised, the treasure buried at sea. He deserved that money, and nobody was going to get in his way. He would use Alex as long as he had to, and once they found the treasure, he would get rid of the whiny little twit.

Nikki's shrill voice snapped Willie out of his trance. "How about it, Willie, I'm hungry. I can go down to the mini-mart and get us a few breakfast burritos and some beer. I just need some cash, baby. Then maybe you can give me a little fix, OK?"

Willie shook his head. "Why don't you clean this place up, you two-bit whore? And clean yourself up. You fuckin' disgust me."

MATT SAT AT HIS DESK AND SCRIBBLED a few notes from his conversation with Katie. The shellfish leases and the proposed legislation had to be connected, the coincidence was too great. But how, and who, and why?

His phone rang; it was the chief.

"Morning, boss, sorry to bother you while you're off, hopefully doing something fun."

"No problem, Chief, I'm just tending to a few personal issues. What's going on?"

"Well, it's probably nothing, but I wanted to let you know that another oyster fisherman was attacked. It happened in Pender County, obviously outside of my jurisdiction, but his lease is in our town limits."

Shit, Matt thought. He didn't want the police to zero in on Covington until he had a better idea of the connection. "You think it's related to Holt Bratton?" he stalled.

Dan walked by the office, and Matt signaled him to come in.

"Could be completely separate events, but it's an awfully strange coincidence." The chief paused for a second. "By the way, the sheriff said he thought he saw you leaving the hospital yesterday with a real pretty lady who seemed a bit distraught. Is everything OK?"

Matt had to think quickly. It's these moments when a con can go south with any sign of hesitation. "Old friend of the family," he said. "She's not from Wilmington but has a family member here who is not doing well, so I told her I would help her out for a few days. Thanks for asking."

"Well, I hope everything is OK. As far as these cases go, I hear the victim is still unconscious. It's the sheriff's case, so I imagine it will be several days before we get together to compare notes. I'll keep you informed as I hear more, as I'm sure you will do the same."

Matt wondered if the chief knew more about him than his town manager persona. If he did, he never said anything. But now he was letting Matt know the clock was ticking on this case.

Dan had made himself comfortable on Matt's couch as he waited for the phone call to finish. His hair was tousled, and he had three days of growth on his face.

"What's the haps, partner?" Dan asked.

"That was the police chief. He's aware of the attack on Aoife's cousin and is starting to wonder if there is a connection with Bratton's death. He basically let me know the clock is running. What's the story with Covington?"

"Tanner and I are going back to his place in just a bit. My guess is he won't be moving until at least lunchtime."

Matt trusted Dan's judgment, so he wasn't concerned that they weren't tailing Covington at the moment. "We don't have much time, so we are going to have to improvise a bit."

"You mean engage."

"Sooner than later if the opportunity is there. I don't want to spook him, but we may have to give this a little push."

"We've done it before," Dan replied.

"Not with a psychopath."

"Point taken." Dan nodded. "When does Shay get here?"

"I expect he will get here sometime later tonight." Matt paused, a realization of the growing seriousness of the situation. "Are you carrying?"

"Do you want to know the answer to that?"

Matt shook his head.

"Tanner and I will be heading out soon," Dan said. "What are you going to do?"

"Research on Majestic Oysters Inc. If what I think is true, we can make a plan moving forward. Let me know what happens out there, and be careful."

Dan smiled as he got up to leave. "Always, my brother."

Dan and Tanner pulled up curbside a few houses down from Covington's place around noon in an old silver Taurus that Dan kept around when he wanted to fly under the radar. Nobody notices a Taurus. The outside paint job had faded, but it had no rust. The interior was slightly worn, but mechanically, it was solid. He knew it was perfect for what they were doing.

Willie's house was one of very few in the neighborhood that

was in shambles. It was missing half of its shutters, and one of the windows was boarded up. Any wood trim still in place was peeling and termite-destroyed. The yard was patchy grass, and the bushes along the base of the house were overgrown. Dan noticed the overflowing trash can at the side of the house, guessing it hadn't been taken to the street in weeks. He could only imagine what the house looked and smelled like inside.

Covington's old pick-up truck was in the driveway, just as it had been the night before. Dan and Tanner sat in the car, eating chicken biscuits and fries they picked-up on the way. It wasn't too long before Covington came out the front door, visibly agitated.

He was followed by the woman. She stood on the porch wearing nothing but a t-shirt that didn't quite cover her panties. Her hair laid flat on her head as if it hadn't been washed in days, and she looked as if the sunlight affected her as it would a vampire. She was yelling at Covington. Dan and Tanner had their windows open, so it wasn't hard to hear the two shouting at each other.

"Ain't you gonna give me a ride, Willie? How the hell am I supposed to get home?"

"I don't care what you do, take an Uber, just get the fuck outta my house!"

"I ain't got no money, you prick!"

Willie stormed back towards the house, and the woman began to step back but it was too late. He hit her with the back of his hand hard, and she crumbled to the ground.

Tanner reached for the car door handle, but Dan grabbed his arm. "Not yet," he said in a quiet but hard tone.

Willie said something they could not make out and went back to his truck, leaving her crying on the porch. He pulled out of the driveway, and Dan let him get the road a bit before he pulled out to follow.

Dan figured Covington wasn't smart enough to know he was being followed, but he didn't want to take any chances. Besides, it wouldn't be too hard to follow him; his truck was a lot like his house, a piece of shit. Two different colored doors were on the driver and passenger sides, and the tailgate was completely gone. There were holes along the quarter panel where rust had eaten away at the metal. Covington was a poster child for the Pathetic Motherfuckers Club.

Dan could tell that Tanner was still upset about what they witnessed. "If I know your father," Dan said as he stared out at the street, "when this is all over, that guy is going to pay for what he's done."

ALEX SPENCER PACED back and forth in his office at Coastal Properties Group. He pulled on his tie as if it was a snake gradually choking the life out of him. He never liked wearing a tie, or a suit for that matter, it wasn't him. He felt like a child playing grown-up. I should be wearing a chef's coat, he thought. Why did life have to be so fucking hard.

Alex had been avoiding his brother-in-law's calls since the day before, but he knew he couldn't do it forever. And now that psycho Willie was coming to his office. Alex pleaded with him to meet somewhere else, but Willie was insistent. Everything was spiraling out of control, and Alex just wanted out. He didn't care about the treasure anymore, if it even existed. He didn't know what to believe, but he knew being anywhere near Willie was a huge mistake. Alex decided he was going to have to put an end to all this, and he was going to tell Willie he was out. Then he would call his brother-in-law.

The more Alex thought about it, the more he got scared. The last couple of days, he noticed large amounts of hair in his sink. Every little noise in his apartment made him jump. He even added a deadbolt lock to his bedroom door. He didn't know how much more he could take.

Maybe I should just run, he thought, but where? He couldn't go to his father, what would he tell him, that he's in trouble with his drug dealer and his brother-in-law? He needed a way out, but he had zero ideas.

Alex sat down behind his desk and hung his head.

Willie didn't have to drive far. He pulled into a spot close to the front door. Dan followed, parking at the next building over where he could still see Willie. He and Tanner watched Willie get out of the beat-up truck and head towards the entrance.

"A realty company," Tanner said, "one that may know about transfers of shellfish leases."

"The same thought occurred to me," Dan answered.

Before Willie could enter the building, he was met by a man in a gray suit. The man was smaller than Covington and seemed nervous while trying to steer Willie away from the door. He kept scanning the parking lot as if looking for witnesses

Dan and Tanner watched the animated conversation dominated by Covington. He threw his arms in the air, occasionally jabbing the man in the suit with his finger. The other guy kept shaking his head, trying to get Covington to calm down. It wasn't working.

Dan and Tanner rolled down their windows, but couldn't

make out what was said. Covington started to walk away, but turned back and shouted loud enough to be heard by Dan and Tanner. "You better have your fuckin' ass there tonight, Alex."

Covington got back in his truck and left, tires squealing.

"What do you think?" Tanner asked.

"Not sure, but I'm gonna find out. You take the car and follow Covington. I'll call you to pick me up when I'm done."

"What are you going to do?"

Dan smiled. "I'm going to engage." He got out of the car, stopping suddenly. "Be careful following this guy, he's definitely on something. Your father will kill me if anything happens to you."

Tanner slid behind the wheel. "We certainly wouldn't want that," he said with a hint of sarcasm.

"Oh, and try not to get pulled by the cops, there's a gun in the glove compartment."

KATIE SAT IN THE HOSPITAL waiting area, a smattering of uncomfortable chairs and a small television mounted on the wall. Very sterile and depressing.

Her parents were standing in the opposite corner of the room, trying to console her aunt and uncle. Frank was still unconscious, and doctors had just told them it was still too early to know the extent of the damage. Katie watched as her aunt sobbed quietly while her mother held her hand.

Katie thought about what happened to Frank, and the other guy, Bratton, knowing they had to be connected. She wondered what could be so valuable that would make the lives of these two men seem inconsequential. She couldn't help but think about the fact that she found herself here at the coast, in the same town as Matt Sheehan, who also had a stake in these conflicts. Coincidence or fate, she didn't know, but she wished Matt was sitting with her.

Her concentration was interrupted by her father's voice. "What was he doing here?" He spat out the word "he" as if it left a bitter taste in his mouth.

Katie didn't want to get into it with her father. "He lives down here, Dad," she said with a heavy sigh. "He just happened to be around."

"Those Sheehans always happen to be around, like cockroaches. The whole damn lot of them."

"Just drop it, Dad, will ya?"

"You left with him last night. Please tell me you're not spending time with him."

"Jaysus, Dad, I'm not your little girl any more. Whatever I did last night is none of your business."

"Matt Sheehan is bad news, always has been."

"He's the town manager of Topsail Beach, for Chrissake. He's not Al Capone."

"He's a conman. The whole family was nothin' but drunken troublemakers, giving the Irish a bad name."

"Not like your lace-curtain side of the family, is that it, Dad? Perhaps you forgot about Mom's side. Maybe I'm more like them than you'd like to believe."

"You watch your tongue, Katie. Men like Sheehan, they don't change. I'm just trying to protect you."

"Like you did thirty years ago?" Tears welled up in her eyes. "How'd that work out?"

Jim Kenny sat down beside his daughter and took her hand.

"He would have hurt you baby, and I couldn't abide that. You should have married Dennis. He is a good man."

Katie looked at him, his face showing his years. She knew he meant well; she could see it in his eyes. But it didn't change the past. "I didn't love him Dad, not the way I loved Matt."

"But you had a child with him. I just don't understand why you refuse to be happy."

Tears ran down her cheeks as she stood. She didn't wipe them away. "That's on you." Her voice caught in her throat. "I love you, Daddy, I do. But the person who took away my happiness is you. Don't get me wrong, I have no regrets as far as my daughter is concerned. She is my world. But you took away what truly made me happy. I'm not going to allow that to happen again."

DAN WAITED A FEW MINUTES after Tanner left to give time for this guy Alex to settle down after his confrontation with Covington. He texted Matt about the connection between Covington and Coastal Properties Group. He left out the part that he sent Tanner to follow a psychopath.

Once he felt like enough time had passed, Dan walked in and headed straight to reception. Behind the computer was a young woman, probably mid-twenties, Dan guessed. She was small but fit with brown hair pulled back from her face. She wore large round glasses with a pink frame, and a slight frown. She did not look up from her computer.

"Can I help you?" she asked.

Dan smiled. "I'm here to see Alex."

"He is unavailable right now." She continued typing, staring at the computer screen, never making eye contact.

Dan noticed a gym bag tucked behind the desk and took a chance. "That's too bad, I was really hoping to see him." He paused for a moment. "I'm sorry if this comes off a little forward, but you wouldn't happen to be a pilates instructor, would you?"

For the first time she looked up at Dan. "Yoga actually, but I'm working on becoming a pilates instructor as well. How did you know?"

Dan smiled and gave his best sheepish look. "You just have that healthy, fit look of an instructor." He hesitated for a beat. "I'm sorry, I hope that didn't sound creepy. I certainly didn't mean anything by it. I've actually been thinking of trying something new."

"Not at all," she said. Her attitude and body language had completely changed. "I didn't take it as creepy." She gave him a little smile, "Unless that was a lame attempt at a pick-up line."

"Oh, uh, no, I…"

She laughed. "I'm kidding, but you should come try my yoga class. It's at night, because I'm here during the day. A girl's gotta pay the bills." She handed Dan a business card. "My schedule is on the website."

Dan looked at the card. "Thank you, Anna, I will definitely do that. I really wanted to see Alex about some shellfish leases, he came recommended. But I guess I can try elsewhere."

"That's odd, we don't really do that kind of real estate, but let me buzz Alex. I'm sure he won't mind."

She picked up the phone. "Mr. Spencer, there is a gentleman here to see you about shellfish leases." There was a pause before she spoke again. "Yes sir, that's what he said." She looked at Dan. "I'm sorry, I didn't catch your name."

"How rude of me. I'm Benjamin Pierce." It was Dan's favorite alias.

She repeated the name, hung up the phone, then faced Dan again. "He'll be right out,'" she said and looked back at her computer as if the previous conversations never happened. He wondered what Alex said to her.

Alex Spencer came down the hallway, hair tousled, as if he had been running his hands through it. His eyes were wild, bouncing inside their sockets like pinballs. Dan assumed he had taken some drug, probably cocaine. Alex scanned the lobby to see if anyone else was there, and then quickly addressed Dan.

"I'm sorry, Mr. Pierce, is it? You must have the wrong place; we deal with homes and property here." He was rubbing his neck, pulling on his collar. His tie was askew.

"Huh," Dan said with just enough confusion to be convincing. "I'm sure Mr. Covington mentioned you specifically."

That got the reaction Dan was looking for: fear and panic. Alex looked at the receptionist, hoping she was not paying attention. "Let's go back to my office," he said quickly. He turned to the receptionist. "Make sure we're not disturbed, Anna."

She didn't look up, just nodded.

Alex led him back to his office, shutting the door behind him. Before they could sit, Alex started talking. "You are mistaken, Mr. Pierce, I don't know anyone named Covington."

"Sure you do. He's probably the one that supplied you with the dope you're currently on."

Alex's eyes went wide. Dan had to decide just how much pressure he could apply without the guy having a complete meltdown.

"Look, Alex, I'm not looking to cause trouble, I just want in."
It was a bluff. Dan didn't know what "in" was, it was his way
of playing the mark.

Alex sunk into his desk chair, and tried to hold on to the lie.
"I have no idea what you're talking about."

Dan pushed back, "Yes, you do. Willie told me everything.
We were out last night with that skinny blonde friend of his."

Alex sank even lower in his chair. "Shit, he told Nikki?"

"I guess so, I mean she was a bit whacked if you know what I
mean." Dan knew he had him.

"Look, we don't know if Blackbeard's gold even exists. I think
buying these damn leases was my brother-in-law's ploy. This
is getting way out of hand. I just want out, but Willie's fucking
crazy."

Dan did his best to show no expression on his face. Blackbeard's gold, he thought, no one believes that story anymore,
except maybe these morons. He knew he needed to get this
information back to Matt, but he also knew he had to keep Alex
on the hook.

"Look, Alex," Dan said in a calmer tone, "I think we can help
each other out, and everyone will be rich and go our own way
afterwards. Are you meeting Willie tonight too?"

Alex now just looked weary. "He wants me to be at the Pelican Tavern tonight, sounds like he's meeting you too."

He is now, Dan thought. "OK, then. See you tonight."

Dan left the building, called Tanner, and told him to pick him
up at the Celtic Creamery. Might as well enjoy some ice cream
while they were there. He let Tanner know not to worry about
Covington now that he knew where to find him later.

His second call was to Matt.

"Covington is connected to Alex Spencer, and there's a meeting set up for tonight. These criminal geniuses are apparently treasure hunters. I'm guessing they think the shellfish leases are where Blackbeard's treasure can be found."

Matt's mind was in full throttle. "Coastal Properties Group has a huge presence here, particularly in the development community. Alex Spencer is a major player in the political arena too."

"You sure?" Dan asked. "This guy didn't seem the influential type."

Matt laughed. "I'm guessing you met Alex the third, his son, by all accounts an idiot."

"That makes sense."

"You and Tanner come on back here. It's time we make a plan."

They reunited later that afternoon at the compound. Katie was back from the hospital. She told Matt that while there was no major improvement, the doctor seemed cautiously optimistic that her cousin would awaken sooner rather than later. What he would remember was more of a mystery. She said her aunt and uncle were holding up for now, but it was clearly taking a toll on them. She left out the conversation with her father.

"I went shopping like you asked," she said with a sly smile.

"Why do I get the feeling there's more to the statement?"

"Well, you weren't clear exactly what the corporate card could be used for, so I got several items to cover most scenarios."

"Meaning?"

"Let's just say I don't need your shirts for pajamas anymore."

God help me focus, Matt thought.

Dan and Tanner walked in, saving Matt from where that was heading. When Dan saw Katie, he immediately went to her.

"Katie," he said as he gave her a hug. "How's your cousin?"

"He's hanging in there." She rubbed his arm. "Thanks for asking."

"Anything we can do; you know we're here for you."

They sat around the big conference table and began to review what they knew, adding what was discovered that day. This was a process that Matt, Katie, and Dan went through years before when they were running a con. It was new to Tanner.

"Understanding the mark is critical, and planning, while never perfect, is vital to success," Matt said as he rubbed his chin. "The problem is, we still don't know all the players. It may be 'marks,' plural."

"So, what's the play?" Katie asked.

"We're going to have to learn as we go, basically do this in phases. Unfortunately, time isn't in our favor, so we don't have the luxury of a complete plan from the start."

"I'll tell you what's bugging me," Dan said, "it's the revelation that Coastal Properties Group may be involved in all this, especially being associated with a piece of shit like Willie Covington. It doesn't make sense."

Tanner agreed, "Something was nagging me about that too, so I did a little digging. Turns out Jack Fleming married into that family."

"Senator Jack Fleming?" Matt asked.

"The same. Unfortunately, most of my contacts are gone for the weekend, but I have a hunch about where the proposed legislation may have started."

"Spencer did say something about his brother-in-law," Dan added.

"That fucking kid is a genius!"

Everyone turned to the booming voice that could only come from one person, Shay Sheehan.

Matt looked up, and there he was, filling the doorway. Right behind him was Brittany, all worked up.

"I asked him to wait, but he said he was here to clean up his little brother's shit, like always." Poor Brittany. Matt wondered if she would ever be the same after this bunch.

"Tanner, I wish you would come help run my ball club. We would have a blast. Screw this nerd stuff, come back to baseball. I have a catcher with a cannon for an arm and rocks for brains. He sure could use your guidance."

Tanner smiled.

Shay scanned the room. "Holy shit, Katie Kenny in the flesh!" He moved swiftly and gracefully for such a big man, and was at Katie in an instant, picking her up in a big bear hug. "How long has it been? You look fantastic."

She grinned from ear to ear. "God, Shay, you haven't changed at all."

"Ah, I'm older, fatter, but still full of the blarney, me love." He said in his Irish brogue. "How's your Mum and Da?"

"They're good. Pretty sure my Da is still not a fan of Sheehan boys, though."

Shay's laughter filled the room. "Can't say I blame 'em." He turned to Dan next. "Danny boy, good to see ya, brother." He gave him a hearty handshake.

"Good to see you too, brother. You ready to boogie?"

"Fuckin A!" He finally turned to Matt. "What's the haps, little brother?"

The brothers hugged. "Life is paradise."

Shay looked to Katie, then back at Matt. "I bet it is," he said with a smile. "Now, why isn't there a whiskey in my hand?"

It took a while before things settled down after Shay's grand entrance. That actually worked for Matt, giving him time to continue formulating the plan. The Jack Fleming information was a game changer, the connection Matt needed to start putting together the pieces. Matt was convinced that whatever was going on with shellfish leases and the proposed legislation was connected to the new dredge, but he knew he needed more.

The treasure hunt angle was confusing to Matt for the moment, but he would likely use that angle in his plan. He had an idea.

"Dan, I need you, Tanner, and Shay to go after Covington and Spencer. We'll use the treasure hunt angle. We need some maps that show where the inlet would have been around the time of the Civil War. It doesn't have to be accurate, just enough to convince our criminal masterminds.

"You guys are going to convince them that you're searching for Confederate gold, not Blackbeard's. But first, I need you to get tonight's meeting aborted. I don't want Spencer and Covington together tonight."

"Confederate gold? You want to clue us in?" Dan asked.

"It's about greed and misdirection. I'll let you know more soon. Just make sure we keep Covington and Spencer separated."

Tanner interrupted, "Why maps?"

"Because props are essential to a good stratagem," Matt answered.

Shay laughed. "Stratagem? Don't you mean con?"

"I'm no conman, not anymore," Matt declared.

ALEX SPENCER STAYED LATE at the office, debating what to do next. Should he call Jack and take more verbal abuse? Should he blow off Willie and risk getting the shit kicked out of him again? This was way more than Alex ever thought would happen.

He was simply looking for something more exciting in his life. He hated real estate; it was boring, and he was terrible at it. He was only in it because his father wouldn't give him any more money unless he worked. His father did try, he had to admit. He wasn't a bad father, didn't ignore or neglect him as a child. It was just that Alex was a screw-up, always was. He knew his father was at his wit's end.

Then there was Jack. What a prick. Alex never knew what his sister saw in him, the power-hungry phony. Jack made Alex's life miserable from day one, never even trying to hide his contempt. Alex was pretty sure Jack was cheating on his sister and had been even before they were married, but he didn't have the guts to say anything. The more he thought about it, the angrier he got. It may also have been the drugs kicking in. As he sat and thought, he mustered up the courage to call Jack.

"It's about fucking time!" Jack said in a tight, angry voice. "Why haven't you returned my calls, and what have you and Willie done this time? For the love of God..."

"Shut up, Jack, and listen." It was the first time Alex ever spoke to anyone like that. "I'm done with you, and this whole stupid thing you got going on, whatever it is. You and Willie can kiss my ass goodbye." Boy, that felt good.

"You moron, do you know what you're doing? You are the one connected to Willie, not me. Who do you think is going down if this goes sideways, huh? Me, a state senator in good standing, or a coked-up weasel and his dealer?"

"I can't keep doing this," Alex said, this time with less conviction in his voice. "I can't control Willie at all. He busted up that guy bad. And now he's got some other guy involved."

"What?!" Jack screamed into the phone. It sounded to Alex like he punched the wall. "Who, how did this happen?"

"I don't know, some guy. He came by the office today saying he already met with Willie."

"The office? Goddammit Alex, that means he can tie Coastal Properties to all this." Jack could feel everything spinning out of control. "I've got to lock this down; Willie has to go." Jack was still on the phone, but really talking to himself. He was quiet for a few moments. Alex was smart enough not to say a word.

Jack finally spoke again, his voice calmer. "OK Alex, it's alright. I'm going to get you out of this real soon. For right now I want you to act like nothing has changed with Willie, just stall him for a bit. Whatever you do, do not visit any more shellfish lease owners. I'll deal with Willie soon, but for now, keep him under control."

"I can't, I don't want to be near him." Alex was back to panic mode.

"It's just for a day or two, I promise. And try to find out what you can about this other person, name, description, anything. Let me know as soon as you do."

Jack hung up the phone before Alex could respond.

THAT EVENING, DAN AND TANNER took off for the Pelican Tavern. It was not in the best part of Wilmington, and Matt wasn't thrilled about Tanner going. Dan reminded him of several facts: one, that he needed someone at his side, and the plan didn't call for Shay to be that person; two, Tanner was the one most likely to physically handle himself if things went south; and three, who was going to stop him? Matt couldn't argue any of those points. Before Dan left, Matt asked him to get in touch with an old acquaintance, Freddy Tosco. Freddy had a special talent that would come in handy that night.

Dan made sure everyone knew he was officially Benny Pierce from this point forward. Katie, Shay, and Matt were very familiar with this alias from years before. "Benjamin Franklin Pierce," he would joke, using the M*A*S*H character name whenever he could. Rarely did the mark pick up on it, which was kind of sad. Shay always used the name Angelo "Babe" Martin, in homage to the Rockford Files. Even fewer people got that one. Matt and Katie used whatever worked best at the time.

Shay was also unhappy with the fact that Tanner was going with Dan and wanted to follow as a back-up, but Matt needed him to make sure Freddy did his job. The big man paced back and forth like a caged animal. He finally stopped and turned to Matt sitting behind his desk.

"I thought you were through with this shit."

"I am, basically," Matt responded. "This is different, this isn't a con."

Shay sat down in one of the chairs opposite Matt. "Why, because it doesn't involve taking someone's money?"

"This isn't a con, it's a stratagem. Think of it as just another means to correct a wrongdoing. Even if the cops could pin the murder on Willie, or the beatdown he did to Aoife's cousin, it doesn't address whoever is profiting from whatever is going on. And something is going on."

"So, you're just doing your civic duty."

"Like any responsible town manager would," Matt said with a smirk.

"Not sure how many of them would send their son in harm's way."

Matt looked like he just took a gut punch. "You think I want him involved? That's the last thing I wanted." Matt stood up, his face reddening. "Fuck, I'm the one who walked away from all this, remember. I didn't want my kids to even know what I did before."

"And yet, here we are."

"Fuck you, Shay."

"I'm not passing judgment, Matt, but you need to face the fact that we are who we are. Deep down, you love this shit. All I'm saying is the sooner you come to that truth, the sooner you can prepare Tanner if he chooses to follow in your footsteps."

"You're wrong, Shay, I don't love this shit. I'm perfectly content living out my days with my toes in the sand. But I can't just stand by when I know something is wrong. And I sure as hell don't want Tanner following in my footsteps. At least not those in the past."

Shay tilted his head. "Good luck with that."

IT WAS CLOSE TO EIGHT O'CLOCK when Alex left his office. He headed straight for his red Porsche Carrera that his father got him to build up his confidence. He got in and backed out, never noticing the man off to the side. He turned and started forward when suddenly the man was in front of him. Alex couldn't stop in time. The man bounced off his car and onto the pavement like a limp noodle. Alex stopped immediately and got out to look. Then he saw the second man running towards the scene.

"Oh my god, you just hit that man," the stranger shouted.

"I never saw him; he came out of nowhere," Alex responded frantically.

The stranger went straight to Freddy "The Flop" Tosco. "It's OK, mister, I'm a doctor. Don't try to move."

Freddy groaned. The man pulled a small flashlight out of his pocket and checked Freddy's eyes, then proceeded to feel around his temples. "This man is likely concussed, plus there could be internal bleeding."

Alex stood there, confused. "Isn't the doctor's office here for an orthodontist?"

The man ignored him as he held Freddy's wrist. "He's got an elevated heart rate; he could be going into cardiomyfibulation. We need to call an ambulance."

"No, I'm okay, I just need a moment," Freddy said. "Besides, I can't afford an ambulance ride, my insurance won't cover it." He began to sit up. A lady was coming across the parking lot from the building next door.

"Is he okay?" the lady asked.

"I don't know, ma'am, but I'm gonna take good care of him, I am a specialist," the stranger said in a dramatic tone. He turned to Alex. "We need to get him inside your building."

"But I thought we shouldn't move him." Alex said.

"Good god, man, it could mean his life."

Alex looked around, hoping not to draw a crowd. "OK, OK, let me get my keys."

As Alex left, Freddy looked up at the stranger and whispered. "Tone it down, Max, we don't want him to get suspicious. What the fuck is cardiomyfibulation?"

"I dunno, I just made it up."

Alex came back, and the two of them helped Freddy up. As they walked to the building, the man called Max looked across the parking lot at a black Escalade and flashed a peace sign. It was the signal Shay was waiting for. He immediately texted *go* to Dan.

THE PELICAN TAVERN was a dump, and that might be kind. The old cinder block building stood by itself between two over-grown vacant lots filled with empty beer cans and cigarette butts. The paint was peeling, and the windows had bars. The outside was poorly lit, and all the trucks parked nearby had seen better days. Most of them had some sort of bumper sticker supporting their right to have guns and plenty of them.

Dan parked his Taurus across the street from the bar in case they needed to move fast. He and Tanner waited until Dan's phone buzzed from Shay's text. He looked at Tanner. "It's showtime, you ready?"

"Let's go shake up some rednecks, Benny."

Dan smiled. "That's my boy."

The two walked in and were not surprised. The interior was dark, but you could see enough to know it was worse inside.

The place reeked of stale beer, sweat, and cigarettes. "Smoke-free laws" didn't apply here. The floor was sticky with spilled beer and other questionable substances. The walls were largely empty, which surprised Dan. He assumed the place would be cluttered with confederate flags or some other supremacist bullshit. Two pool tables with worn felt crowded half the space. There were a couple of booths along the wall, each with torn vinyl-covered seats and scarred laminate tabletops.

Dan saw Willie sitting in the last booth, a scowl on his face. He looked up at a clock on the wall, then scanned the entrance as if expecting someone. He looked like he was having a bad day. Dan was about to make it worse. He took a quick inventory of the situation, particularly making sure Willie's hands were where he could see them. Dan moved in that direction, and Tanner grabbed a seat at a nearby table while Dan slid into the booth opposite Willie.

"Howdy, Willie. Where's Alex?"

Willie went from annoyed to confused. He looked around the booth and then the bar, trying to figure out what was going on. "Who the fuck are you?"

"I'm Benny, your new partner. Didn't Alex tell you?"

Willie leaned across the table, eyes narrowing. Dan could smell his rancid breath. "I'm having a bad day, buddy, and would like nothin' better than to have an excuse to stomp your ass back to hell. You best get out of my booth and this bar real quick."

Dan smiled. "Now that ain't at all hospitable, Willie. I'm just here to have a beer and get to know you a little better."

Willie looked up and signaled to someone at the pool tables. "I ain't generally hospitable to some fuckwad I never met. I did try to be nice and give you a chance to leave my booth peacefully, but now time's up, dumbass. My friend here is gonna take you outside, and if you're lucky he won't cut you and your friend there too badly."

A man was walking over towards the booth, pulling a switchblade out of his pocket. He was skinny with a shaved head and tattoos down both arms and along his neck. Now that's what Dan expected.

"Problem here, Willie?" the man asked.

Before he could say anything more, Tanner was on him. He moved so fast that no one saw it coming. He grabbed the man's arm with one hand and wrapped his other hand around the back of his neck. He slammed the man's face into the wooden frame of the booth, then spun him around and threw him across one of the tables, twisting his arm behind his back until he dropped the switchblade.

Dan saw Willie start to move his right arm below the table, but Dan quickly grabbed him. "Don't be stupid, Willie, I'm trying to help." Willie tried to jerk back, but Dan's grip tightened.

The man with Tanner groaned. "I think my nose is broke. This fucker's gonna break my arm." Dan nodded at Tanner, who lifted the man by his collar and tossed him into a chair at the table. Tanner never said a word.

Dan finally let Willie go. About that time the bartender came over to the table. He was older with a white beard and a scar across his nose. He made sure his sidearm was visible. Clearly a man not to be messed with. "We ain't gonna have no trouble in my place." He looked at Dan and then Tanner. "I don't know you two boys, and I don't want to. Say what you came to say and git."

Dan put his hands up in surrender and smiled. "We don't want no trouble, friend; we'll be on our way." He turned to

Willie. "I know about the leases and what you fellas are up to. I can guess what happened to that ole boy that drown too. I don't give a shit about it, I just want in. I'll be in touch."

Dan and Tanner got up, and Dan reached into his pocket to pull out two hundred dollars and gave it to the bartender. "For your troubles, sir."

"I'll be keeping the blade," Tanner said to the bloodied man.

As they walked out the door and towards the car, Dan looked at Tanner. "Damn, son, I had no idea you could move that fast."

"I always had a good pop time from my catching days."

"I knew you were strong, but that was certified badass, brother." Dan laughed as he got to the car door. He held two fingers up in the air for peace. Shay pulled away from the curb.

Saturday, October 15

SUNLIGHT FOUND ITS WAY between the cracks of the blinds. The open window allowed the rhythmic sound of the crashing waves to fill the room, nature's white noise. Matt had spent the night in the guest house with Katie, again. This time, he watched her as she slept beside him, wondering if this was moving too fast. After all, he thought, I wasn't all that happy to see her when she first showed up. Now he couldn't stand not having her around. He knew he should be careful, but this was way more fun.

Matt never spent much time in the guest houses, and he had forgotten how nice they were. The first floor was built as a rec room, but also had a bedroom/bathroom suite. No frills, since it was most vulnerable to flooding. The second floor had a kitchen/dining room, living room, and a large master suite with French doors that lead out to a balcony overlooking the pool. The pool was surrounded by dunes, creating some privacy from the three public trust areas: the ocean, the inlet, and the sound. Matt generally didn't have much use for the pool. Why bother when he could swim in the ocean or the sound? But the grad students liked it, and it was nice to have at night sometimes.

Matt brewed coffee for Katie and laid out some fresh fruit, bagels, and cream cheese, but mostly, he let her sleep.

Matt called Dan to check in on the previous night's meeting with Covington, but he primarily wanted to make sure Tanner was safe. Dan gave him the lowdown, telling him he got Covington's attention. Dan covered the highlights from the evening, although he left out the part with Tanner and the switchblade guy. No point in getting Matt worked up, Dan figured.

Dan also told Matt what he got from Freddy Tosco and his partner: "Apparently, they fleeced Alex Spencer for more money on top of what we paid them. Leave it to Freddie to play a con within a con."

Matt wasn't surprised. "That's alright, it did exactly what I wanted, which was to separate Willie and Alex until you could set the trap. Mission accomplished."

"Now what?" Dan asked.

"Gather the troops. It's time to go to work."

Katie came into the kitchen in the flannel pajamas she got the day before. It was not exactly what Matt was expecting when she mentioned not needing his shirt anymore.

"All I said was I didn't need to wear your shirt for pajamas. How you took that is on you, perv," she joked. "Nights get chilly now, and I need something comfy."

She stretched her arms high and gave Matt a big smile. "You made me coffee. You *like* like me." She sat in his lap and cupped his chin in her hand, giving him a long kiss, then she jumped back off his lap and went over to get a bagel. "What's next?"

Matt stared at her, baffled. It was like trying to keep up with a pinball. "I'm not sure...what?" he said, fumbling his words.

"Easy, cowboy. I mean what's next for the con, not whether or not we should practice making babies."

"OK, first of all, I knew that," Matt replied. He didn't. "And second, everyone needs to stop calling this a con, it's a stratagem."

"So, what's the difference?" she teased.

Matt sighed. "A stratagem is a ruse used to outwit your opponent. A con is a swindle. Completely different. We are not running some game here; we are trying to right a wrong, in somewhat unconventional ways."

She smiled again, staring deeply at Matt with those big emerald eyes. "You are so cute when you're frustrated," she said. "OK, what's next for this not-con-stratagem that we're doing?"

"Eat your breakfast, then we'll meet with everyone else at the main house and talk about next steps."

"Hmm, OK, I'll just take my bagel and head back to the bedroom to get ready. She unbuttoned her pajama top. "I don't want to get crumbs on my new pajamas." As she walked by, she gently dragged her hand across his chest.

Matt closed his eyes. "What the hell, they can wait for just a bit." He followed her like a puppy into the bedroom.

JACK FLEMING WENT THROUGH his emails at his kitchen table, coffee in hand. Most of them were from constituents wanting help with some nonsense he had absolutely no interest in. He usually had his assistant respond to these emails with some sympathetic bullshit like *Senator Fleming is deeply concerned with* (fill in asinine problem) *and is looking into the matter with great urgency. God Bless America and the good people of North Carolina.*

He was looking for any emails from fellow senators that might need his assistance on some issue or another. As he was finishing, his phone started to vibrate. He grumbled under his breath, but answered.

"Good morning, Senator Denton, what can I do for you this morning?"

"Well now, son, I was just checkin' in to see how our project was comin' along." Hearing Senator Denton's pretentious drawl was like fingernails on a chalkboard to Fleming.

"Ah, it's good, coming along quite well. I've been working on lining up support for the bill, and I'm confident we are going to be good to go." Fleming nervously tapped his fingers on the kitchen table.

"That so?" Denton asked. "Well, I have to say that I'm relieved because when I did my own canvassing, I got a bunch of 'I don't know anything about it' answers from the boys in the mountains."

Fleming felt the tension in his shoulders build as he squeezed his free hand into a fist. "Senator, you know how those people in the mountain region are. I'll wheel and deal with them as we get closer to the vote. I've already spoken to Bixby Lamont. I'm not concerned at all."

"How long you been in state government, boy? Are you a child or just plain stupid? You need them boys in the mountains. Those liberal cocksuckers from the middle of the state don't give one good goddamn about your dredging. In fact, they think the money is better spent on some never-gonna-work social bullshit." Denton's voice was getting louder as he spoke. "Show me you can be a governor and take charge."

"Is that all, sir?"

"No, that's not all. I got a call earlier from the Pender County Sheriff's Department. Seems they think there might be a connection between the drowning down there and the boy who's laid out in the hospital, since both had oyster leases."

Fleming froze for a moment. "I thought you said they believed the death was accidental drowning."

"Sweet Jesus, you dumbass, they did when it was just one incident. I can fix some things, but I ain't a fuckin' miracle worker." There was a pause as Denton caught his breath. When he spoke again, his tone was calmer, but still forceful, "Now this is the second time I'm telling you to clean up your mess. There won't be a third. No more oyster leases, and you need to eliminate the weak links."

Denton hung up.

He didn't know what was worse, that he just got his ass handed to him by some pig-shit farmer, or that his moronic brother-in-law couldn't follow simple instructions. He rubbed his temples, attempting to ward off the massive headache that was coming.

"Honey," a voice called out to Fleming. "You need to get ready soon. I don't want to be late for Daddy's birthday party."

"OK, OK," he called back to his wife. He hated the idea of going to an old man's birthday party, but his father-in-law was an extremely influential man. He needed his full support for his run for governor.

As he stood up, Fleming had another thought. "Hey sweetheart, do you know if your brother is going to be there?"

"Which one?"

"Alex."

"I guess. I haven't heard from him the last few days. Why do you care, you don't even like him."

I don't like any of you dipshits, he thought. "I just want to make nice with him, darling, that's all."

EVERYONE WAS ALREADY GATHERED when Matt and Katie arrived at the main house. Dan looked at his watch and gave Matt the side eye, eyebrows cocked. Tanner looked down at his feet, trying not to smile. Matt knew he and Katie had been the talk of the moment. Shay was not nearly as subtle.

"We need to get this discussion underway before our little rabbits here get distracted again."

"Give the lad a break, Shay, it has been a long, lonely stretch after all," Dan chimed in.

"Well, that explains a lot," Katie added.

"Et tu, Brute?" Matt turned to the rest of them. "That's quite enough from the peanut gallery. We've got work to do.

"This one is a little trickier than past hustles. For one, we have no clear mark. What we know is that Willie Covington and Alex Spencer have been trying to buy up shellfish leases as part of some Blackbeard treasure hunt. I believe this led to the murder of Holt Bratton and the assault on Frank Kenny. They are target number one. The second part of this centers around the new state-owned dredge."

"The dredge?" Tanner interrupted. "I thought it was the proposed legislation."

Matt shook his head. "Without the dredge, the proposed legislation, and all the bullshit that goes with it, is useless. All the money and all the mandates are tied to that dredge. We need to find out who benefits most from all this."

"We need a connection between the shellfish leases, Covington, and the dredge," Dan added.

Tanner snapped his fingers. "Jack Fleming."

"Bingo," Matt replied. "Jack Fleming is Alex Spencer's brother-in-law, and he has the connections and the influence to get legislation passed. He may also have enough pull to bypass regulatory processes."

"Like shellfish public hearings?" Tanner asked.

"Exactly."

Shay had been sitting quietly, listening to the conversation. "So, what's the play?" he asked.

"Divide and conquer," Matt replied. "We need to first confirm my theory about the connection between Covington and Fleming. We need to convince Covington and Spencer the Blackbeard treasure doesn't exist, but that there is something bigger. We have to get them to want to partner with us.

"We can use stories of past attempts to show them it's not true. We can also use the old maps that show the landscape before the Intracoastal was constructed. Neither are that bright, so I'm sure you guys can convince them that the different location of the inlet and waterways makes tracking Blackbeard's old movements impossible."

"But if we do that, isn't it game over with them?" Tanner asked.

"It would be, except you guys are going to convince them there is another treasure to be found."

"I don't follow," Tanner said.

"Aw shit." Dan smiled. "Bait and switch."

"The C.S.S. Phantom," Matt said. "A Confederate blockade runner during the Civil War."

"Jayus, Mary, and Joseph, this is the part where Matt gives us a history lesson," Katie said.

"It's about attention to detail in a good stratagem. The Confederate Army used the Phantom to get lead ingots from Bermuda to bring back for making cannon shot and bullets. The Phantom could slip through the Union Army defenses and get to the Wilmington port. It was successful at first, but eventually got chased down by the U.S.S. Connecticut.

"In an effort to keep from falling into enemy hands, the crew of the Phantom ran the boat aground and set it on fire, avoiding capture and destroying the ship's cargo," Matt explained, "and they ran it aground at Topsail Inlet. Or at least where Topsail Inlet existed in 1865."

"Thus, the need for the old maps," Tanner remarked, nodding.

"That's a great story, Mark Twain, but how does that help us?" Katie asked.

"Well, rumor has it that this particular trip also included a couple hundred pounds of gold. It was supposedly taken from the ship before they set it on fire but had to be ditched somewhere in the sound. Truthfully, there is no official verification that this gold ever existed, just some found letters from one of the crew. But that should be enough to convince our two friends to continue the search."

"What do you hope to gain?" Shay asked.

"Well, y'all are going to get more information on why the shellfish leases are important, so I can make the connection I need. But more importantly, you're going to confirm that Willie was responsible for Aoife's cousin, and he will pay."

"You got a plan, partner?" Dan asked.

"I need you, Shay, and Tanner to meet with Covington and Spencer tomorrow night, after hours at the Salt Marsh. It needs to be on our territory. Shay, I mean *Angelo*, will be the money behind the effort, preferably organized crime money. I'll get you more information on the C.S.S. Phantom to review, we'll get together beforehand to go over specifics."

"And what will you and Katie be doing in the meantime?" Shay said with a smile.

Matt shot him a dirty look. "We're going to follow up on a theory Aoife came up with involving Majestic Oysters, Inc. On Monday we're going to Wanchese to see a man about a dredge."

The rest of the day was research and discussion, finalizing Matt's plan. Tanner detailed his research on the state's new dredge, the *Chinquapin*. "It's the brainchild of former Senator Orville Denton. The Corps of Engineers has a limited fleet that serves the entire Atlantic and Gulf coasts, so Denton wanted a dedicated dredge for North Carolina. Specifically, he wanted a split-hull hopper dredge designed for use in shallow draft inlets."

"Why would that matter?" Katie asked.

"That design prevents the dredge from being used in the larger ports like Wilmington or Morehead City," Tanner answered. "The plan was to create a public-private partnership with the state providing twenty million dollars from the Inlet Recovery Fund towards the construction of the dredge. The private company, Nautical Dredging Services, LLC, became the owner once it was built. The deal is that they provide dredging services to the state for ten years at a discount rate. After that, they set the prices."

"I never heard of Nautical Dredging Services," Matt said.

"You would know them better by their parent company, Simmons Dredging and Marine Construction."

"Jaysus, are you serious?"

"Sadly, yes. And as Chris mentioned to you earlier, Dean Filben was put in charge of this new business."

"Denton's lackey," Matt said, rubbing his chin. "And Simmons is notable for overcharging and underperforming."

"That's a nice way of putting it. I would say they're fucking criminals. It's why we've taken them off the bid list for any of our projects."

"Let me get this right," Katie said. "This enterprise is mixing FEMA, state, and local government monies into a private company? This is a forensic accountant's wet dream. Is there any government oversight?"

"There is a group called the Shallow Draft Task Force that is supposed to review projects," Tanner answered. "Largely friends and appointees of Denton before he retired."

"Why doesn't the Coastal Commission handle that?" Matt asked.

Tanner shrugged. "Too honest a group, I suppose. While Chris and I didn't initially see this as a threat to our program, the proposed legislation changes all that."

"This is why we're going to Wanchese, isn't it?" Katie chimed in.

"If my guess is right, Mr. Filben will be our biggest help to follow the money."

DAN CALLED COASTAL PROPERTIES on the chance that Alex might be in the office. He figured Saturdays would be a prime time to show properties, and Alex might want a distraction from recent events. Dan had always been adept at getting people to do things they didn't want to do. He knew this was going to be the case with Alex, so he needed to find a way to keep from spooking him again.

"Coastal Properties, how may I direct your call?"

"Is that you, Anna? It's Ben Pierce, how are you?"

Anna's monotone changed quickly. "Hi Mr. Pierce, how are you today?"

"Come on now, it's Ben, and I'm just fantastic. Why do they have you working on a Saturday, you need to be helping people like me get fit."

She laughed. "I offered to help. My classes aren't until later tonight. Do you want to speak to Alex?"

"Please," Dan said, "and if he says he's busy, tell him I'll just come to the office instead."

It took a few minutes, but Alex finally got on the line. "Can't you just leave me alone? I don't want any part of whatever you're doing."

"No can do, Alex, not yet anyway. I need you to get in touch with Willie and tell him the three of us are meeting tomorrow night."

"Nope, I'm not doing it. Willie is fucking crazy. He screamed at me all morning about you and your gorilla. He thinks I sent you there."

Dan couldn't help but smile. "Hey Alex, I get it. I don't want anything to do with that psycho either, but unless you have a better option, we're stuck with him."

Alex hesitated, but finally responded, "Nope, I'm out."

Dan gave an audible sigh for effect. "Alex, do this one thing, and it will soon be over. If you do, you'll be a rich man. You'll never have to see Willie again; I can promise that." Alex didn't respond right away, so Dan continued, "I'm talking millions, Alex."

"Millions?" Alex whispered.

"You and Willie, tomorrow night at ten o'clock, the Salt Marsh Restaurant. Don't disappoint me, Alex." Dan hung up.

With that kind of money, Alex thought, I could start my own restaurant. I could be head chef and owner. Better yet, maybe I'll just buy a food truck and drive as far away from Willie and Jack as possible. I can finally get away from this shitty real estate job.

For the first time in a long time, Alex smiled. He sat in front of his computer and went straight to the Johnson and Wales website.

JACK FLEMING WANDERED around his father-in-law's palatial home, thinking there was no way he made that kind of money honestly. The house was actually three homes in one, connected by elegant corridors. There was the 5,000 square-foot main home on the Intracoastal Waterway, with views of Wrightsville Beach and Figure Eight Island. The huge living room, with its pine flooring and custom tray ceilings, was perfect for entertaining, as was the oversized screened-in porch and the outdoor living space. Connected to that was not one, but two 1,600 square foot Nantucket-inspired guest houses, each with three bedrooms and baths.

The guests at Alex Spencer II's party were a who's who of Republican heavyweights. Fleming was spending time pressing flesh, as it were, because he knew he would need their support in his run for governor. Despite the fact he had been in the senate for several years, he was still considered wet behind the ears by the old guard. His father-in-law didn't seem to push for Fleming's advancement as much as he would like either. That's why he was having to count on Orville Denton as much as he did. God, he hated that.

Fleming searched for the old man's half-wit son, Alex the Third, near the firepit. Fleming needed to make sure that Alex and Covington were completely out of the way before they could do any more damage. Alex hadn't returned Fleming's calls, and Jack feared he might be going rogue.

"Jack," a voice called. "What are you doing out here?" It was Fleming's wife. "Daddy wants to introduce you to Wellington Cavenaugh."

Fleming tried to hide his shudder, thinking he heard her say "Willie Covington." He gathered himself and answered, "I was just looking for your brother, but I haven't seen him here yet."

"Alex? He's not coming. Daddy said he called earlier to apologize, but he was working on a big sale. I think that made Daddy happier than any gift Alex could give him. You know he's been waiting for Alex to finally make something of himself."

That fucking worm, Fleming thought. What is he up to now? If this family is waiting for that moron to make something of himself, they'll be waiting until hell freezes over.

It was after five o'clock when Dan and Shay walked into Matt's office. Katie and Tanner were already there. Dan gave the thumbs up; Shay was already at the liquor cart.

"It's the night before, Matty-Boy, you know what that means." Shay grinned as he spoke.

Katie grimaced. "No, no, no."

"We have a firepit, a perfect backdrop," Dan added.

"Jaysus, Mary, and Joseph, do we have to?" Katie whined.

"What?" Tanner asked.

"It's tradition," Shay asserted. "The night before a con truly started we used to sit around and have a few drinks, cigars. To loosen up."

"But do we have to listen to Jethro Tull?" Katie whined.

"You bet your sweet ass, darling," Shay replied.

The five of them spent the evening sitting around the firepit having a few drinks and lots of laughs. It was an important part of the process; from this point forward, everything would get much more serious. While Matt continued to emphasize that their scheme was not a con game, it certainly had elements of one.

"There's something I don't get," Tanner said. "Why go through the trouble of tricking Covington and Spencer with the Confederate gold? Why not just pay them off for the information?"

Matt sipped his drink. "You always make the mark do some work. You don't dump all the information out; you make them come and get it. Look like you're holding something back, that way they think they outsmarted you. That's when they're hooked."

"That's why your dad is a genius," Dan said with a chuckle.

Shay folded his arms across his chest and closed his eyes. He saw that Matt was falling back into old habits.

As the gathering broke up and Tanner and Dan walked towards their cars, Tanner stopped and turned to Dan. "What we're about to do here… this is some serious shit."

Dan nodded.

"Look, I know you and Dad could bend the rules a bit when you ran the consulting firm to get things done. But this seems more serious than working the system to get a small-town sheriff an assault vehicle. I feel like you and Dad may have a little more experience in…" He paused, searching for the words. "Creative approaches. For that matter, so does Katie. What's the story?"

"I think you need to talk to your dad."

"I'm talking to you. You know damn well he's not telling me."

Dan shook his head. "Your father's gonna kill me, but OK. Your dad has an amazing ability to get people to like and trust him, almost immediately. You already know that. He can come up with ideas and plans like no one I've ever met, changing and reacting on the fly. Years ago, we used those talents to run confidence games on people."

"You're conmen."

"No, we *were* conmen. Past tense. Your father is a good person, almost to a fault." Dan hesitated. "When we were young, we would run a scam on occasion. 'Conmen' makes it sound like we were lowlifes, taking advantage of the elderly or the incredibly gullible, but we never ran a game on innocents. Every mark was chosen because they were shitty human beings that hurt others. If there was money made, most of it went to the asshole's victim."

"Modern-day Robin Hoods." Tanner smirked.

"You say that like it's a joke, but yeah. The shit we did was to benefit others, not us. I know that doesn't necessarily make it right, but don't ever question his motives. Believe me, there were times I badly wanted to use his talents for our gain."

"Does that include Slaggers? Seems like a multi-million-dollar business is a convenient benefit."

Dan's face flushed, words spilling from his mouth: "You want to know about Slaggers? OK, yeah, we ran a huge con on those bastards. They killed your mother. Your father gave up his life of hustling for Hannah and you and Sedona. When your mother died, he did what he knew best, but believe me he would have killed those sons of bitches had I let him. That con was his way of revenge, and since then, he's tried to use Slaggers as a way to honor your mother. He's tried to make amends."

Dan caught the confusion in Tanner's face and realized he didn't know the full story. Dan buried his face in his hands.

Tanner responded, "I knew Dad suspected Mom was murdered, but I had no idea he knew who was responsible."

"Fuck me." Dan looked up and took a deep breath. "I'm sorry, this isn't the way you should find out. You have a right to know, and I hope you have this conversation with Matt."

"Does Sedona know?"

Dan shrugged. "I doubt it. She wasn't exactly interested in Matt's theories at that time."

"Where does Katie fall in all this?"

"She's a whole other story. I don't know if anyone can love a person more than Matt loved Hannah, your mom I mean, but Katie is damn close. She was our roper for the most part, a damn good one."

"Roper?"

"The person who would get the mark involved in the con. She was the lure, setting up the mark for our scam. She would also cool the mark after the con was over. They never knew she was part of the con, usually they thought she was a victim."

"But she was more than just a partner," Tanner pushed.

"'Thick as thieves', as it were. But one day Katie up and left, and that was that."

"This is a lot."

Dan sighed. "Whoever said 'The truth shall set you free' didn't know your dad."

SHAY STOOD ON THE BALCONY of the other guest house, a tumbler of Jameson in one hand, cigarette in the other. He had a bad feeling about what was to come. Violence was not part of his brother's life, certainly not since the Sampson con, but Shay knew: it was coming.

What Matt was planning felt different. They were dealing with a psychopath, not the usual marks of the past. He was also talking about hustling state and federal government officials. Shay worried that Matt might be biting off more than he could chew. Shay was afraid that maybe he couldn't rescue his brother this time.

He also worried that Dan was too eager to get back in the game. Dan always enjoyed the thrill of the hunt, the danger of getting caught. It was an adrenaline rush for him.

But he mostly worried about Tanner. Why in the name of God did Matt bring Tanner into this.

Shay went back into the kitchen to refill his tumbler and grab a beer chaser. The whiskey warmed his cheeks, but it also awakened the spiders that resided in his head. He stared at his Glock and his Sig Sauer sitting on the table. He had never actually shot anyone; they had always been for show, to deter violence. But he knew this could be that time.

I'm here for a reason, he thought, to have their backs. That's exactly what I'm going to do.

III

It Doesn't Always Go As Planned

Sunday, October 16

MATT WALKED TO THE BEACH for a quick swim. The tide was rolling out, the waters relatively calm. He knew the cool water and the chill of the morning air would help clear the cobwebs from last night's drinking. With the stratagem officially started, the potential for failure, and the consequences, weighed heavy on Matt's mind. The swim did nothing to ease that.

As he headed back to the compound, Matt ran into Dan, who could sense Matt's misgivings. "It's a good plan, Matt."

"It's got holes."

"They always do, that allows us contingencies. You taught me that. What's really bothering you?"

Matt looked down at his feet, shaking his head. "It's been a long time since I did this kinda shit, Dan. I dread it. I dread that we'll fail, that someone will get hurt. You and Shay seem to think it's in my blood, and maybe it is. Regardless, you seem to want this more than I do. And what's worse, so does Tanner."

"Sure, Matt, maybe there is a thrill to this for me. Maybe life is getting a little stale. But I also know that Frank Kenny is laying in a hospital bed, and some assholes are about to grift funds from communities that need it. So you can spare me the self-righteous bullshit."

After a moment, Matt looked back up at Dan. "Aoife and I are going to leave for Wanchese shortly. I want to get settled before going to the dredge in the morning. Are you guys set for tonight?"

"It's all copacetic, partner," Dan said.

Matt frowned. "I wish I had your confidence."

TANNER LOOKED AT HIS WATCH and wondered: is Montana two or three hours earlier? Sedona and Jed get up early to do that hunting crap, he thought, so she should be up by now.

Sedona answered on the third ring. "Twice in less than a week. What's wrong?"

"How is that a remotely acceptable greeting?" Tanner asked. "Did social graces die in that frozen tundra you live in?"

"I call you all the time, occasionally even getting a response. If you call me, there's something wrong. Or you need something. Which is it this time, TJ?"

"Can't a brother call and check on his pregnant sis?"

"A good brother can." She laughed as she said it.

Tanner laughed too. "How are you, really?"

"I'm good. Cold, but good. Honestly, this may be the last year we do this. I can't see bringing a baby up here every winter."

"Pops will be ecstatic to hear that."

"Please don't tell him, I don't know if I could take listening to him go on about that all winter."

"Dad's actually part of the reason I called."

"Is he okay?" There was a touch of panic in her voice.

"He's fine. I'm curious though, did he ever mention anyone named Katie or Aoife?"

"I certainly don't recognize that second name. Don't remember any Katies either. Why?"

Tanner chuckled. "Not sure, but I believe he may finally have a new love interest, or more like a blast from the past."

"How long past?" Sedona asked, suspicion in her voice.

"Long past, like pre-Mom." But Tanner picked up on the question in Sedona's voice. "Why, do you think he cheated on Mom?"

"No, never mind."

"Come on, Sis, you're leaving something out. Does this have anything to do with you leaving?"

"Let's just drop it, okay?"

"Sedona, this lady showed up a few days ago. I don't know who she is. Now it seems to me that you're suggesting that she was part of whatever went down after Mom died. What's going on here? What really happened?"

There was a long pause on the other end of the line. "Dad was drinking a lot after Mom died," Sedona finally said.

"Duh."

"Shut up and let me get through this. I was pulling him out of dive bars on the regular, trying my hardest to sober him up." Her breath caught in her throat. "I was seventeen for chrissake." She paused again, but eventually continued, "Anyway, during one of these benders, I caught him hustling some loser so he could pay his bar tab. I always suspected he was into something illegal, but that's when I finally knew for sure. I thought maybe this lady you mentioned was part of that time.

"Anyway, when I got him home that night, he told me that he and Uncle Dan used to run con games. But all that changed when he met Mom, according to him. He broke down, saying he was lost without her."

"Shit Sedona, that was a lot to dump on you."

"I was pissed. I told him that you and I lost our mother, and he was abandoning us. I told him he better clean up his act or he would lose us too."

"And that's when you left."

"Yeah, I had to. I felt it was the only way he would get the message." Sedona paused. "Why are you really asking about this Katie lady?"

"Just keeping an eye on the old man. On another note, what do you know about Slaggers Inc.?"

"Nothing," she said abruptly. "And I don't want to know. Does Dad have you involved in something shady?"

"If you're asking me that, you must think he's capable of something shady."

"Goddammit, TJ, quit playing games. What are you up to?"

"Nothing, Sedona, really," Tanner lied.

"He promised me he was done with con games."

"I swear, we are not running any con game." He figured it wasn't a lie; it was a stratagem. "Dad has been honest to a fault since I've been involved with his business. He loves you Sedona, and does not want to ever disappoint you."

Tanner heard Sedona sniff. "I know," she said. "But I swear to Christ, if you two are doing something stupid, I'm gonna come back there and brain both of ya."

WANCHESE WAS UP THE COAST from Wilmington, a three-and-a-half-hour drive to the Outer Banks. Matt booked two rooms at a hotel in Manteo to give the appearance of a working visit. Attention to detail was important. They rented a car from the Wilmington Airport since they would be pretending to be from Texas. That was Katie's idea; she wanted Matt to wear his Stetson. He was happy to oblige.

On the ride up to Wanchese, they went over their back story, the possible scenarios they could face with Filben. Based on the intel, he was a greedy but dull individual that could be manipulated easily.

They were quiet for a while after strategizing, but Katie eventually broke the silence.

"Why do you still call me Aoife?"

"It's your name, isn't it?"

"You know what I mean. Everyone calls me Katie, always have, except you and my grandfather. I know why he called me that, but I always thought you did just to get in his good graces. And mine at the time, I guess."

"I know you were close to your grandfather."

She looked out the window, but he saw a tear in her eye. He could hear the sadness in her voice. "I was so close to my Daideo, he was my world. Don't get me wrong, my parents are great, but I had such a special bond with him. I still miss him so much."

"If I remember, you were the center of his universe."

"Oh God, and did he love you. It really pissed my dad off. Daideo was so mad at me when he found out we weren't together anymore." Katie paused, wiping a tear from her cheek. "You still haven't answered my question, why are you still calling me Aoife?"

The memories came flooding back to Matt. He could feel the adrenaline course through his body, like it did when he first met her. "I have to tell you the whole story."

"I'm sure you do." She rolled her eyes.

"Well, it really all started at the beginning of your first semester at Charlotte when Dan and I were watching the new students arrive. Dan was already making plans for which of the new coeds he would invite to our house parties. Then I saw you." Matt paused and smiled. "You were wearing that yellow sundress, an absolute goddess."

Matt peeked over and noticed she was blushing. He continued, "When I found out you were going to be in the same dorm, I knew I was done. I had to know more about you, so I started to follow you around."

Katie giggled. "You mean you were stalking me."

"I guess you could call it that. It started at dorm orientation. Your presence in that room dominated everyone and everything. I think everyone was watching you."

She interrupted, "If I remember right, you and Dan were the focus of attention, particularly for the girls. All the guys followed your lead."

"Dan and I lived in the dorm the year before, a great position to be in, I suppose. Anyway, I spent the next few weeks asking about you, watching you come and go. I knew your class schedule, what you drank at our Thursday house parties, and even what you liked to dance to."

"Perv," she said with a smile. "You really were stalking me!"

"I remember it was Parent's Day, and your grandfather came. You seemed so excited to see him. It was then I heard him call you Aoife. I thought it was the most beautiful, exotic name I ever heard. It fit you perfectly.

"I figured since my mom came from a huge Irish Catholic family, she might have heard the name before, so I called her. I can still hear her laughing at me, saying she knew I would fall for an Irish lass. I guess she knew even before I did.

"She told me the name meant *beautiful* and *radiant*. She also told me in Irish mythology Aoife was a warrior princess encouraging people to embrace their inner power and strengths."

Katie was quiet, but Matt could feel her staring at the side of his face as he drove. "Some people don't believe that you can find the right person so easily, but at that moment, I knew I loved you. Calling you Aoife was not about your Daideo, it was always about a name that represented everything you were, and still are, to me. Even now, all these years later, you are beautiful and radiant, and a warrior. That's why I call you Aoife."

She looked away, but grabbed his hand and gave it a squeeze. "You're such a sappy fecker," she said quietly.

DAN CALLED EMMA and told her to make sure that everyone was gone from the Salt Marsh by nine thirty that evening, customers and staff. He told her that he would take care of locking everything up. She offered to stay and help, but Dan said no.

Dan and Tanner arrived at the Salt Marsh a little after nine, but parked across the street to make sure Willie hadn't shown up early. Covington was a wildcard, and Dan wanted to make sure he could limit problematic surprises, including anyone else Willie might bring. The stratagem had more risk than usual since the normal prep work was cut short.

Shay was already inside the restaurant. He parked his black Escalade in the back, so it would be less conspicuous. He searched the perimeter before he went inside and took a seat at the bar. He wore a gray herringbone Boston Scally Cap and a black Di Lusso casual coat. He did not look like a local, and that was the plan. He ordered a Jameson neat and a Sam Adams, immediately flirting with the bartender. She didn't seem to mind; he had that kind of charm.

The last of the customers filed out by 9:05. The kitchen staff had already started clean-up and were done shortly thereafter. Shay walked out the front door and quickly flashed a peace sign, letting Dan know all was clear.

Dan pulled his car to the front and parked near the entrance. The only other car in the lot was Emma's, as she waited for Dan to come in. Dan and Tanner entered through the front door, but Tanner hung back to keep watch for Willie and Alex, hopefully no one else. Dan found Emma at the hostess stand, pretending to do some paperwork.

"Thanks for the help, Emma, but it's time for you to go home."

"I'm happy to stay and help, maybe serve drinks to you and whoever you're meeting with."

Dan's smile faded. "I appreciate it, I really do, but not this time."

Emma looked at him closely and saw the anxiety in his face. "Is everything OK?"

"It's fine, but you need to leave. Please."

Emma grabbed her coat hanging near the hostess stand. She

turned back to Dan, eyes pleading. "Please be careful." She turned and left.

Dan could hear the car doors slam.

"They're here," Tanner said.

"They come together?" Dan asked.

"Separate vehicles. Looks like Willie brought his friend from the bar, though."

"Squash it," Shay said as he came in from the bar.

Dan and Tanner stepped onto the porch near the steps as Willie, Alex, and the other man approached.

"Mr. Spencer, Mr. Covington, welcome," Dan said. "Sorry to say your friend is not."

By that time, they were up on the steps. Willie and his friend smelled of beer and weed. Alex looked terrified. The other man still wore the wounds from his earlier confrontation with Tanner. His nose was bandaged, both eyes were black.

"My boy doesn't come in, we walk," Willie said, trying to sound as tough as possible.

Dan smiled. "Then walk, I don't give a shit. I have a business proposition for you, but that asshole doesn't come into my establishment. And neither does the piece you got on you, Mr. Covington." He nodded at Tanner who moved towards Willie.

"Fuck this. We're out." Willie was out of his element but felt he needed to establish some level of control.

Alex finally spoke up, "Willie, we're talking serious money here." He gave a side glance to the man with the smashed face. "Leave him out here, and let's at least see what they have to say."

Willie was torn between his greed and his need to be in charge. Dan was counting on greed.

"Fine." Willie looked over at the man. "Go wait in the truck, Merle."

"But Willie, they ain't in charge," he said.

"Shut the fuck up, and do what I say. I can handle these guys."

The man looked at Tanner with hate in his eyes. "This ain't over, bitch. I'mma get my blade back and then some."

Tanner smirked. "For your sake, you better hope it's over, dumbass."

As Merle went back to the truck, Tanner looked at Willie and stuck his hand out, palm flat. Willie scowled and handed his gun to Tanner. "Don't shoot yourself with it, boy."

"I wouldn't worry about me being the one who gets shot."

The four men walked into the restaurant and went to the back where a long table was set up. At the head of the table sat Shay, who looked up at the men coming his way, but didn't move. The first to notice Shay was Alex, who immediately stopped in his tracks.

"Who's that?" Alex asked.

"What the fuck's goin' on?" Willie asked defensively. "How come Merle had to stay outside, but this guy is in here? This is bullshit." Willie looked around for an exit strategy, but Tanner blocked his path.

"Relax, Mr. Covington," Dan said. "This is Mr. Angelo Martin, and he is bankrolling our project."

Shay looked at Willie, then Alex, then back at Dan. "This is what you brought me down here for, Benny?" Shay spat out the words in disgust. "These two don't look like they can wipe their own arses."

"I think they can be a big help to us, Mr. Martin."

Willie spoke up: "Fuck this old man. I'll wipe my ass with him. Let's go, Alex."

Shay stood up, all six-foot-seven of him, and grabbed Willie in one quick motion, throwing him up against the wall. "I swear to God, Benny, I don't have time for this. I'm disappointed in you." Though he addressed Dan, Shay never broke his stare from Willie.

Dan immediately got between Shay and Willie. He didn't want this to get out of control, they needed Willie to cooperate. "Mr. Martin, I assure you these gentlemen can help. Let's just everyone take a breath and regroup."

Shay let go of Willie, who staggered. Dan turned to steady Willie, who pushed him away. Dan then turned to Alex. "Alex, I need you to get your partner to understand we are doing this together."

Alex looked at Willie wide-eyed but didn't say anything. Willie gathered himself. "Who is this guy?" he finally said.

"Mr. Martin is in the salvage business," Dan said. "Let's leave it at that. Please, let's just everyone have a seat, and I'll explain everything."

Willie took a wide berth around Shay and sat at the opposite end of the table. Alex took a seat in the middle. Dan signaled to Tanner, who brought out a set of maps and rolled them out. The first map showed the locations of the current shellfish leases in the Topsail Inlet superimposed on the area as it existed in the 1800's. The leases owned by Majestic Oysters, along with the Bratton and Kenny leases, were highlighted in red. Alex noticed them but didn't say anything.

"We've laid out where we believe the treasure could be given changes in tides, location of the inlet, addition of the Intracoastal Waterway, things like that. This map shows where it may have been dumped and shifted over time."

"What do you mean, *shifted over time?*" Willie asked. "It should be right where Blackbeard buried it, we don't need you for that."

Shay leaned forward. "Benny, what the fuck is this eejit talkin' about?"

Dan looked at Willie. "There is no Blackbeard's treasure, that story is for kids. We're looking for the Confederate Army's gold."

Alex frowned. "No, no, it's Blackbeard's treasure. It's just not in the Gold Hole on Topsail Island."

"Not sure where you got your info, Alex, but that's been debunked for years now."

Willie piped in, "Goddammit, Alex, your fucking brother-in-law had us on a wild goose chase."

"What are these two talkin' about?" Shay asked.

"His brother-in-law, Senator Some Fuck, I don't know his name, had us get these shellfish leases," Willie answered, pointing at Alex. "We thought for treasure, but now I don't know. That sumbitch."

"I'm not sure what's going on, but the gold that's out there is from a Confederate ship that sank in the 1860's," Dan clarified.

"What good is fuckin' Confederate money to us now?" Willie asked.

Shay looked over at Benny, hands up in the air. "Where did you find these fuckwads, Benny?" He turned to Willie. "It's gold, you moron, not Confederate money. It doesn't matter who owns it, it's still gold."

"Wait, I know about this wreck, somewhere near the inlet," Alex added. "Divers have been all around it and never found gold. This is just another lost cause."

"Officially, you're right, Alex," Dan said. "But we have letters from one of the sailors on the ship that talks about how they took the gold before the Union Army could get to the vessel. Unfortunately for them, they had to dump it before they could get away."

"How much we talkin' about?" Willie asked.

"Based on our calculations, it's probably worth anywhere from eight to ten million dollars, maybe more."

"And you need our leases, don't you?" Willie sneered.

"Wrong again, Willie. See, you've been using the wrong maps the whole time. Some of these leases you've been trying to buy up are in cut-throughs that wouldn't have existed in 1865, because the Intracoastal didn't exist then. You have to remember that the shoreline didn't look the same 150-plus years ago. You follow?"

He didn't.

"What I need you for," Dan continued, "is to tell me why you're really buying up these shellfish leases."

"What do you care if it ain't for the gold?"

"Because, Willie, I don't need your Senator Some Fuck to get in our way when we do finally pinpoint the gold. And thanks to you, I now know there is a senator involved."

Everyone's eyes went to Alex.

"You want to shed light on this for us, Alex?"

Alex got up from the table and started pacing. "I swear, I don't know anything other than Jack said the path to Blackbeard's treasure was getting the shellfish leases."

"Then you said he told you there was no treasure," Willie said angrily. "That's what you told me."

"Well, which is it?" Shay asked menacingly. "You may want to think real careful before the next words come outta your mouth."

Alex was in full panic. "He did say there was no treasure—I mean, at first he said there was, and then he said there wasn't."

Dan went to Alex and put his arm around his shoulder. "Relax, Alex, take a deep breath. You see, my boss, Mr. Martin here, he has a lot invested in this venture, and he only wants to make sure there are no hiccups, understand? He has people who fix hiccups for good. Now, he's a very fair man, but he is also a businessman. We just need to know who and what we're dealing with."

Alex looked at Shay, then back at Dan. "I'm telling you the truth; I don't know why he wants those leases. You have to believe me."

Shay emptied his tumbler of Jameson. He stood up, adjusted his hat, and straightened his coat. "Benny, the equipment will be here in the next day or two. The boat better be out on the water and the project underway. If these two fucking mopes are gonna be a problem, let me know." He looked at Willie and Alex. "If you can help, which I seriously doubt, but if you can, it's worth ten percent of the take." Shay started for the door.

"Fifty percent, mister, that's fair," Willie said.

Shay looked at Dan. "I like this guy, he's funny. Dumb as fucking rocks, but he's got balls of steel." Shay then looked at Willie. "You'll get ten percent and say 'Thank You, Sir' when you get it. Anything else and I'll cut your goddamn tongue out and feed it to the fish outside." Shay walked out the door.

Willie was fuming, but he was at least smart enough not to say anything until after Shay was gone. "Ten percent ain't shit. We can find our own treasure, Alex."

Dan glared at Willie. "You don't have a clue about where it is, how to get it, or what to do with it if by some miracle you did find it. Mr. Martin offered you a fair deal, and he is not a man you want to cross. We don't need you to finish this job, I'm just hoping you'll make it easier."

"If you didn't need us, then why are we here?" Alex asked. It wasn't much, but he finally had at least enough courage to ask the question.

Dan sighed with resignation. "Your brother-in-law is up to something; I just don't know what. He wanted you to get those leases for a reason, maybe for treasure, or maybe for something else. I'm trying to make this a flawless job, and I don't need anyone messing it up, especially the government."

"I don't know why he wants the leases if there's no gold," Alex said.

"Think, Alex, did you ever hear your brother-in-law say anything, talk to anyone about the leases?"

Alex shook his head. "I don't know, he was on the phone about dredging when I was in his office once."

Willie interrupted, "Shut up, Alex, don't tell him nothin'."

"It wasn't anything, Willie, just that the leases would help with some new dredging law and federal money. Nothing to do with gold."

"Godammit, Alex, don't say nothin' else." Willie looked at Dan. "We want on the boat when you go searching. We'll let you know all you need to know when we're on the boat."

"No."

"I ain't asking. You should check with the last few guys that said no. Oh wait, they can't answer no more." Willie smiled an evil smile.

Dan ignored Willie on purpose and told Alex, "I'll be in touch with the details. In the meantime, let me know if you think of anything else. And don't say a word of this to your brother-in-law, you got me?"

Dan turned back to Willie. "If you're not ready to go when I say, we leave your ass behind, and there is no deal."

Willie folded his arms across his chest and stared at Dan for a moment. "We'll be ready. Let's go, Alex." The two walked out the front door.

Once they were out of earshot, Tanner looked at Dan. "That moron didn't even ask for his gun back."

Willie walked toward his truck but stopped and grabbed Alex by the arm. "When this is over, we're gonna take all the gold, and I'm gonna kill those cocksuckers." He smiled that cruel smile. "You better make sure you're on the right side of all this."

Once Willie and Alex left, Dan and Tanner followed. As they walked out the door, Dan flashed the peace sign. Shay pulled out from his hidden spot.

Monday, October 17

MATT WAS UP BEFORE SUNRISE, sitting on the hotel balcony overlooking the Roanoke Sound. He recounted his conversation with Dan the night before about the meeting with Alex Spencer and Willie Covington. As expected, Alex was simply a pawn in a larger scheme, and he had no idea what was really at play. Willie Covington, on the other hand, was a mystery. Matt assumed he was either there to provide muscle, or he was a mistake that Alex's brother-in-law, Jack Fleming, hadn't counted on entering the equation. It was likely the latter, which made Covington all the more dangerous.

Matt heard Katie stir in bed. They had connecting rooms for both appearance and safety purposes, but she spent the night in his room. It was becoming a very comfortable and familiar feeling. That worried Matt. He felt guilty, like he was betraying Hannah and their kids. Plus, he had to stay focused on the task at hand.

He was watching the sunrise when Katie joined him, hugging herself against the cool morning air and sea breeze coming in off the ocean. Matt watched two brown pelicans fly by, heading to the ocean for breakfast.

"The sunrise is beautiful," Katie offered.

"Yep."

"Are you still beating yourself up over getting back into the confidence game?"

"It's a stratagem." He sighed. "I hate that I'm dragging my son into this world."

"He's old enough to make his own decisions. As far as what we're doing, they're the bad guys, Matt. Remember that. You're just using the best way you know to bring it to light."

"Maybe, Aoife," Matt said without conviction. He wanted to be done with his past, the hustling, the con games. He wanted to be someone his children would be proud of, not some matchstick man.

Katie shifted the conversation. "What's on your mind?"

"Something Dan said. He mentioned a comment Alex Spencer made about the phone call regarding dredging and federal dollars."

"What about it?"

"As hard as it is for me to believe that an elected official would be so brazen to launder federal funds, I'm beginning to think your theory has merit. The proposed legislation would require any community to use the *Chinquapin* if they wanted to dredge in federal channels, or to have access to the state's Inlet Recovery Fund, plus any potential FEMA resource money that goes through the state."

"So?"

"That likely means there would be no bid process, so Nautical

Dredging Services, and Dean Filben, could set their price. FEMA would review any damage and provide a maximum benefit amount, but NDS could still pad the actual costs."

Katie's eyebrows raised. "And an audit could expose that excess money."

"Exactly. The feds aren't just going to turn over that amount of money without some accountability. The question is, where else is the money going? Shellfish leases aren't enough."

"You paid attention to my layering theory," Katie goaded.

"I did. Alex's comments point to Jack Fleming's involvement."

"What do you hope to find out today?"

"I'm hoping Dean Filben will be just stupid enough to confirm my beliefs."

They showered and took off for breakfast. They dressed for their parts. Matt wore a pair of jeans, a crisp white shirt with a chestnut-colored sports coat, and Ariat boots. And, of course, his Stetson. Katie wore a sculpted gray pantsuit and a dark-colored blouse. Her black-strapped heels added to her five-foot-six frame.

The plan was to show up at NDS offices around nine in hopes of getting a meeting with Filben. It was a risk without an appointment, but Matt counted on Filben's curiosity. How the meeting went would determine how Matt and Katie would play the mark. Matt's instincts, and what he knew of Filben, made him believe Filben would be much more interested in Katie. This would play in their favor, as he was more likely to open up to someone he thought was in the private sector than a government official. It also didn't hurt that Katie was more than qualified to set the trap.

Matt and Katie walked up to the receptionist, just getting settled. She appeared annoyed that they were there so early. She first looked at Katie and then Matt, not sure what to make of the apparent cowboy and business woman standing in front of her.

"Can I help you?" she asked with a tinge of aggravation.

"Howdy, ma'am," Matt answered with a slight drawl. "I'm William Johnson, but really everyone calls me Billy Buck. This here is Miss Maggie." He nodded to Katie.

"It's Maggie Duvall," she said as she rolled her eyes to show her frustration to the receptionist. "We're here to see Mr. Filben."

"He doesn't have an appointment scheduled with you this morning."

"That'd be my fault, ma'am," Matt responded. "See we're coming from Texas, and I just clear forgot to call earlier. We had a couple of stops to make, and, well, I just messed up the schedule."

"I'm sorry, sir, but Mr. Filben is a busy man."

"It's Billy Buck. No need to apologize for my mistake." He adjusted his hat. "Any chance he has time later today?"

Katie spoke to Matt. "Another waste of my time, Mr. Johnson. You should have had this scheduled weeks ago."

The receptionist looked at Katie with a scowl, and then to Matt. She looked at his eyes, and suddenly softened. "You say you're from Texas, huh? I always wanted to go there, ride horses and such. You have a horse?" She was completely ignoring Katie now.

Matt gave her his biggest smile. "Can't call yourself a true Texan without one. I got me a beautiful Appaloosa that's just a sweetheart, and a good ole quarter horse. You ever get down my way, we can surely go ridin'."

Katie, showing her impatience, interrupted, "Mr. Johnson, may I remind you that we are on a tight schedule." She looked at the receptionist. "Is Mr. Filben available or not?"

The receptionist looked back at Katie coolly. "Can I tell him the purpose of the meeting?"

"Yes ma'am," Matt said. "We want just a bit of his time to talk about your dredge here. See, I'm with the Texas Department of Transportation, and Miss... Ms. Duvall here is with Fiscal Dynamics."

"Let me see what I can do."

"That's so kind of you, I sure would be obliged." Matt grinned at her again.

They walked away from the desk as the receptionist called up to Dean Filben's office, apparently on the second floor. Matt and Katie stood in front of one of the oceanscape paintings pretending to be interested. It gave Katie a chance to give Matt a little dig. "You're such a flirt," she whispered, "but you are kinda hot in that hat. Later tonight, I'm goin' all cowgirl on your ass."

"Stop it, we need to focus." Matt really meant that he needed to focus, and she was his biggest distraction. She giggled at him.

DAN SAT ON THE BALCONY, a cup of steaming coffee in his hand. The breeze was coming in from the south, keeping the temperature moderate for October. He stared out at the ocean as a fisherman dragged his gear and his beach wagon towards the inlet. He wasn't paying attention, thinking about the meeting with Willie and Alex the night before, contemplating next steps. He didn't hear Shay walk in.

"I smell coffee"

"Help yourself."

"Perfect, I brought bagels. Is the Irish Whiskey there too?" Shay walked towards the bar cart. "Never mind, found it."

"Jesus, Shay, It's not even noon."

"Hey, some pussies take sugar and cream. I like mine with a little more punch."

Shay sat beside Dan, handing him a Taylor Ham, egg, and cheese bagel.

"I thought last night went OK."

"So far so good," Dan agreed.

They sat there in silence, sipping on coffee and chewing on bagels.

"Do you remember the hustle we ran on that frat douchebag back in college? The one that was telling freshmen girls that if they slept with his brothers they could skip rush for the Deltas?"

Dan laughed. "Yeah. Man, I loved driving that guy's BMW around, until Matt made us sell it."

"Fuckin' A," Shay snorted. "We were young and carefree back then."

"Mm-hmm."

That sat there quietly for a few minutes before Shay spoke again. "What the hell are we doing, Trek? This isn't thirty years ago, and it sure the hell isn't some stupid frat boy we're rolling. I thought Matt was done with this."

"This is different, Shay. We're trying to right a wrong. What's the problem?"

"The problem is, we're dealing with a psychopath, a rich and influential family, and the government. It's one thing to drag me into this, but Tanner? Katie? Tell me that you and Matt aren't bored and looking to walk the tightrope again."

Dan stared at his hand, opening and closing his fist. "Seems like the pot calling the kettle black, Shay. You do have some interesting associates, after all."

"What I do, I do on my own. I don't bring family into it."

"Matt didn't want Tanner anywhere near this. It was Tanner, and maybe some of me."

"That's insane. Tanner doesn't need to be like the rest of us Sheehans. He's young enough to go another way."

"Are you wanting out?"

Shay sighed. "You know better than that, Dan. I always have my family's back. And I sure as hell ain't gonna let anything happen to Tanner. He's the future. We're the past."

"I still don't see the issue here."

"The issue, Dan, is that we are trapped in this cycle of self-gratification, and probably self-destruction, constantly looking for the next hustle and score. I accept the fact that it's too late for me, but I thought Matt broke free after the Sampson scam." Shay frowned. "I sure as shit thought the next generation of Sheehans would be better people."

"It's not like that, Shay. This is a one-time thing, and for the right reasons."

"I see it in your eyes, the excitement. Hell, I can even see it in Matt's eyes, although his conscience is fighting him."

Dan held up his hands. "You have to trust Matt, Shay. He knows what he's doing.

"I sure as hell hope so."

DEAN FILBEN'S HAIR was thinning, so he combed it back to look younger than his forty-plus years. He sat at his desk with his coffee, going through emails when the receptionist called. He was abrupt as he picked up. "What is it?"

"There is a man and woman here to see you, Mr. Filben. They came from Texas wanting to talk to you about the *Chinquapin*."

"Hang on just a second." Filben looked over at his security monitor, checking the views from each of the three lobby cameras, scouting who was here to see him. A silly-looking cowboy he was not about to waste his time with on a Monday morning. But then he caught a glimpse of Katie.

"Texas, huh," he said back to his receptionist. "I see a lot of potential there. Make our visitors comfortable in the conference room, I'll be right down."

The receptionist knew what Filben meant and shook her head. She found him detestable but needed the job.

"Yes sir," she answered and hung up. She turned to Matt and smiled again, this time a little forced. "Mr. Filben will be with you shortly. You can wait in the conference room, it's more comfortable. Can I get you anything to drink?"

"Water please, in a bottle," Katie said abruptly.

Matt tipped his hat. "Nothin' for me, ma'am, but thank you kindly."

The receptionist went to get the water. Matt put his hand on Katie's arm.

"The conference room looks like it's set up to record everything," he whispered. "So, from here on in it's strictly business, OK?"

She winked at him. "You are no fun."

It wasn't long before Dean Filben made his grand entrance, chest puffed as he swung the door open. He went straight to Katie, a smile pasted on his face.

"Dean Filben, CEO of Nautical Dredging Services, pleased to meet you." He took Katie's hand, holding it longer than necessary.

"Maggie Duvall. It is a pleasure to meet you, Mr. Filben." She smiled. Filben's ego was reaching its peak already.

"Billy Buck Johnson." Matt broke in, shoving his hand to force the release of Katie's. "Texas DOT. Man, I'm sure glad you're willing to meet with us."

As Filben took his hand, Matt gave it a little squeeze, not enough to hurt, but to gauge his response. Filben tilted his head and squeezed back a little harder, as Matt expected. "Mr. Johnson," was all Filben said. He had to look up at Matt, which made him more agitated.

"Are you with the Department of Transportation as well?" he asked Katie.

"No, I'm with Fiscal Dynamics, a private corporation interested in a potential partnership with the state of Texas, particularly the DOT."

"That's correct," Matt added, knowing Filben would not engage him. He sat down and took his hat off and placed it crown down on the table. "The state is interested in building its own dredge, just like North Carolina."

"Let me stop you there. It's not North Carolina's dredge, it belongs to NDS. We just have an agreement with the state."

"Really?" Matt answered. "I thought the state gave something like $20 million to have it built specifically for its use."

"I'm afraid you have some bad intel, Mr. Johnson."

"It's Billy Buck, we're all friends here."

Filben sighed. "I assure you, it's our dredge. Why is Texas DOT asking anyway?"

"Great question, Deano. Can I call you Deano, like the great Dean Martin?"

"I'd rather you not. Dean will be fine."

Matt nodded. "Gotcha, big man. Anywho, in Texas the DOT has a Maritime Division, focusing on things like port access, supply chains, and the like." Matt waved his hands around, getting a little animated for effect. "We believe that more promotion of waterborne transportation leads to much greater economic impacts for the state, especially when maximizing the Gulf Intracoastal Waterway."

"Fascinating, but what does that have to do with our dredge?" Filben responded blankly.

"The waterway needs to be passable. We can't have it shoal up. If we had our own dredge, the state wouldn't have to count on the availability of the Corps."

Katie's eyes narrowed before she spoke. "What Mr. Johnson and I are hoping to find out are some of the details, pros and cons if you will, of what you went through getting a dredge. Fiscal Dynamics may be interested in a similar arrangement."

"I'm not familiar with any Fiscal Dynamics in the dredging industry." It was the first time Filben questioned any part of the story. "I know pretty much everybody in the business."

"We're not in the dredging industry, not yet. Fiscal Dynamics is interested in investment potential. We diversify our holdings in order to maintain a strong balance sheet. I'm sure you can understand."

Filben looked skeptical. "Dredging as an investment option? That would be a long-term investment."

"Maybe," Katie responded, "depending on how it's done. You said North Carolina loaned you the money to build the dredge?"

"I don't believe I said that, but yes, that's true. It's a forgivable loan."

Katie cocked an eyebrow. "Forgivable loan? That's very interesting, Mr. Filben. If you have the time, I would love to hear more."

"Don't you think we should focus on the actual dredge, Miss Maggie?" Matt asked.

Filben couldn't take his gaze off Katie. "I think I can clear my schedule. Perhaps I can get one of my staff to give Mr. Johnson an overview of the technical end of the dredge while you and I discuss the business end."

"I think it's best if we stay together, so we're gathering the same data," Matt replied.

"Nonsense, Mr. Johnson. Divide and conquer," Katie responded.

Filben looked at Matt and gave him a smug smile. "If you don't mind waiting here, I'll make the necessary arrangements." Filben left to make his call.

Matt leaned over and whispered to Katie. "You sure you want to go this route?"

"If I can get past his body spray, I think I'll be OK," she answered.

"We don't want to push him too hard. We need to see if they are planning to defraud the government, but I don't want him to get suspicious and contact anyone else. Filben may be an idiot, but I doubt whoever is truly behind this is."

"Don't worry, if I think he's getting suspicious I'll just sleep with him."

"You take great joy in tormenting me, don't you?"

"It's just so easy," Katie teased.

"Seriously, see if you can get him to show you the dredge with me, then maybe the two of you can go to lunch as I dig around."

"OK, but why?"

"I think we may be able to embarrass him a bit so that he will want to impress you later," Matt answered.

Filben came back to the room, and his scent was even stronger. "Alright, Tony Hillman will be joining us shortly," he said. "He will take you to the dredge, Mr. Johnson, and answer any questions you may have. Ms. Duvall and I can discuss the business aspect of the public-private partnership." He leered just a bit.

"Please, call me Maggie. Is the dredge actually here and not out working?"

"It is. It's getting a little maintenance and should go back out later this week."

"That's fantastic. I'd like to go see it first if you don't mind, Dean. Then maybe we can discuss the partnership over lunch."

Filben frowned. "Well, I'm not sure I'm going to have time to have lunch with the two of you."

"Not the two of us, just me." Katie smiled. "I just want to see the vessel; I'm sure Mr. Johnson will want to stay longer for more details."

Filben perked up but tried to play it off smoothly. "I'll see if I can move some things around. I'm sure we can help our friends in Texas."

Matt pushed his Stetson back on his head a bit. "I suppose that'd work; we can catch up later this afternoon."

Tony Hillman walked into the conference room, nearly as tall as Matt, but considerably younger. He looked very annoyed to be there.

"Tony, this is Ms. Duvall and Mr. Johnson from Texas, the ones I told you about."

"Pleasure," he said, joylessly. "I don't mean to be rude, but we're in a bit of a time crunch trying to get the *Chinquapin* back out to the Inlet."

The group made its way out to the *Chinquapin*'s dock. Hillman kept looking Matt's way. It was starting to make him nervous.

"You look awfully familiar, Mr. Johnson," Hillman finally noted. "Do we know each other?"

Matt knew there was a risk of being recognized, but it needed to be taken. Now he had to deal with it.

"I don't reckon we do, unless you've spent some time in Texas. But my mama always said I have one of those faces."

Hillman shook his head. "No, I'm sure I know you from somewhere."

Matt snapped his fingers and pointed. "It was probably at one of those beach nourishment conferences. You go to the one down in South Padre Island a few months back?" Matt kept talking, hoping to create confusion. "That one was a hoot, alright. Margaritas flowing, and those tacos, did you get one of those? Big as my head."

"We're all busy here, so let's move on," Filben snarked.

The *Chinquapin* was a thing of beauty, a little longer than 150 feet, with a red hull, black trim, the bridge in white.

Matt whistled. "Now that's a thoroughbred right there. She's a real beaut. I assume she's a TSHD."

"Nope, it's a hopper dredge," Filben said confidently.

"He's asking if it's a Trailing Suction Hopper Dredge," Hillman snapped, "and, yes, it is, as a matter of fact. Do you know much about dredges, Mr. Johnson?"

"Please, it's Billy Buck. I know just enough to be dangerous. What's its capacity?"

Filben interrupted again, in hopes to rebound from his misstep. "It can accommodate a crew of five."

"I'm pretty sure he meant how much spoil it can handle. Full load displacement about 565 tons, hopper capacity of 512 cubic yards."

"Damn, son, that's impressive. That's gotta mean it's drafting near on ten feet when full. Y'all run that deep?"

"It's not a problem at all. The *Chinquapin* can handle anything." Filben just couldn't shut up, exactly what Matt hoped.

"Actually, it is a problem, which is why we are time sensitive right now. Our water depth in some areas is less than seven feet, so we have to get the Corps to come in with a sidecaster first to get us a workable depth."

"Can you two speak English here?" Katie demanded.

Matt smiled. Katie set up Hillman to do what Filben couldn't: give a quick Dredging 101.

"A hopper dredge is built with suction pipes, collecting sand and silt which it deposits in the 'hopper' or hull of the ship," Hillman explained. "The sand is then transported and either dumped elsewhere or pumped back onto the beach for reconstruction. The sidecaster dredge simply sucks up the sand and shoots it out into the ocean, but eventually it comes right back."

"Think of it like a lawnmower," Matt said. "The sidecaster is like when you don't have the bag on the mower, sending clippings everywhere. You eventually have to rake it up. The hopper adds the bag so you can dump the clippings wherever you want."

"That's just stupid," Filben snorted.

"Actually, not a bad analogy," Hillman said.

"No, it's stupid. Who wants to keep grass clippings?" Filben doubled down. "Anyway, Maggie, shall we move on to lunch and discuss financials?"

Filben and Katie left, Filben clearly flustered, exactly as Matt hoped. Filben needed to redeem himself in front of Katie and was now likely to show off.

Hillman let out an audible sigh. "C'mon, Mr. Johnson, I'll show you around."

"It's Billy Buck, please. And that won't be necessary, I know you're a busy man. I appreciate the info, Tony. You mind if I call you that?"

He smiled back weakly. "Sure, Billy Buck, if that's your real name."

Matt stopped in his tracks. "Meaning?"

"I'm pretty sure you're not from Texas, unless you moved there in the last month or so. And we didn't have margaritas or tacos in South Padre."

Matt had no choice but to bite. "Who do you think I am then?"

Hillman rubbed his chin. "Not sure of the name, but pretty sure you're a town manager from one the beach communities further south. You're usually with Chris Taylor at the quarterly meetings we have with the Corps." He raised his eyebrows. "Am I close?"

Fuck, fuck, fuck. "Matt Sheehan," Matt confessed. "Topsail Beach."

"Well then, Mr. Sheehan." He looked straight at Matt. "You want to tell me what the hell this is really about?"

At this point, Matt felt like he had nothing to lose. If his cover was blown, the stratagem was over. "I believe there's a plan to use this dredge for something questionably legal and definitely unethical."

"That would explain a lot. Ever since the *Chinquapin* arrived, I felt like it's been misused. I swear it's like when I worked for Simmons Dredging."

"It's the government way, isn't it, partner?"

"It's worse than that. I got a clueless boss who doesn't know starboard from port. We have a vessel that is top of the line and grossly underused, and now I hear rumor it's going to be pimped out like a high-priced hooker to the top bidder. We could make serious improvements to our waterways if we just used this dredge as it was intended."

"'Pimped out'? I don't follow."

"I overheard Filben talking one day about how they're going to assign the dredge to the highest bidders, basically pitting local governments against each other. They would eliminate competition by forcing towns to use the *Chinquapin* in order to qualify for state and federal funds. Filben laughed about setting the prices high and milking all three levels of government for top dollar."

"That's some comic-book-villain-type bullshit. Do you think there is any chance Filben recognized me from any of those meetings?" Matt asked.

"Not a chance. His head is way too far up his own ass. No offense, but he would see you as a waste of his time, unless Topsail Beach had the money to bid on the dredge."

"Thanks for your time. I have to ask, could you keep my identity secret?"

"Sure. Hell, you're the one taking all the risks. Whatever you're up to, I sure hope it works. For once I would like to see a good, honest project."

"You and me both," Matt replied, a touch of regret in his voice.

FILBEN WAS FUMING. He was starting to think he might as well cut his losses now. They went up to his office, and he plopped in his chair behind his desk, winded from the walk. "I've got a full schedule today, Ms. Duvall. Perhaps another time."

"I can see you have your hands full," Katie replied, "dealing with the responsibility of the business end of this venture and employees who can't manage their time properly. I've been dealing with mergers and acquisitions of companies for much of my career, so I can spot the good ones and the duds pretty quickly. Seems to me you got this on the right track even with an incompetent staff."

Filben rubbed his chin. "Tony's not bad, just young. I'm sure I can mentor him." He was starting to catch his breath. "Not like that clown you're with."

"Billy Buck? Typical bureaucrat, he just happens to be a good ole' boy clown as well. Trapped in the same thought process, you know? We need to think outside the box, like you obviously have." She didn't need to sink the hook any further, but she leaned over his desk just close enough for him to smell her perfume. "I'm just sorry we can't finish this conversation over lunch."

Filben looked down her blouse, as Katie expected. He caught himself, then looked away as he cleared his throat and checked his watch. "If you don't mind an early lunch, we can drive up to Manteo. I know a place that has a great grouper sandwich." And happens to be across the street from a hotel, he thought, pleased with both his improvisation and foresight.

As they walked through the lobby, he made it a point to call out to the receptionist, "Colleen, reschedule my appointments for the next few hours."

"You don't have any," she responded.

 Tanner's office just as he hung up the phone. He had maps spread across his desk so he could finish preparing them for Dan before their meeting with Covington and Spencer.

"Hey, what's goin' on?" she asked, her voice almost singsong.

"Working on a project for a client. Nothing special."

She walked over to where the maps were laid out. "Why do you have old maps? The inlet positioning is all wrong, and it doesn't show the Intracoastal Waterway."

"Research. Looking at past and present conditions."

"Why? Is it environmentally related?"

"It's just a project," Tanner snapped. He walked over to the maps and folded them over.

Brittany leaned back, surprised at Tanner's reaction. "OK. Sorry I asked."

Tanner winced. "I'm sorry, Brit. This particular project has me a little wound up."

She walked over to him, standing toe to toe. She put her hand gently on his chest, staring at it for just a second before looking up into his eyes. "Why don't you take me to lunch? You can tell me about the project, maybe I can help."

Tanner knew there was no way he could tell Brittany about any of what was going on. He wished he could confide in someone not involved, though.

When he didn't immediately answer, Brittany put her arms around his neck. "These last few nights have been unbelievable.

I love spending time with you downtown...especially at the condo."

Tanner's brow wrinkled for a half a second, but he kept eye contact. Maybe Pops was right, he thought. He slowly moved Brittany's hands away from his neck. "I'm afraid I can't have lunch right now. I've got a few calls to make and a lot of work to do."

Brittany's face dropped, a hurt look in her eyes. "I see. I better get going, I've got to get to the lab." She turned for the door.

"Hey, Brit," Tanner called back to her, "when this job is finished, why don't you and I take a trip, maybe to the islands?"

She looked back and smiled. "Do you mean it?"

He smiled back weakly. "Yeah."

FILBEN TALKED ABOUT HIMSELF the entire ride to the restaurant. He made sure Katie knew how influential he was with the NC General Assembly, and while he wasn't an elected official, he practically handled all the key legislation regarding dredging himself. For Katie's part, she acted interested without appearing too impressed. She wanted to make Filben feel like he needed to show her more.

They stopped at a restaurant called The Sand Dollar, where Filben asked for a booth in the corner so they could have some privacy.

"They make a great dirty martini here," Filben hinted.

"It's a little early for me," Katie said, lips pursed. "Just water for me, please, with lemon if possible," she told the waiter.

"Same," Filben said.

"I need to freshen up, Dean, I'll be right back." Katie gave him a little smile so he wouldn't shut down.

Katie went to the bathroom to check her phone and Matt's whereabouts.

"I took the liberty of ordering us a dozen oysters on the half shell," Filben said with a smile as she returned.

"I love oysters." She changed the subject, "So, you mentioned earlier that the loan the state gave you to build the dredge is forgivable. How does that work?"

"Oh, that. Yeah, that was something I insisted upon," he lied. "We promised to provide dredging services at a discounted rate for ten years. Once that's up, the dredge belongs to NDS free and clear. We make no payments during that period. Pretty sweet, right?"

"I don't know," Katie said, a little disappointed. "Seems to me that you're eating up some valuable hours on that dredge at a discount rate. I would think you would want to maximize its billable time while maintenance is at a minimum."

Filben wasn't ready for any real questions. "It's the long game we're playing," he countered, hoping that made sense.

About that time the oysters arrived. Katie took one and brought it to her lips, slightly tipping the shell and sliding it into her mouth. She put the empty shell face down back on the iced platter. Filben watched, his mouth slightly ajar, eyes wide, as if discovering porn for the first time. She grabbed a second oyster. "Aren't you going to try one?"

Filben stammered, "Oh, a yeah, absolutely." He fumbled with one, ultimately dropping it. He quickly picked it up, trying to salvage some dignity.

"Anyway," Katie continued, "Fiscal Dynamics isn't interested in a long-term project. Our investors are looking for a quicker return on investment.”

She grabbed another oyster. “Which is too bad.” She peered at him with those large, emerald eyes. “I was looking forward to spending more time here, you know, going over things with you.”

Filben’s brain hit overdrive. He had to figure a way to keep Katie around for what was sure to be his conquest. He had to tell her about the bigger plan, even though he had been ordered not to say anything to anyone. It was OK, he thought, she’s from Texas and would be gone soon anyway. Denton and that other senator, the arrogant one, would never know.

“There is more to it, something I haven’t told you.” He was trying hard to play it cool. “Maybe we can continue this conversation later this evening—over drinks, perhaps.”

“I’ve got an afternoon call scheduled with the board chair of Fiscal Dynamics. Honestly, he’s been opposed to this project from the start. I doubt he’s going to want me to pursue this further based on what I know.” She picked up another oyster for effect.

“What if I told you that there is a ton of money to be made right away?”

“Based on what you’ve told me, I don’t see how. If you have to give discounted rates for ten years, how are you going to make a large enough profit margin?”

“Let’s just say I’m about to get legislation passed that will funnel federal, state, and local dollars to this dredge with minimal oversight.”

“I would say no way. Federal money in particular requires a ton of oversight alone, especially now.”

“My legislation requires communities to use the dredge if

they want access to these funds, meaning no competition from other dredge companies. I set the price."

"OK, let's say that's the case," Katie conceded as she leaned in. "You still have to account for these funds. FEMA isn't just going to give you millions of dollars without justifying costs. Don't they require a bid process? And even if you get it past them, where does the excess money go?"

Filben didn't have the answer to any of these questions, mostly because he was an idiot. But he did know enough to deflect.

"We have ways, other enterprises." Filben didn't know the ways, he was not in that loop, but he couldn't admit to that. "I've got a senator in my pocket to help deflect government interference."

"I don't know, that may work, but I need to know more for my chairman."

"More tonight. That should be enough for you to convince your chairman to investigate a little further." He smirked.

Matt sat in the parking lot of the restaurant. He was thinking about the stratagem, and how easily everyone seemed to play their roles, as if they never stopped. Even Aoife, he thought. For someone who supposedly dumped Matt to escape the con life, she was still damn good at it.

His phone vibrated as he was waiting. It was Tanner calling.

"What's up?"

"I found out some info you might like to know. According to Strickland's legislative assistant, the proposed legislation was not written by anyone in her camp. It came from Fleming's staff."

"Not surprising," Matt responded. "The question is, why is Strickland putting his name on it?"

"I asked the same question. She said it was strange, because she and several others recommended Strickland pass on it. But get this, she did say she walked in on Strickland and former Senator Denton last week, and they got real quiet. She thinks they were discussing the legislation."

"Denton's name is popping up a lot for a former senator."

"He's been responsible for several people getting key subcommittee chairs, including Strickland. Some are speculating that he may be positioning Fleming for a gubernatorial run. This shit reeks, Pops."

Matt thought for a moment. "Do you know if Chris is finished putting together his analysis?"

"I think so, why?"

"I may have someone who can help and is not indebted to Denton as far as I know."

Matt's phone buzzed, a signal from Katie. "I gotta go. It's showtime."

Matt walked into the restaurant and caught Katie's eye. She gave him a quick nod, so he strolled to the table. "Howdy, you two, I thought I saw you from across the room." Matt gave them a big smile. "Startin' out with oysters, huh? Bet they're not as good as what we grow in Texas. Mind if I sit down?" Matt was already taking a seat beside Katie.

"We are trying to have a private conversation, if you don't mind," Filben replied, barely controlling his anger.

"Well, about that, Mr. Filben, I reckon I do mind." Matt took a more serious tone. "See, me and Ms. Duvall have been asked to research options together, so that the public and private sector have the same information going into this venture. You know, for transparency sake. I'm sure you understand."

Matt reached over to grab one of the remaining oysters. When he did, Filben grabbed his arm.

"I will let you know when we're done here," he said in what Matt assumed was supposed to be his menacing voice. Matt looked at his arm and back to Filben's face.

"If you don't want to share your oysters, just say so." Matt's voice got low, almost guttural. "But son, I would suggest you remove your hand, unless you enjoy spending time in traction." Matt glared directly at him.

Filben quickly removed his hand.

"The State of Texas appreciates your help," Matt said with a smile, "but I believe it's time we hit the proverbial dusty trail." Matt stood and held his hand out to Katie. "Ms. Duvall."

She took his hand and stood up beside him. She leaned towards Filben and said in a low voice, "Meet me in the lobby of the hotel across the street at eight tonight. We'll finish this then." She gave him a smile and a wink.

They walked out to the car, and Matt handed Katie the keys. "Will you drive? I need to make a few calls."

"Sure, cowboy."

As he opened the door for her, Matt asked, "Why did you tell him to meet you later? We'll be long gone."

"I want the little prick to think he's getting some tonight and then be embarrassed when he's left standing there, dick in hand. The fecking gobshite."

Matt laughed. "I hope I never piss you off."

As they drove back to Topsail Beach, Matt asked Katie about her conversation with Filben. "Did he say anything that would lead you to believe they're moving money around?"

"He all but confessed to it, or at least as much as that dipshit knows. He said they have 'other enterprises'. My take is he doesn't know what they are."

"I think I do. Fleming's father-in-law is a huge developer. Real estate would make a great investment."

"It's got to be something more specific than just real estate, babe. It would have to be a project, probably a big one."

Matt rubbed his chin. "If we assume Majestic Oysters and the shellfish leases are the initial step in laundering the money, it's possible they could be an outlet to layer money to a bigger investment. Since Fleming and Spencer are involved, then the obvious connection is Coastal Properties. But why would a company with their reputation get involved in something that risky?"

"The usual answers are greed and power, but that doesn't seem to make sense here."

"I need to find out more."

"It's a three-hour drive, slick. Start reaching out."

Matt called a few of his contacts to see if anyone was aware of a big project on the books for Coastal Properties, but no one did. Out of desperation, he called the town manager of Holly Ridge, a small but growing town just north of Topsail Beach.

"Hi Gretchen, it's Matt."

Gretchen Tolliver had a huge crush on Matt and wasn't shy about letting him know. "Please tell me this is a personal call, Matt, not business."

Matt couldn't help but smile. They had a one night stand a few years back, while at a conference in Winston-Salem. It was one of the few times Matt had been with a woman after Hannah died. He held a soft spot for her, but Matt felt she was too young for him, and too energetic in bed.

"Sorry, this call is business."

She let out a dramatic sigh. "OK, your loss. I have some pent-up energy I need to exercise."

Matt had no doubt. He chuckled. "The thought alone could

give this old man a heart attack, Gretchen. What I really need to know is if there are any big development plans for Holly Ridge."

"You're going to have to be more specific, handsome. We've got a lot going on here. Are you looking at residential, commercial, or industrial?"

"Anything by Coastal Properties, or anyone associated with them."

"Well, that would be residential or mixed-use, I would suspect. Short answer is no, but what do you mean 'anyone associated'?"

"I'm not sure, just fishing, I guess. Anything out of the ordinary going on in terms of large land sales?"

"I think I did hear something about a rezoning request around Stone's Bay in Sneads Ferry. It's a lot of swampy land, but something could be going on there. You should call Onslow County's Planning Department."

"Thanks Gretchen, I owe you."

"I'll take a nice bottle of wine and a night of pure passion." He heard her giggle as she hung up.

Katie gave him the side-eye. "Gretchen sounds nice."

"Jealous?"

"You wish, cowboy."

Matt called Onslow County Planning and confirmed the rezoning petition for over three hundred acres along Stone's Bay. The applicant was the property owner, however, with no additional information on future plans. That didn't make much sense; rarely would someone rezone that much land without a plan or contract for sale in place. Then the developer usually acts as the agent for the property owner on the application.

Matt took a chance and called Coastal Properties, asking for the development division.

"How can I help you today?"

Matt tried to sound young and frazzled. "I sure hope you can help. This is my first job out of law school, my wife and I just had a baby, so I'm getting no sleep. Now this."

"Take it easy, honey. We've all been there. Now, what is it you need?"

"I can't find the file on the Stone's Bay rezoning, and I need to know how long the contingency is for our client to make sure we get this done on time. If I mess this up, I'm toast."

"I'm really sorry, sir, but we don't have any projects for Stone's Bay."

Damn, Matt thought. If not Coastal Properties, then who? He took one last shot. "I could have sworn my client said he spoke to Alex Spencer."

The silence at the other end was deafening. When the woman finally spoke, her tone had changed to frustration. "I suppose you mean young Alex. I'd like to help you, but that's not us. My guess is that's the property Alex was bothering us about for some other company. Not even a developer as far as I know, Royalty Something-or-Other."

Matt's heart skipped a beat. "Majestic Oysters, Inc. by chance?"

"Yeah, that sounds right."

Bingo.

When they got back to the compound, Matt found a copy of Chris' analysis on his desk. There was a note from Tanner that simply read: 'Do we ever let you down?'

After reading the analysis, Matt called Senator Geoff Carson. He had met Senator Carson once early in his career through

Hannah and felt he was honest, smart, and genuine. He was one of Hannah's favorites too, always willing to hear her environmental concerns, mostly supportive of her initiatives. Carson was younger and destined for bigger things, like the Governor's Mansion, or US Congress, but didn't seem tied to any particular lobby. It was refreshing.

Matt told Senator Carson his concerns about the proposed legislation and what it meant to the coastal communities. They talked about how the money was to be handled and the suggested improprieties from Dean Filben. Matt also explained his belief that the legislation had more devious intentions. They talked about Majestic Oysters, Inc. and the breaks they seemed to be getting regarding shellfish leases. Finally, Matt traced it back to Senator Jack Fleming.

"These are pretty serious allegations, Mr. Sheehan," Carson said. "It seems like a stretch, although I will admit I wouldn't put anything past Fleming."

"I know it sounds improbable, sir, but there is just too much going on to be coincidental. I have what I believe to be damning information that I would be happy to send if it helps."

"Send me what you have, Mr. Sheehan. I have to be honest though, this is something I normally wouldn't do, but your wife was a straight-shooter, so I'm hoping you are too."

Matt couldn't help but smile. Hannah was still helping him out.

Tuesday, October 18

THE WINDS SHIFTED, coming from the northeast, so the morning was noticeably cooler. Dan anticipated the waters would be a little rougher than normal, which may be an advantage. He didn't imagine Willie Covington was much of a boater, so choppy waters could make him uneasy. He was going over maps and listening to the Beatles as Matt walked in.

"No headphones?" Matt asked.

"I figured you were coming. What's the haps, partner?"

"We good to go?"

"I'm getting ready to call Alex to set up a meeting for this afternoon, then out on the boat tonight," Dan answered. "The box has been dropped near Frank Kenny's lease, ready to be found by Tanner."

The box was the prop they were using for the Confederate gold, filled with rocks and shells to give it weight, appropriately water fatigued to fool Willie and Alex at first glance. The team had added a few markings to make it look authentic, certainly enough to fool those idiots.

"Who'd you get for the professor?" Matt asked. The professor was their expert on Civil War artifacts.

"Nigel Thornburg."

"You got a Brit to play our Civil War history buff?"

"Sure, he can play an arrogant academic better than anyone. I'll make sure he dials down the British accent."

"Jaysus, Mary and Joseph, it's a wonder we've gotten this far," Matt said, shaking his head. "Somehow, we have to get them to believe in the gold, get them on the boat, and convince them to take it back to the compound. And then, Shay and I have to somehow get them to admit to murder. Nothing to it."

"Relax, Matt, it's a good play you came up with. You do your thing, and let me do mine. It's gonna work. Have you thought who's gonna cool the mark?"

"This isn't a con, there is no mark to cool. I don't want to cool Covington, I want his ass in jail."

"So you said last night. By the way, what's Katie doing if not cooling the mark?"

"Nothing. I don't want her around when this goes down."

Dan snickered. "I bet that went over well."

Matt took a deep breath. "When we did this years ago, it was a game. Everything was safe, there was never a risk of violence when Aoife was involved. It's gonna stay that way."

"I hope you can pull that off," Dan said, smiling.

"You and me both, partner. I gotta go." He paused at the door as he was about to leave. "You guys be careful today. If shit goes sideways, you bail."

Matt walked to his office and placed a call to the police chief. If everything went as planned, they would need the police to be ready to take down Willie Covington. The trick for Matt was to make sure he knew exactly what to say to the chief, and what not to say.

Chief Phillips answered on the first ring. "Hey Boss, how are you enjoying your time off?"

"It's been interesting."

"I bet. By the way, we have an APB out for a guy named Willie Covington. He's the top suspect in the Holt Bratton case."

"Yeah, about that," Matt responded, "I may be able to help you there."

The chief hesitated. "Before we go too far, remember I am a law enforcement officer, first and foremost, so don't say anything that could come back on you or me."

"Understood. I think you're right about Willie Covington, and I think we can help get you the proof you need."

"Who's 'we'? Don't tell me Dan's involved too. If you know where Covington is, you need to tell me now."

"I don't know where Covington is right now. But I'm pretty sure I know where he will be tonight."

"Is he involved in the assault on the other guy? The Pender County Sheriff said he saw the same lady you were with a few days ago visiting the victim. Is that the family member you mentioned?"

"Yeah."

The chief blew out his breath. "That's something you should have told me earlier. What have you gotten yourself into? Whatever it is, let me help."

"I'm fine, Chief, really. But I do need your help. Covington should be at the Slaggers compound tonight. Probably armed, possibly with others. Alex Spencer is likely to be there too."

"The real estate mogul?"

"His son. I promise I'll explain it all later, but I need your guys to be at the south end of the island tonight."

"You are putting me in one helluva spot, Matt." The chief never called Matt by name, always Boss, or Mr. Sheehan. "All my training says I should bring you in right now. You are interfering with an official investigation."

"I know, but you have to trust me on this."

"I'm gonna trust my instincts on this one, for now. Please don't make me regret it."

WILLIE AND MERLE were the first to show at Alex's office. Willie wanted to confront Alex ahead of time to ensure Alex wasn't going to blow the deal. He really wanted to frighten Alex more than anything else.

When Willie and Merle walked in, Alex jumped from the receptionist's desk and hustled them into a conference room. Willie motioned to Merle to take a spot in the corner of the room where he could keep an eye on Willie for protection. Willie told him earlier to try and look menacing but not to speak. The bandage across the bridge of his nose didn't help. Willie took a seat at the table in the middle of the room while Alex paced.

"What exactly did he tell you, Alex?" Willie demanded.

"Nothing, just to get you here to discuss a move tonight."

"What kind of move?"

"I don't know, Willie, he didn't say." Alex wanted out so bad, but he just didn't know how. He felt he was in too deep.

"It's OK, Alex, just remember we've been partners from the start. I got your back, and you got mine. These assholes are going to lead us to the gold, and we're gonna get ours. Then they're gonna get theirs." Willie cracked his knuckles and grinned, exposing his yellowed teeth.

"Yeah, I'm gonna even the score with that one prick," Merle added.

"I thought I told you not to speak, Merle," Willie spat.

"No, Willie, no more violence. I won't be a part of it," Alex asserted.

"Take it easy, Alex, I ain't gonna hurt no one. Those other two guys, well that just happened. Besides, you're the one that hit that first fella. That's what likely kilt him." Willie's eyes narrowed as he spoke. "I just mean we're gonna make sure they deal with us fairly, you know, even split."

Alex knew it was a lie, but he didn't protest.

"Stay with me here, Alex, and you're gonna be very rich." Willie was already thinking about how he was going to get rid of Alex, and probably Merle once he took care of the others.

Dan, Tanner, and Shay rolled up to the Coastal Properties building. They took Shay's Escalade for effect, Tanner driving. Nigel Thornburg pulled in right behind them. They walked into the building without saying a word.

Willie and Alex watched from the hallway just outside the conference room. Even Willie was a little bit in awe. Alex hurried to greet them.

"Alex," Dan said with a warm smile. "Thanks for hosting us and getting everyone together."

"I didn't have many options, did I?" Alex responded bitterly.

Dan kept smiling. "Nope, you sure didn't."

As they walked into the room, Tanner spotted Merle in the corner. Merle scowled at him, but Tanner just smiled and shook his head.

"Who the hell is this guy?" Willie sneered, pointing at Nigel.

Dan started to speak: "This is—"

"I'm a visiting professor at UNCW, an expert on Civil War history and artifacts," Nigel interrupted. "One of my main areas of study has been blockade runners, particularly the C.S.S. Phantom."

"I don't like this, Benny," Alex protested. "You keep bringing in new people. How do we know we can trust him?" He turned to Nigel, "What's your name?"

"I have concerns too," Nigel replied. "What I'm doing with you all is highly irregular and could cause me to lose tenure, so no names, just call me 'Professor,' OK?"

"The professor can authenticate whatever we recover," Dan offered. "He also knows how to handle the goods properly, so we don't compromise the find. He is vital to this operation."

"What the hell are they talkin' 'bout, Willie?" Merle asked.

"I told you to shut up, Merle." Willie glared at Shay. "How much is this guy's share?"

"None of your fuckin' business, asshole," Shay answered, then looked to Dan. "Benny, I still don't know why the fuck we're dealing with these guys. They bring nothing to the table."

"I think I know, Mr. Martin," Alex spoke up. "What you need from us is our knowledge of the shellfish leases and probably to keep a certain state senator out of the way. Isn't that right, Mr. Pierce?"

Dan was impressed. Alex was wrong, but it was a logical response to the question. "He's right, Mr. Martin." Dan signaled to Tanner. "Get the maps."

Dan took back control of the meeting. "I know we don't all get along here, but we need to work together if we're gonna be successful. Once it's done, we can say 'Fuck you' and go our different ways."

"Not at ten percent we can't," Willie said. "Seems to me Alex brought up a good point. You need us. I want half, and the professor's share comes outta your end."

Shay lunged at Willie, but Dan intervened.

"You listen here, shitbird. When I'm done with you, they'll be lucky to find any pieces," he growled. "On second thought, we're done here, Benny. I'm going back to Chicago to find someone who can get this job done."

"Please, Mr. Martin, just give me a moment." Dan turned to Willie. "Let's be clear, I don't need you, or Alex, or his brother-in-law senator." Dan turned to Alex. "You have a chance to make an easy million bucks tonight, but hand to God, I will drop you now if y'all don't get your shit straight. You morons can take your chances with Mr. Martin." He let that last part hang in the air. "You and your band of misfits need to make a choice, and make it right now."

"Fine. What's the fucking plan?" Willie said.

"I was talking to Alex," Dan admonished.

"We're good, we're in, let's proceed," Alex replied.

Tanner rolled out the maps. The first was of the Topsail Island area from the 1800's, the second was the current geography.

"Experts believe the C.S.S. Phantom ran aground right about here." Nigel pointed to the edge of what was the inlet. "When the Union Army closed in on these blockade runners, the Confederate sailors would do their best to destroy the ship and its contents before it fell into enemy hands, which was the case with the Phantom. But on that particular trip, they also had gold pieces they didn't want to destroy, so they took it with them."

"So that's why divers never found anything at the wreck site," Alex added.

"Exactly," replied Nigel. "But the Union Army was fast on their heels, so the Confederates had to ditch the gold. My research suggests they buried it in the marshes, and by all accounts, it would have been here, near the mouth of what is now Howard's Creek." He pointed to the map.

"Are you just making a guess, like a wild goose chase?" Willie asked. "I mean, that's a long time ago, someone was bound to find it."

"It's not an exact science, but I have been researching this for over twenty years. I've met with coastal engineers, mapping experts, and other Civil War historians. I know more about tides and water shifts than I care to think about. It's somewhere within a three-to-five-mile radius of that spot."

"Then why don't you just get it? Why do you need these motherfuckers?" Willie asked Nigel.

"Anyone who finds this treasure is required by law to turn over any valuables to the state," Dan explained. "If you want to keep it, you need someone able to fence the goods without the government finding out."

"The government. You mean like my brother-in-law," Alex said.

"Among others, yes."

"As you can see on this map, the marsh that existed in the 1800's isn't there anymore, it's underwater." Nigel pointed to the map.

"Hey Alex, haven't we been there before?" Willie asked.

Alex shook his head violently.

"Yeah, we have. That's the lease the guy didn't want to sell. You know, the guy we busted up," Willie sneered, glancing at Shay.

Dan took a deep breath and let it out slowly. "What the fuck did you just say?"

"Did I stutter? We can play rough too, you know."

"What you did, you imbecile, is bring this to the cops' attention."

Shay got up and put on his coat. He looked at Willie and Alex, shaking his head. "I'm leaving, Benny. Here's the deal, you deliver me the gold by tomorrow, or you are the hook for all that I got invested in this…plus twenty-five percent. Be happy it ain't worse." He looked back at Willie and Alex. "If I was you two, I'd pray to God he finds the gold. That may be your only saving grace."

Finally, he turned to Tanner. "Give me the keys to the Escalade, son."

Tanner reached into his pockets and handed him the keys. "Excuse me, sir, but we came with you."

"Not my fuckin' problem." Shay walked out the door.

Dan sat down and stared at the maps. After a few minutes of awkward silence, he looked up at the group. "Professor, I hope you're right. We got one shot at this, and it has to be tonight. We'll take the boat out later tonight, once it gets dark enough. It'll be the five of us."

"Six, counting Merle," Willie added.

"Hell no, I don't want that asshole anywhere near this project," Dan answered. "Two fuck-ups are already too many."

"How come that gorilla gets to come?" Willie pointed at Tanner, who just smirked.

"He's our diver, unless you want to put on the scuba gear."

Dan waited a second before he continued, "I didn't think so. We meet at Bush Marina on Topsail Beach at nine. I leave without you if you're not there."

"It is critical that if we find the box, we get it to the lab before we open it," the professor added. "Any prolonged exposure to the salt air will devalue the gold. We probably have less than an hour to get it in a controlled room."

"How are we going to get it to the university in that time?" Alex asked.

"We're not," Dan answered. "The university has a facility at the end of Topsail Beach. The professor has access to the facility. We can use their dock for the boat and get the goods inside quickly."

"This sounds a little too convenient," Alex said, questioning the plan for the first time.

Dan stood up and walked over to Alex, getting right in his face. "'Convenient'? It's not at all convenient, Alex. It's six months of detailed planning and work that you and your partner have fucked up in a matter of days. If this works, and that's a big if now, you walk away with a million bucks. If it doesn't, we're all likely dead. Sound convenient to you?"

Alex swallowed hard. "No."

"We're done here. Boat leaves at nine." Dan, Tanner, and Nigel got up to leave.

"I'll show you out," Alex offered.

"I'm sure we can find the way." Dan gave Alex a hard stare. "Don't fuck this up."

"Ya did good, Alex," Willie said after they left. "We're all gonna be rich as hell when this night is done. Better than the lousy million they're offering."

"Let's take the money they're offering, Willie. A million bucks is serious dough."

"Ten million is a shitload better, Alex. Plus, nobody threatens me like that. Don't worry, I won't get your soft little hands dirty."

Willie and Merle left the building, and Willie told Merle, "I want you to be at this facility tonight. Don't let anyone see you, but be sure you're there. And bring some guns."

Merle smiled a crooked, half-toothed smile. "You got it, boss."

MATT SAT ON THE DECK, staring at the ocean. The sea oats on the dunes swayed, their hypnotic motion stealing Matt's thoughts. The serenity was shattered by the ring of his cellphone.

"I read the information you sent," Senator Carson said. "I had one of my staff check into Majestic Oysters, Inc. It's all very disturbing.

"I have a meeting set for tomorrow with Senator Strickland regarding the legislation since he is listed as the sponsor," Carson continued. "I have a strong feeling he will kill it before it gets to committee. I also believe there are grounds for an ethics hearing for Senator Fleming, but that's going to take more time and more evidence."

"I may be able to speed up that process, Senator."

"You are tenacious, I'll give you that. A lot like Hannah was."

Matt's chest tightened. Hannah. Was. The past tense. But still here, present in the conversation. Even a decade later, the pain was palpable. His eyes welled up.

"You still there? Sorry if I shouldn't have brought her up. It's just in the political world, a person like Hannah comes around once in a lifetime. She made a lasting impression. The two of you must have made quite the pair."

"Thanks, Senator," was all Matt could muster.

JACK FLEMING SAT at the hotel bar, nursing his second appletini. He thought the young bartender was interested in his witty banter, but of course she was only interested in the possibility of a good tip. She rolled her eyes as she whispered to one of her coworkers, "He thinks he's a ladies' man, but he sure drinks like a girl."

Fleming looked at his watch and grumbled. Late as always, he thought. It's about time to move on from this mistress, maybe find a redhead. Not tonight, though, he needed a good tumble in bed after the past few days. While she may not be punctual and talks way too much, she was good in the sack. But after tonight, it's over.

A blonde woman sat two seats down and ordered a Gin Gibson. She looked over and gave Fleming a little smile. He took that as an invitation to join her. No harm in a conversation while he waited.

"You look like you're having a tougher week than me," he said with a half chuckle. "Maybe I should buy you that drink."

"Save it, Romeo, I'm not a hooker." She stared straight ahead without looking at him.

"You got it all wrong, Miss. I'm waiting for someone, so I just thought I'd make conversation. I'm not looking for anything else."

She sighed and faced him. "I'm sorry, but you can't imagine how often I get hit on in a bar. Hazard of the job, I guess."

"What do you do?"

"Pharmaceutical lobbyist, the entire southeast, so hotel bars are a necessary evil."

"I understand." He sipped his drink. "Lobbyist, huh? Have you been to the legislative building yet?"

"Oh yeah. I think I've camped out in front of every door there is, but I can't seem to get an audience with anyone."

"Well, you missed a door." Fleming stuck out his hand. "Senator Jack Fleming, nice to meet you."

"That sounds like a bullshit line."

"It's true." He reached into his coat pocket and pulled out his card.

"Oh my God, I'm so embarrassed. I'm Jen Cavendish, J&G Pharmaceuticals."

Fleming laughed. "Don't be, Jen, it's an honest mistake. Why don't we meet tomorrow night for dinner to discuss your company?"

"Dinner? I don't want to intrude in your personal time, Senator."

"I'm booked all day tomorrow, so dinner is the only time I have...assuming you want to state your case."

"No, no. Dinner tomorrow is great." She smiled. "It will actually be nice to have a charming, young escort for a change."

As she turned, she knocked her clutch off the bar. They both reached for it at the same time, bumping shoulders in the process. They laughed as they stood back up.

"Just like in the movies," he said, his eyes lingering on her for just a beat too long.

"Jack?"

Fleming looked up to see his mistress.

"Oh, hey Kendra. I've been waiting for you. I think our table is ready." He turned to Jen. "It was very nice to meet you, Ms. Cavendish. I'm sure we can discuss your concerns at a later date."

"Thank you for your time, Senator."

Fleming took his mistress by the arm as they walked towards the dining area of the hotel bar. "I just can't get away from lobbyists," he whispered to her.

He didn't realize his phone was missing.

AROUND 8:30 P.M. Dan pulled his Sportsman Heritage 251 up to the outside slip at Bush Marina. Being October, Dan knew the outer slip would be empty. He chose the Sportsman because it included an insulated bow storage for the treasure chest and a side dive door, perfect for the night's activities. They added a portable winch to help lift the decoy box of gold.

Tanner was already on the boat with Dan; Nigel showed up around 8:45. Alex and Willie followed about five minutes later. Alex looked skittish, scanning the area to make sure no one else was around. Dan noted his nerves and Willie's arrogance, not surprised but vigilant. Dan stepped off the boat to intercept Willie and Alex on the dock. "Before anyone boards that boat, you gotta get rid of any weapons."

"Fuck you," Willie responded. "I'm keeping my piece."

"Then you aren't coming." Dan looked him in the eyes, unwavering.

"What about those guys?" Alex asked.

"Same went for them." Dan signaled for them to come to the dock. "Feel free to frisk them, because we're gonna do the same to you." They hid guns on the boat earlier in the day.

"You mean to tell me we're going out on the water at night, unarmed?" Willie didn't like the water or the thought of what was out there. He didn't want to be left unarmed in case of alligators or sharks.

"No, there's a shotgun on the boat, but that's all we'll need. Make a choice, Willie, make it now."

Willie grumbled but slowly handed his pistol to Dan. He knew Merle had more weapons at the compound anyway. Dan tossed the pistol in the water.

"What the fuck you do that for?!" Willie shouted.

"Quiet down, Willie, people live around here," Dan hissed. "I'll buy you a new one when we're done."

Alex was actually relieved after the pat-down, not wanting any further escalation. They all got on the boat, and Dan maneuvered into Banks Channel. They headed towards Howards Creek until Dan pulled up and let the engines idle.

"Before we go any further, let's talk about how this is going down. Thanks to Mr. Martin, this vessel is equipped with sonar that detects metal. Based on the professor's information, the chest with the gold is likely to be wooden but with heavy cast iron hinges and a lock. When the sonar pings, Warfield will dive the site to see if there is anything there, and if so, we will use this winch to bring it up to the boat."

"We need to immediately get that chest into this space," Nigel added as he pointed to the bow storage. "That will keep the chest pressurized until we get it to the lab." Nigel knew people will believe anything if it's said with conviction.

"Is that where we split up the gold?" Alex asked.

Dan shook his head. "No, the gold is likely to have very specific markings that will identify it as Civil War artifacts. There's not a fence around who will touch that. We're gonna need to melt it down, otherwise the government will look to confiscate it."

"And it's going to weigh a lot, probably more than two people can carry," the professor added.

"I've got a UTV with a flatbed ready at the site," Dan answered.

"You guys sure have this planned out," Alex said. "Almost too good."

"We've been working on this for a long time," Dan said. "I don't know what you guys were doing when you planned your big Blackbeard heist, but this shit is serious to us."

"He didn't mean nothin' by it." Willie glared at Alex. "We're good." Willie was thinking of his big score later in the evening and sure as hell didn't want Alex to ruin it now.

They cruised Howard's Creek and Banks Channel. The marshes were alive with birds rustling in the grasses, every sound amplified in the night air. The musky smell of decaying plant matter, pungent and distinctive, filled their nostrils. The cool mist tingled their bare skin. Dan loved the marshes at night.

As expected, the water was choppier than the last few days, so navigation was a little tricky. He triggered the console ping a few times and sent Tanner down in his scuba gear, who came up empty or with bits of sea trash.

Willie was getting agitated. "Are you sure we're even in the right place? I thought you fuckers knew what you were doing."

"My calculations show this is the general area," Nigel answered. "But if you take into account hurricanes and nor'easters, it's possible the shift was greater than anticipated."

"Makin' me feel you don't know shit, Poindexter. This better not be a big waste of my time."

Dan made the console ping. "Shut up for a second, Willie," he snapped. "Listen, Professor." Dan hit the ping twice more, each time a little louder. "Whatcha think?"

"There's something significant down there, no doubt."

"Get ready to dive, Warfield."

The water was only about twelve feet deep, but appeared deeper because of the choppy waters. Tanner used the opportunity to surface periodically as if he was searching for the chest, though he knew exactly where it was. After his fourth time down, Tanner surfaced and removed his regulator.

"I found something, Mr. Pierce. Looks sizable."

"Can you get the winch around it?" Dan shouted back.

"I think so. It looks like I can at least get it around one end and loosen it from the sand."

"You need to be very gentle," Nigel shouted. "We don't know the condition of the chest. If it's not properly secured, the bottom can drop and everything goes."

Alex looked around. As a teen, he and his friends would look for sandbars at low tide to anchor their boats and mess around with girls on vacation. Occasionally, they would pretend to snorkel to impress them. In all that time, no one ever saw anything the least bit interesting, let alone sunken treasure. He grabbed Willie and pulled him aside.

"Something doesn't feel right, Willie," he whispered. "I think these guys are playing us."

Willie was wired, thinking about the millions worth of gold he was about to get. "No way. Too many people and expensive equipment involved for this to be fake. We are so close I can taste it."

"I'm serious, Willie. I've been in these waters for years and never saw anything close to valuable. It's a scam. We need to bail."

"Look," Willie seethed. "I know you think this is gonna end bad, but you got nothin' to worry about. We're gonna be home free soon, and you won't be part of no violence."

Willie held up his hand to stop any response. Tanner had resurfaced, and Willie wanted to hear what he said.

"I got the harness underneath one end of the chest," Tanner called to the boat. "Start lifting the winch so I can secure the other side."

"Slowly," Nigel called as Dan turned the winch.

Tanner dove back under for effect. He had already secured the chest since it wasn't deep in the sand. The delay gave Alex more time to think.

"Isn't this where the town dredges sand for beach nourishment?" he asked Dan with an accusatory look. "How is it possible something like this wasn't found before?"

Dan knew even the best planned cons can fall apart at the last minute, and this was dangerously close. What surprised Dan was that it was Alex who was figuring it out.

"I don't know, Alex, I'm not an expert in dredging. What exactly are you asking me?"

"I'm just wondering…"

Alex was interrupted by Tanner, "All secure. Bring her up!"

Tanner climbed back on the boat through the dive door and started to shed his gear. Dan called for Willie to help as the chest rose out of the water. Once the chest was lifted high enough, they swung the winch around and gently lowered the chest onto the deck. Nigel searched it closely, and waved for the others to come over.

"There it is!" he said excitedly. "Come take a look."

"What the fuck we looking at, Professor?" Willie asked.

Nigel pointed to markings he engraved on the chest earlier. "See those markings? That's the C.S.S. Phantom insignia. We've got to get this back to the lab right away and get it pressurized properly."

Alex watched as the end of the treasure hunt unfolded. He considered the events of the past several days. This guy Pierce shows up at his office unannounced. The night he was supposed to meet with Willie and Pierce he hit a guy out of nowhere with his car. Some mobster shows up. Why did they even need Alex and Willie if they knew where to look for the treasure? They said it was to sidestep the government, but the more Alex thought about it, the more it didn't add up. He tugged at Willie's shirt. "Don't you see? This makes no sense. Pressurize a box? Willie, think about it."

Willie hissed, "These guys ain't hustlers, Alex. I know some of the best, and these guys ain't like them. Why would they hustle us? We ain't got nothin' for them. Besides, the box got some serious weight to it."

Once the chest was secured in the bow storage, Dan started the engines and headed back to the compound.

"Let's load up the chest on the hand truck," Dan told the others as he pulled up to the dock. "Then onto one of the UTV's and take it to that first building. Warfield, once you get out of your wetsuit, bring the other UTV. We'll need your help getting the chest into the building."

This was perfect, Willie thought. They could take the UTV with the gold on it and never go in the building. Get it to Merle's truck, and they were home free. He texted Merle while everyone was busy: *Head to building by water we comin now.*

Willie figured they could take care of the asshole and professor before that other clown showed up. Or maybe he would let Merle cap his ass, though he wasn't sure Merle had it in him.

Dan pulled the UTV up close, so they wouldn't have to carry the chest any farther than necessary. Willie looked around for Merle, but didn't see him. As Dan and Nigel walked around to the back of the UTV to get the chest, Dan called to Alex and Willie. "Let's go, you two, this damn thing is heavy."

"Just hold on," Willie said and then shouted out, "Merle, get your ass out here!"

Merle came around the corner, pointing a gun at Dan and Nigel. "Here you go, Willie," he said as he handed him a Magnum revolver. "I figgered you might want this baby."

Willie grinned as he pointed his gun at Dan. "I believe we'll be taking that gold. No need to take it off the vehicle, we're taking it too. Your mistake, smart guy, was the whole no guns on the boat thing. You wasn't countin' on me outsmartin' you."

"You got that right, Willie."

"I'm gonna take great pleasure blowin' you're fuckin' head off, Benny. I only wish that big fucker was here too." He threw his head back and roared.

"Fuck, Dan, you said this would be an easy job, no guns!" Nigel cried.

"Shut up." Dan didn't take his eyes off Willie.

"Hold on, I thought your name was Benny." Alex shook his head. "I knew we were being played!"

Nigel started talking fast. "He's playing you," he said, pointing to Dan. "There's no gold, it's all made up. I didn't want to do it, but they made me. Please don't shoot me, I swear I won't say a word."

Willie looked back and forth between Dan and Nigel, his

confidence waning. "Bullshit. There's gold in that chest, you're just stalling." Willie was unsure, trying to convince himself.

Dan shrugged. "Look for yourself."

"Keep your gun on that motherfucker," Willie commanded Merle. "If he twitches, shoot him."

Dan looked to Merle, eyes narrowed and head tilted, challenging him to shoot. He then turned his gaze to Alex.

"It's over, Willie, let's just get out of here," Alex pleaded.

"We're ain't done here yet, Alex."

"It's over. You already killed that one guy on the boat, and maybe the other guy. It's got to stop."

"I am so goddamn tired of hearing your whiney voice, Alex." Willie shifted his aim and fired, hitting Alex in the chest. Alex fell backwards, landing in a heap. He groaned as the blood began to seep through his shirt.

"Alex!" Dan shouted as he ran towards him. Both Willie and Merle started shooting, but neither were exactly expert marksmen.

More shots came from behind. A blast hit Willie square in the shoulder, spinning him to the ground, forcing the gun out of his hand. He looked up in shock at Tanner, holding Willie's own Glock.

Merle aimed his gun at Tanner, but his luck ran out: Shay's shot hit him in the temple. Merle was dead before he hit the ground.

"You motherfucker," Willie said to Tanner as he struggled to stand.

"Just stay there, Willie, for chrissake. You can't be that stupid."

But he was. Willie reached for his gun. This time Tanner shot him in his kneecap. Willie fell again with a loud cry. Tanner shook his head. "Moron."

Matt came running out of the building, followed closely by Chief Phillips and several officers. Some converged on Willie and Tanner, while the rest searched the perimeter.

Shay was gone.

Matt ran to Dan, who was at Alex's side. Fortunately for Alex, Willie was not a great shot, especially with the Magnum. The wound was high, away from the heart, though he was bleeding badly.

"Stay with me, Alex," Dan said, trying his best to comfort him. "We'll get you help."

Alex looked up, confusion and pain in his eyes. "Why?" was all he said.

"You were supposed to get them inside the building, Dan," Matt shouted over to where Dan was crouched beside Alex.

"Dipshit over there had other plans."

Matt's eyes got wide as he reached Dan. "Shit, you're bleeding."

"Yeah, well, that happens when you get shot." Dan winced as he spoke.

The EMT's were on site quickly, a contingency Matt had in place with the chief. Medics on the scene prioritized need; first Alex, then Dan, and lastly, Willie. Only Alex's wounds were considered life threatening. They were quick to get Alex off the island and to a hospital, no easy task.

Matt stayed with Dan as they bandaged his side where the bullet had gone through.

When the EMT was out of earshot, Matt turned to Dan. "See, I told you we shouldn't do this. I knew someone was going to get hurt."

"I never got shot when we ran cons, Matt, only when you insist on a stratagem."

"Not funny, asshole."

"It's a little funny." Dan smiled.

Once Dan's wounds were dressed, he too was taken to the hospital for further attention. When Matt was certain Dan was OK, he walked over to Willie. One of the medics had bandaged his shoulder, and was trying to stabilize his knee. Willie kept crying out in pain, and cursing the medic.

"Give me something for the pain, you cocksucker," Willie howled. He looked up to see Matt. "Who the fuck are you?"

Matt turned to the medic. "Can you give us a minute?"

The medic nodded. "Take your time, I've had enough of this guy."

"I said, who the fuck are you?" Willie asked Matt again.

Matt stared at Willie for a moment. "You shot my friend, Willie. You beat another man senseless who was just trying to make a living. It's time you paid the price for your sins."

"I ain't done yet, motherfucker. You just got added to my list."

"Look over there, Willie." Matt pointed to Merle's dead body, lying covered with a sheet. Matt's voice got eerily calm. "You asked me who I am, but I think you know. I'm the Grim Reaper, even if I don't wanna be. Pay for your sins in jail, or join your boy in Hell. Doesn't matter to me either way."

Willie looked into Matt's eyes for the first time and shuddered. He saw the cold shroud of death, and for the first time since it all began, Willie realized he was in over his head.

Matt walked away, trying to shake a level of hatred he hadn't felt for anyone since the Sampsons. It scared him.

Chief Phillips gathered Matt, Tanner, and Nigel, in an effort to get some idea of what happened.

"What's in the chest?" he asked.

"Some seashells, rocks, stuff like that. We thought maybe the grad students could use it for research," Tanner explained.

The chief looked at Matt. "Why did Willie think it was gold? How did he know to come here tonight? More importantly, how did you know he would be here?"

Matt shrugged. "Frank Kenny is a friend of the family. I got word someone was trying to buy his lease. Word may have gotten out that there was gold to be found."

The chief turned back to Tanner. "Where did you get the gun, or do you just happen to walk around with one?"

"I found it on the ground when I got here. I think it might be Willie's."

"Quite the marksman, wouldn't you say?" Nigel said, his British accent returning for the first time.

Matt gave him a sharp look. "I'm just saying," Nigel mumbled.

"Assuming Spencer lives, we'll get statements from him and Covington." The chief rubbed forehead. "I have no idea how this will play out."

Matt and the chief walked together back towards the building. "You gotta do what you gotta do, Rob. I'm not going to interfere. But you at least have Covington on attempted murder of Alex Spencer, right?"

"I believe we have more than that."

Matt stopped and looked at the chief. "I'm supposed to go to Raleigh tonight, but I'll be back tomorrow. I swear I'll answer whatever questions then, but I do have one more favor to ask."

The chief raised his hand. "You want me to deal with the mayor, don't you?"

"I'll owe you."

The chief shook his head and walked away.

TANNER SAT OFF TO THE SIDE by himself, replaying everything. It happened so fast: the shooting, a dead man, cops everywhere, Dan taken to the hospital. He could still see the look in Willie's eyes before he shot him the second time. It was a look of a wild animal, desperate but still cold and hate-filled. Tanner noticed for the first time that his hands were shaking, so he started rubbing them together.

Matt came over and sat down beside him. "You OK?"

"Well, there's a dead man over there." He pointed to Merle's body. "Dan's hurt, and I shot someone, even if he is a piece of shit. So, no, not so much."

Matt nodded and sighed. "I'm sorry, son, this is exactly why I didn't want you involved."

"Is Dan going to be alright?"

"Yeah, the medic said the bullet went clean through. No major organs hit."

"Who killed Merle?"

Matt paused for a moment. "I don't know."

"I think you do, Dad. Where's Uncle Shay?"

Matt didn't say anything, just shrugged. He lowered his head, and stared at his feet. He knew Tanner's life would never be the same.

It was Tanner that put his hand on Matt's shoulder. "Come on, Pops. We still need to head to Raleigh. A plan's a plan, and we need to see it through."

Matt and Tanner drove up to Raleigh that night because Matt wanted to be at Jack Fleming's office as early as possible the next morning. He needed Tanner to run interference.

It was about a two-hour drive to Raleigh, and they rode in silence for the first hour until Tanner finally spoke, "So, is Katie going to be my stepmom?" He chuckled.

"That's funny, smartass. Is Brittany going to be my daughter-in-law?"

"Touché." His smile faded. "Pops, just how much of this did you and Dan, and I guess Katie, do when you were younger?"

"The person I was before I met your mother is not who I am now, or who I want to be. That past is buried and needs to stay that way. I'm a town manager of a small beach community, that's it."

"I think what we've been doing for the past several days says otherwise," Tanner pressed. "There is a part of you that came alive and for a damn good reason. Sometimes you have to get creative to get the right things done."

"And look what it got us, Tanner," Matt replied somewhat angrily. "I dragged you and Aoife into danger. Dan's been shot, and people are dead. Jaysus Christ, you shot somebody. And for what, some stupid piece of legislation."

Tanner looked out the window. "You know better than that, Dad. This isn't just about some stupid legislation, it's about what's right. And as far as involving Katie and me, we did it willingly."

Matt shook his head. "It's the wrong path, Tanner. I should have left this side of me in the past."

"You know that's not true. How many other Franks or Holts would be in the hospital or dead if Willie was still out there? And what about Jack Fleming?"

Matt didn't say anything. He hated it when his kids were right.

"We are who we are. It doesn't make it wrong, especially if it's for good."

"You're the second person to say that to me. But the end doesn't always justify the means."

"Does that buried past, never to be seen from again, include Katie? Because if it does, that would be a shame."

Matt gripped the steering wheel a little harder. "That's complicated."

Tanner laughed. "God, raising you is a 24/7 job. You like her, she likes you. Hell, I like her, and I'm sure Sedona will too. What's so fucking complicated?"

Matt didn't have an answer, so he changed the subject. "By the way, where did you learn to shoot?"

"That was a pretty awesome couple of shots if I do say so myself."

They pulled into a small condo complex and parked. "A friend is letting us spend the night," Matt told Tanner.

"Two bedrooms, I hope. You snore like a train, old man."

"Only when I've been drinking."

"Keep telling yourself that."

The key was under the doormat as instructed. They walked in to find a woman sitting on the couch, glass of wine in hand. "I was wondering if you were going to show up."

"Hi Jen," Matt responded, "I wasn't expecting you to be here."

She walked over to Matt, placing her hand on his chest, a little pout across her lips. "Aren't you happy to see me?"

Matt blushed. Jen had a way of making men do that. "Of course I am, it's just—"

"Relax, sweetie, I'm not staying. I just wanted to give you this in person." She handed him Jack Fleming's cellphone. "You were right, it was an easy job. What a schmuck. By the way, I disabled the password protection so you can access whatever you want."

"You're the best. I owe you."

"I'll take it in trade. I want a week at one of your guest houses at the beach, with all the frills. That includes a cabana boy."

"Sorry, but I'm kinda in a relationship, I think."

"You think?" She laughed. "Men. But honestly, I wasn't talking about you, I meant that stud you came in with." She winked as she headed out the door.

Wednesday, October 19

MATT SAT AT THE KITCHEN TABLE, contemplating his up-coming showdown with Jack Fleming. This was his strength back in the day, finishing off the mark. His favorite part was seeing their faces when they realized what was happening. There was satisfaction knowing the marks were getting what they deserved. He didn't want to admit it, but part of him craved this action. Maybe Shay and Tanner were right, we are who we are. He spent the last few years successfully repressing that desire. Now he wanted nothing more than to finish the job.

Tanner walked into the kitchen. "It's go time, Pops."

They walked to the legislative building, stopping at a coffee shop for Tanner. He came out with two cups of coffee in his hand. Since Matt didn't drink coffee, he assumed Tanner needed a double jolt of caffeine.

"When we get to the legislative building, it will be locked," Tanner said. "Follow my lead, and we'll get in."

As Tanner predicted, the building was locked, but there was a security guard inside. He was a squat gentleman in his early sixties with graying hair and a sparkle in his eye. He opened the door and stuck out his head.

"Tanner Sheehan, what are you doing here this early? You know we aren't open for business yet."

"Hey Ernie, what's the haps?" Tanner smiled. "Ernie, this is my old man, Matt Sheehan. He's the town manager of Topsail Beach."

Ernie shook Matt's hand. "Pleasure to meet you, Mr. Sheehan. Step on in here where it's warm. That second cup of coffee wouldn't be for me, would it?"

Tanner handed him a cup. "You know it is, Ernie. I can't have you drinking that swill they have here."

"You speak the gospel, my brother. But again, why are you here so early?"

"My dad has an early meeting with Senator Fleming. You know how he is about early starts."

Ernie rolled his eyes. "Yes, I do. You know, I hope the guy gets elected to governor or some federal spot just to get him out of here." He looked down at his shoes, a little embarrassed. "I shouldn't have said that. I didn't mean no disrespect."

"Shouldn't have said what, Ernie?" Tanner winked. "Do you think it would be OK if I took my pops up to the senator's office?"

"For you, sure thing."

The apple really doesn't fall far from the tree, Matt thought.

Tanner led Matt to the senator's office on the second floor. The legislative building was a maze, but Tanner knew exactly where to go. Matt realized that Tanner had established his own reputation in Raleigh as part of his job and was clearly quite influential. Maybe Dan was right, Matt pondered, I have been clueless for too long.

Tanner dumped his coffee in the trash at the elevator. "Don't you want that?" Matt asked.

"Props, old man. Didn't you say they were critical to any con... I mean 'stratagem'? Besides, I need an excuse."

When they got to Fleming's office, his administrative assistant was already there, but he was not. Tanner rapped lightly on the open door, and she looked up, not expecting anyone that early.

"Good morning, Sylvia."

"Tanner, what are you doing here?" She perked up immediately at the sight of Tanner. Matt shook his head, wondering if there was anyone who didn't like this guy.

"I want you to meet my dad."

"The manager at Topsail Beach!" She smiled. "It's a pleasure to meet you."

Matt tipped his Stetson. "Likewise."

"If you're looking for the senator, he should be here in just a few minutes. But I don't have you down as an appointment. Senator Fleming is particular about his schedule, you know that."

"I certainly do, but my dad just wants to make the introduction for future contact. You know how it is."

"I do, but, well, it's Senator Fleming, and he does not like any unscheduled visitors."

"Hmm, what if my dad was just hanging around while you and I go get a cup of coffee? That way, it's a meeting by happenstance. My treat on the coffee."

Now Matt understood the whole coffee thing.

Sylvia looked at Matt with a sheepish grin. "Not too many

women in this building pass on the chance for coffee with Tanner."

I'll bet, Matt thought.

The door separating Fleming's office from the reception area was locked, so Matt picked it and went in. Certain skills never go away. Plus, it was an old building. The locks weren't that difficult.

Despite hearing about Fleming's ego, Matt was still surprised at the sheer arrogance of the office. The monstrosity of his desk was one thing, but even the chair behind it was a luxury leather high back, worth a couple grand, easy. The pictures on the wall were mostly of Fleming with high-ranking political figures or B-List celebrities filming in Wilmington. The photo on his desk was him and his wife on their wedding day. Neither looked especially happy. Nowhere was any sign of the people or places he represented. Quite the show for a man of the people.

Matt stood near the desk, holding the framed wedding picture when Fleming walked in. He was fit, tailored, and well-groomed. He looked the part. He stared at Matt for a second, looked back into the reception area as if looking for someone, and then back at Matt.

"Who are you, and what are you doing in my office?"

Matt removed his Stetson, placing it crown down on a corner of the desk. "Why, Senator Fleming, I'm Matt Sheehan, town manager of Topsail Beach. You know, one of the towns in your district."

He looked at Matt as if he was a curiosity. "Sylvia!" he called out to no one.

"She's not here, Jack." Matt paused, suppressing a smirk. "Do you mind if I call you Jack?" Before he could respond, Matt continued, "Anyway, she took a break."

"I don't believe we have an appointment. Mr. Sheehan, is it?"

"It is, although I would figure in all the time you've been our representative you might have taken the time to see who was handling the day-to-day needs of your constituents."

"I'm a busy man, Mr. Sheehan, and you don't have an appointment. I would suggest you get in touch with my assistant to make one. I will be more than happy to meet with you at that time." He paused for a moment; then a realization: "Sheehan. There's a young lobbyist by that name."

"Yep. That would be my son, and he 'lobbies' for the coastal towns you claim to represent. Perhaps you should have taken the time to meet with him when you had the chance."

Fleming's face changed again. "The environmentalist woman from several years ago."

"That woman was Hannah Sheehan, Senator, and she was my wife, so I would advise you to tread lightly."

"Sylvia!"

"Still not here, Jack."

"I'll call security myself."

He reached for the phone, but Matt snatched the receiver from his hand, gently placing it back in its cradle. "You might want to hear what I have to say, Senator. It won't take long, and then I'll be out of your way."

Fleming sat in the big chair behind his desk, trying to take control of the conversation. "You got two minutes, Mr. Sheehan."

Matt laughed. "Your proposed legislation is dead on arrival, Senator. I just wanted to be the one to personally deliver the news."

"I don't know what you're talking about," he said.

Matt noticed a slight nervous twitch. "Sure you do, Jack. It's the one that has you getting local governments to grab their proverbial ankles while you shove it up our arses."

Fleming's back stiffened. "This is the office of a North Carolina State Senator, you don't need to be vulgar."

"OK, we'll do it your way. The draft legislation that requires, among other things, that local governments use the *Chinquapin* if they want access to funds that are rightfully theirs to begin with. It's the legislation that greatly limits access to spoil islands, sand sources in federal channels, and FEMA Recovery Funds. It holds local governments hostage. Any of this ring a bell?"

"I think you're confused, Mr. Sheehan, I have no idea what you're talking about."

"Come on, Jack, this has your fingerprints all over it. But that's OK, because I know you sent this to Senator Strickland for his sponsorship. Problem is, Senator Carson is meeting with him right about now to persuade him to drop the idea. And he has some very convincing arguments."

Fleming took off his glasses to clean them. "This is all very interesting, Mr. Sheehan, but your time is up."

"But I didn't even get to the part about my conversation with Dean Filben."

Fleming sat up in his chair a little straighter. "He was very helpful," Matt continued, "even if he didn't realize it. Seems he likes to impress people, especially the ladies. Not very bright, though, I'm sure you agree."

"Legislation comes and goes, Mr. Sheehan. If anything, this is just a slight delay."

"Try to convince Orville Denton of that." Matt knew he had

his full attention. "You are working with the former senator, or am I wrong? He doesn't seem to be one I would want to disappoint, especially if I had greater political aspirations. You know, like the governor's mansion."

Matt could see panic in Fleming's eyes. He knew it was time to go for the kill. "Oh, I almost forgot about Majestic Oysters, Inc. Seems that they've been getting some preferential treatment. Some may even question the validity of its Articles of Incorporation. I'm pretty sure there's going to be a full ethics review about that one. Of course, without Majestic Oysters, how do you get money to fund the Stone's Bay Development?"

"What the fuck!" Fleming jumped to his feet.

"Language, Jack, this is a North Carolina State Senator's office after all." Matt tried to suppress a smile, but he was enjoying every second. "Laundering money, especially federal government dollars, is a tricky business to say the least. You should really leave it to the professionals."

Fleming's face reddened. Backed into a corner, he needed to come out swinging. He went with what he knew best, threats. "You have no idea who you are messing with, Sheehan. You got nothing on me. I didn't get where I am without some very powerful friends. I'm going to bury you."

Matt had a bemused look on his face. "'It is a tale told by an idiot, full of sound and fury, signifying nothing.'"

"You're going to quote Shakespeare to me now?"

"Very good, Jack. *MacBeth* to be exact. But hey, I haven't even gotten to the best part yet." Matt took Fleming's cell phone out of his pocket and laid it on the desk.

"How did you get this?"

"A friend. A lot of people were looking for you last night, Jack. Seems your brother-in-law, Alex, was shot last night, along with a guy named Willie Covington. Your wife and your father-in-law left several messages according to your phone, but I guess they didn't have your mistress's number. Don't worry, they do now."

Fleming stood there, staring at his phone like it was a bomb. "What's in this for you? Whatever it is, I can give you more."

"Don't you even want to know if your brother-in-law survived?"

"Fuck him, he's a moron. Why do you even care? Why do all this?

Matt picked up his hat and placed it back on his head. "I thought you would have figured it out by now. I don't like you, Jack. My son doesn't like you, and my wife definitely didn't like you. You are a fecking gobshite." That last one was for Aoife.

Jack Fleming sunk into his chair. Matt was nearly at the door when he heard Fleming speak again.

"My grandfather once said to me, 'Boy, it ain't the darkies or the Jews that are gonna ruin this country, it's the filthy Irish gypsies. I thought the senile old bastard was just crazy, but it looks like he was right."

Matt turned to look at him and shrugged. "Perhaps you should consider that for your political epitaph... *Here lies the political aspirations of Jack Fleming, destroyed by a filthy Irish Gypsy... Rest in Fucking Pieces.*"

MATT JUST WANTED TO SLEEP for the next few days, but of course that wasn't going to happen. He and Tanner hung around Raleigh for a couple more hours to see how long it would take for the rumor mill to ignite. It wasn't long.

Tanner first got a call from the legislative aide for Senator Strickland saying that the draft legislation would be dropped immediately, and the senator's name was no longer associated with it in any way, shape, or form. She said that Strickland was pretty animated about it, blaming staff for not giving him more of a heads-up on its content, which they had tried to do on several occasions.

Next, the grapevine was buzzing with rumors of a big ethics investigation tied to shellfish leases and a business named Majestic Oysters, Inc. The rumor was that several elected and appointed officials were under scrutiny, but no names as of yet.

They left Raleigh mid-afternoon, getting back to Topsail Beach around five that evening. They were pulling into the compound when the police chief called Matt.

"I thought you might like to know that Alex Spencer is going to make it. He lost a lot of blood, but he is currently in stable condition."

"That's good to hear," Matt answered.

"His father has him lawyered up. It sounds like for the right plea deal he will hand over Willie Covington on a platter—who, by the way, is going to be fine as well."

"I honestly don't give a shit about his well-being."

He chuckled. "Not many of us do. Funny thing, he keeps saying that he needs protection from the mob. He thinks Dan and Tanner are somehow connected, as well as some really big guy and the Grim Reaper, who apparently just showed up last night. I wonder what that could be about."

"Beats me. Probably some drug-induced hallucination."

"That's one theory, I suppose. I still need statements from you and your son."

"Can it wait until tomorrow, Chief? We just got back from Raleigh."

"First thing would be great." It really wasn't a request.

Matt dropped off Tanner at the compound. He went back to the guest house where he and Katie had been staying. She wrapped her arms around his neck and squeezed tight. When she let go, she punched him in the chest.

"You could have been killed, you little shit. And then you take off without even talking to me? You are such an arse, Matthew Patrick Sheehan!"

"I'm sorry, Aoife, I really am. But can you yell at me tomorrow? I want to go to the hospital and check on Dan."

She looked at him, her emerald eyes moist with tears. "OK, but I'm coming with you."

It was after visiting hours when they got to the hospital. It took some persuading, but they finally talked their way into Dan's room. He was sitting up in the bed, watching Andy Griffith reruns.

"If it isn't the man who got me shot," Dan joked.

"If you followed my simple instructions, this never would have happened. How you feeling, partner?'

"Hell, I'm fine. They're releasing me tomorrow."

A nurse popped her head in. "Two more minutes, then you have to go."

"The least they can do is let her give me a sponge bath before I go."

"Jaysus, the two of you are pathetic," Katie snapped. "What you need to do is ask Emma out."

"Emma? She wouldn't go out with me."

"Yes, she will."

"I'm not going to ask her out."

"Why? Because she's younger than you, or because she's black?"

"Emma's black?" Matt asked.

"Her dad is," Dan answered.

"What did you think?" Katie asked.

Matt shrugged. "I don't know, just that she's really pretty."

Katie looked up at the ceiling. "Oh my God, you two are hopeless. I'm going to wait outside. You eejit." With that, Katie walked out of the room.

Dan started to give Matt a hard time, but the look in Matt's eyes was that of conflict deep in his soul. Dan knew that Matt was taking the events of the previous night to heart, blaming himself for what transpired.

"Don't do this to yourself, Matt. What happened last night is on Willie Covington. He dealt the play."

"People were shot, Dan. You were shot. A man is dead. My son is involved in my mess. There is blood on my hands, partner. Blood I can't wash off."

Thursday, October 20

MATT AND TANNER MET WITH the chief and his lead investigator first thing in the morning. Their stories were consistent with the others. The police were able to confirm that the gun Tanner used to shoot Willie Covington belonged to Covington. What they didn't know was that Willie had actually handed it to him the night they met at the Salt Marsh restaurant. Tanner told them he found the gun while coming back from the dock. He stumbled upon Willie and Merle holding Dan and Nigel at gunpoint. When the shooting started, he just reacted as any normal person would. Both the chief and the investigator were impressed that Tanner could give this statement with a straight face.

The one thing they couldn't quite square was Merle. The detective believed that there must have been another shooter. They found tracks that lead back to the shoreline, but lost them from there. They were sure ballistics would confirm the bullet was from a different gun than any found on the scene.

"Maybe Willie had a third person there who fucked-up and made a run for it," Matt suggested. He knew they were never going to get Shay; he was too good.

"Maybe," the chief said. "My guess is there won't be a huge push to solve that one. Merle Washburn had an extensive rap sheet."

As they finished up, the chief asked Matt to hang back for a moment. Matt told Tanner to wait for him at his town hall office.

"You sure there isn't anything you want to add to all this?" The chief looked tired, and Matt felt bad for his part in all this.

"I'm not sure what you want me to say, Chief."

"You just happened to know that Willie Covington was going to show up at the Slaggers compound last night with enough time to warn the police, yet the official statements coming out of your camp is that it was a shock to them."

"Maybe we call it an anonymous tip."

The chief frowned and let out a big sigh. "Boss, you've been the best manager this town has had in all my time here. I'd like it to stay that way. The DA wants Covington for murder, and he really doesn't care about the rest of it. Let's hope Alex Spencer gives him what he needs."

Matt stood up and smiled. "I like it here too, Rob. Have a little faith."

Matt walked back to town hall. The morning was brisk, with a strong breeze coming off the ocean. He stopped for a second to enjoy the smell of the sea and the feel of salt on his skin. It gave him a feeling of serenity, even if only for a moment. "This beats mindful yoga any day," he said to himself.

He walked into town hall and was greeted by several of the staff, all wondering why he was there.

"I thought you were off until Monday," Kelly said.

"I'm not here, you didn't see me," Matt said back.

"Good luck with that. FYI, the Pickleball Mafia is looking for you. It seems they feel like you're not taking their suggestions seriously. Looks like you might be going to the mattresses."

Matt heard her laugh as he headed up the stairs to his office. He didn't know what he would do without her.

Tanner was sitting at a table in Matt's office. "What do you think, Pops, are we done?"

Matt knew what he was asking, and his initial thought was to tell him that it was all good, but he was done shielding his son. "I don't know. It really depends on Alex Spencer and the DA."

Kelly buzzed Matt. "You have a visitor, says it's critical that he sees you."

"Who?" Matt asked.

"Senator Orville Denton."

The former senator sat down in one of the chairs on the opposite side of Matt and Tanner. His large frame filled the chair, which creaked as he leaned back. Matt sat up straight, laser-focused on the man.

"What can I do for you today, Senator?"

"Relax, son, I just wanted to meet the man who, in one giant swing, undid all my hard work."

"I'm sure I don't know what you're talking about, sir."

Denton smiled. "Sheehan. Lawd God, that name seems to make grown men wet their pants." He turned and looked at Tanner. "You know, your mama could be a pit bull in battle. She was a pistol for sure."

Tanner moved quickly, but Matt grabbed his arm. "All due

respect, Senator," Matt said, eyes burning, "you need to be real careful choosing your next words."

He laughed, almost nonchalantly. "Easy, boys, I meant it as a compliment. You have to excuse my simple country phrases. I meant no disrespect. Miss Hannah and I had our disagreements, that's for sure, but she was a sharp lady, a worthy adversary. I had nothing but admiration for her. That's the God's honest truth." He paused long enough to shift his massive weight. "What happened to her was tragic. I am truly sorry 'bout what happened."

"You need to state your business, Senator, and move on." Matt was losing patience.

"I used to know this ole boy, Elijah Sampson. Big donor of mine. Got into some trouble sometime after your missus passed." Denton looked at Matt, hoping for a reaction. He didn't get it. "Ended up losing his entire fortune before having a heart attack. I hear his boy is in jail."

"What's your point, Senator?"

"Forgive me. Sometimes my mind wanders. Topsail Beach, Slaggers Inc., you showing up as town manager. Got me thinkin' is all."

Matt saw where this was going. He needed to shut it down. "Get to the point of your visit, Mr. Denton, or I'll have to ask you to leave."

"Fair enough. I wanted you to know that the dredge legislation that suddenly died was a personal interest of mine. Not in that form, mind you, that was Fleming's doing. I just hope when a new, more reasonable proposal comes forward I don't have to worry about any interference."

"My sole interest is Topsail Beach's program, Senator. If it's intact, I won't have a dog in the fight."

Denton's folksy persona went dark quickly. "I have my doubts, Mr. Sheehan. It seems that we are destined to butt heads in the future." Denton turned his head and looked at Tanner. "Honestly, boy, it's you I worry about most."

As Denton got up to leave, Matt couldn't help but ask. "You're a very smart man, Senator, so why have Dean Filben involved with the *Chinquapin?*"

He shook his giant head. "Sadly, that boy is my wife's kin. But next time you see him, he'll be managing a dollar store in the most remote location I can find. Hopefully, he won't fuck that up."

Late October

A WEEK WENT BY SINCE the showdown at the compound. Dan was back home recovering from his gunshot wound. He still hadn't asked Emma out for a date, although she did go by and check on him daily. Nigel Thornburg took off to God-knows-where, but before he left, he told Dan to never call him again. Once the chief felt like he no longer needed him, Tanner took Brittany to some Caribbean Island for a long weekend as promised.

Shay surfaced back in Charlotte. Matt gave him a call.

"What's the haps, Matty-Boy?" His voice was booming and jovial, as usual.

"You disappeared before I could give you a proper goodbye, brother."

"Yeah, well, you know how it is. Sometimes a man just has to boogie."

"Uh-huh. Did you know that some guy was shot and killed down here? Apparently, some small-time loser with enemies. Cops think it was probably one of his associates, maybe a failed robbery attempt."

"I think I did hear something about that," Shay replied. "Pity. But you know, sometimes there is a price to pay when you point a weapon at a Sheehan. It's karma." Matt knew he was referring to Merle's attempt to shoot Tanner.

"Shay…"

"Enough said, brother, it's all copacetic," Shay said. "You just tell Tanner to come work with me running a baseball team and leave the nerd shit behind."

Matt smiled. "Thanks, brother, I can always count on you."

Matt spent as much time as he could with Katie. They decided to move out of the guest house and stay at Matt's condo. It was closer to the hospital, so Katie could spend time with Frank. It was also farther away from other distractions.

Frank regained consciousness but couldn't remember much of anything about the night he was assaulted. His hands were a mangled mess, with several surgeries still ahead. Dan had arranged for a friend to take care of his shellfish lease as long as necessary, compliments of Slaggers Inc.

They ran into Katie's parents at one of the visits. "I'm pretty sure your dad still hates me, Aoife," Matt said. "I guess that part of his memory is still strong even as he gets older."

"There's no doubt that he still hates you, sweetie. But that hasn't stopped me from getting naked with you, so don't worry about it."

They spent the next few days exploring Wilmington and enjoying each other's company. They would end each day at Mad

Mole Brewery, or the Blind Elephant, and then home. Matt wanted it to last forever.

Katie was up early on a Sunday morning. Matt found her on the balcony, coffee in hand, staring out at the Cape Fear River. A sudden panic gripped Matt, sensing the end was near. He didn't say anything, because he thought if there was no conversation, she couldn't say she was leaving.

"It's time for me to go home, Matt," she said quietly.

Dammit.

He looked down at his feet. "I know."

"I never wanted to leave you back then," she said, her eyes tearing up. "My father thought it would be best..." her voice trailed off.

"Stop." He held her hand. "I know. It's OK."

She looked at him, her emerald eyes wide, tears streaking down her cheeks. "I'll never be able to replace Hannah in your heart, and I won't try."

Matt looked at her, a sad smile exposing what was in his heart. "I'm not asking you to, Aoife, any more than I asked her to replace you. I've been blessed to have both of you in my life."

David Gray's "Shine" was playing in the background. Katie looked into Matt's eyes. "Do you think this song is a sign?" she asked.

"Yes," he said. "But I see it as a song of hope. I know it starts with acknowledgement of a fading love, but to me it's about letting go of the past and embracing the journey towards a brighter future, being true to yourself. I'd like to believe you and I will shine together at some point, not apart."

They went back to Topsail Beach so Katie could get her car and the rest of her things from the guest house. That afternoon they took a long walk on the beach, making plans to see each other on a regular basis. They sat in the sand by the inlet, watching waves crash along the shoreline, until sunset arrived, a panoramic view of purple and orange reflecting off the wispy clouds above. And just like that, she was gone.

Matt went into the main house and up to the second deck. There was Dan, sitting there staring at the night sky. He handed Matt a tumbler of whiskey.

"I visited Alex in the hospital today," Dan said. "Do you know that little fucker actually figured out we were scamming them? Fortunately for us he was a little too late."

"They actually let you see him?"

"I pretended to be a doctor. People aren't too smart. You know, I kinda like the guy. I mean, he's an idiot, but not really a bad guy. All he ever wanted to do is be a chef. I think I'm gonna offer him a job at the Salt Marsh.

"He told me he's got a plea bargain that his daddy's lawyers set up. Probation as long as he testifies against Covington for the murder of Holt Bratton and the assault on Katie's cousin. Oh, and attempted murder on him. Apparently, that's all the DA wants."

Matt nodded.

"But get this, Daddy and his lawyers also want to go after Senator Fleming. Shouldn't have cheated on the man's daughter, I guess."

That made Matt smile. Between Senator Carson, Orville Denton, and Alex Spencer II, Fleming was done.

They sat there quietly for a while before Dan spoke again. "What about you? You gonna be OK?"

Matt leaned back, took a sip of his drink and smiled. "You know what, partner, it's not that complicated after all."

Acknowledgments

I always pictured the novelist hunched over the typewriter, all alone, writing the next great story. A solo act for sure. What I learned is that while this is partially true, it doesn't happen without a little help and a lot of support. Thirty-five plus years in public service allowed me to meet all sorts of people, see many noble acts, and the occasional head-scratcher or two. If you just pay attention to what is going on around you, the stories flow.

For me, writing this book was fun. It was sitting outside with my dog, listening to music in the background (special thanks to David Gray and Norah Jones for their musical inspiration!), telling the stories that have lived inside my imagination for years. Characters and places, events and moments, all the things that left an indelible mark on my psyche coming to life. It was a blast.

But to get to this place, to have a book that would actually entertain people other than myself, took a lot of help. This book doesn't get published without the hard work and dedication of my developmental editor and jack-of-all trades, Bryan Jewell. Bryan helped me take a good story and make it infinitely better. He taught me more about writing than I knew existed. He smoothed out the wrinkles, made the critical connections, and got me to the next level. If there are any mistakes in this book, they are all mine.

The cover is the artistic renderings of Karen Snave. I gave her no help, and she still came up with exactly what I was looking for. Genius. Tristan Steffe took my scribbles and turned them into a professional looking product, no small feat.

I can't thank the three of them enough.

Much of this story takes place at Topsail Beach. While the story is fictional, I assure you the town is very real. It is filled with wonderful, kind people who made me feel welcome the entire time I worked there. Because of their hard work and commitment, it is the best beach around, hands down. And sunsets are magnificent!

Then there is family, immediate and extended. I've been blessed with uncles and aunts and cousins that made me laugh, but I also knew they were always there for me, even though we lived far apart. My best friend since the fourth grade (and later college roommate) is a major influence in this book. Thank you all.

Special thanks to my mother, who believed in everything I did, almost to a fault. And to my four brothers and their families. There were more good times than I can remember.

Finally, to my daughter, Amanda, her husband Jason, and their boys Easton and Carter, my son Matt, his wife Taylor, and their son Townes. You are my world. It's Amanda's skills in marketing and social media that keep me relevant. Matt was my early sounding board to see if what I was writing was the least bit interesting.

But mostly I want to thank the love of my life, my wife, Susan. Every day I am amazed that you are willing to put up with my nonsense. You believed even when I didn't. I can't thank you enough.

www.ingramcontent.com/pod-product-compliance
Lightning Source LLC
Chambersburg PA
CBHW040858010826
48978CB00013BA/1065